An Angel for Maxey

RONALD C. WINTERS

WestBow
PRESS

WestBow Press books may be ordered through booksellers or by contacting:

WestBow Press
A Division of Thomas Nelson
1663 Liberty Drive
Bloomington, IN 47403
www.westbowpress.com
1-(866) 928-1240

Because of the dynamic nature of the Internet, any Web addresses or links contained in this book may have changed since publication and may no longer be valid. The views expressed in this work are solely those of the author and do not necessarily reflect the views of the publisher, and the publisher hereby disclaims any responsibility for them.

ISBN: 978-1-4497-0275-5 (sc)
ISBN: 978-1-4497-0276-2 (hc)
ISBN: 978-1-4497-0274-8 (e)

Library of Congress Control Number: 2010929972

Printed in the United States of America

WestBow Press rev. date: 10/1/2010

An Angel for Maxey is a work of fiction. But it is a story based in harsh realities of social, biblical and spiritual truths. It explores the message of Christianity, touches on the opposing tenets of Islam and other religions, looks at Israel's present and future state and portrays a realistic scenario of the dangers inherent in global religion and corrupted ecumenism. "Angel" manages to be informative and faith building while unfolding as a five-star rated thriller.

For by Him all things were created that are in heaven and that are on earth, visible and invisible. Whether thrones or dominions or principalities or powers. All things were created through Him and for Him.

Colossians 1: 16

ACKNOWLEDGEMENTS

Much appreciation for my wife Sandra who saw the writer in me even before I did. And who supported me all the way with this project. Who plied me with healthy snacks as I worked and always had a delicious dinner waiting at the end of a long writing day. Love ya' Sandra!

CHAPTER

1

The man appeared suddenly and unexpectedly. Reese had just closed the driver's side door of his Santa Fe SUV, and before his first step, the man was standing near the rear of his car.

"Good day to you, sir!"

A cheerful, friendly voice. He stood there looking at Reese. He had the impression the man was waiting for him. There was something unusual about the man, but Reese couldn't quickly define what. He started toward the rear of his vehicle and into the enclosed parking lot's driveway.

"And a good morning to you ... sir," he replied, uncertainty in his voice.

"Can you tell me, sir, where the Christian bookstore is?"

Reese relaxed a bit. "So happens I'm going right past it. Tag along," he said, smiling, pushing past his slight discomfort.

The man was as tall as Reese—a couple of inches over six feet. He wore an open white-collared shirt, dark dress pants, and polished, nondescript shoes. In a subtle, quick glance, Reese took in the man's face: unlined, serene almost to the degree of the mannequins on display in the shopping center they were entering. The man carried an expensive-looking walking cane. Reese did not detect a limp.

There was little traffic in the multilevel parking lot this time of morning, so they walked in the driveway, side by side.

"You know, a man should make his calling and election sure."

The man had a highly euphonic voice, a dialect Reese could not place. The words echoed a recent sermon of Bishop Padduck's as he had called sinners and backsliders to, and back to, the Lord. Reese had felt a prick of discomfort at the time.

"Sounds like good advice there," was all Reese could think to say. He wasn't quite sure what the stranger meant.

Midway down the drive, they turned right and opened the two large doors leading into the mall. Reese saw the Christian bookstore two shops away on his right.

"I believe that's the store you are looking for. It's the only Christian bookstore in the mall that I know of."

There was a strategic island of books on display just inside of the store, along with a handful of customers and browsers milling about. Reese stopped and turned toward his guest.

"Have a nice—"

"I thank you, my good man, for your help." He looked at Reese for a second. "Keep your faith in God, Mr. Ma—"

"Maxey. Reese Maxey." He could have sworn the stranger was about to say Maxey and regretted having spoken too soon.

"Mr. Maxey. There are many diversions in life. But with God's direction, we arrive at our true calling. Usually God's help comes through people. In the time of your troubles, Mr. Maxey, remember the chosen. Have a very, very fine day."

With that, the man turned and, instead of going into the bookstore, started back the way they had come. An odd man. A real odd ball. But Reese felt the impact of the man's words, a lingering effect. There was more to the man's words than the mere sermonizing of a lunatic.

He started into the mall. Customer traffic was light this time of day. Some shops were just opening, sales staff setting up displays, arranging products for maximum eye appeal. He stopped briefly at the window display of Lenny Horshak's. It was a drool thing. He admired good fashion and style. And he understood the difference.

He looked at the two suits on display. A nailhead pattern gray suit next to a dark navy pinstripe. One by Oxxford, the other, Hickey Freeman. They contoured to the mannequins almost as if tailored for them. One suit was cut with a shorter, tight-fitting jacket, the other, a fuller cut. Youth to senior citizen. Horshak covered the demographic spectrum. Reese glanced at his Tag Heuer. Ten minutes to go until his marketing research interview. He continued walking to the other side of the mall and entered the skywalk connecting the mall to the office complex of Fountain City Incorporated.

As he walked the skyway, he looked out and down at the traffic passing beneath him. It was still heavy with commuters going into downtown Kansas City, Missouri, on a beautiful fall day.

At the elevator, Reese pushed the lobby button and emerged a few seconds later in the vestibule. He passed through two heavy glass doors, then down a few steps to the lobby of FCI, Inc., where he discovered an attractive lady behind the desk. She reminded Reese of Shirley McClain—Shirley McClain back in the day.

"Good morning. How can I help you?" She had a pseudo-friendly voice.

"I have an appointment with Al Wolf."

"Is he expecting you?" Brusque. Reese stared at her for a second. At six feet two, 195 pounds, and with racially ambiguous good looks, Reese occasionally felt targeted. He knew he was paranoid by nature. He had majored in psychology in college and was given to analyzing his interpersonal relations—too often, he knew. And he was too sensitive. Intellectually he knew this, but still, he wondered if people found it difficult to categorize him. And he wore no wedding band (divorced ten years). He wondered if the absence of a wedding band made him suspect.

"Well, let's see. If I say I have an appointment with Alan, do you think that maybe he is expecting me? Maybe?"

Reese saw the expression on the receptionist's face and immediately regretted his sarcasm. He gave her a soft, genuine smile.

"Oh, you did say that you do have an appointment, didn't you? Silly me."

"Well, I probably didn't say it loud enough. I tend to mumble sometimes. I am sorry." Two smiles. She picked up her telephone, hit a button.

"Marie, this is Julie. Mr ...," a look at Reese.

"Maxey."

"Mr. Maxey is here to keep his appointment with Mr. Wolf. Oh, okay." She disconnected the call. "He is expecting you, Mr. Maxey. Marie said you know the way to Al's office. There's your badge. Let's see, you signed in, okay. They're looking for you!" Julie returned to her magazine, still smiling.

Reese caught his reflection in the glass of one of the pricey pieces of artwork that decorated the many walls in the complex. He thought he was appropriately attired. Tall and tan, he had black and gray hair that was slightly receding and neatly combed back. He wore a black blazer over gray slacks, an open-collared, button-down shirt, and well-polished Cole-Haans. A few years ago, a tie would have been expected, but not so in today's business world.

Reese felt bad about his sarcasm with Julie. At his center, he had a soft, good-willed heart toward people in general. All people—he didn't see race. Or he saw it, but it made no difference with him. Red, yellow, black, or white—all were precious in God's sight, and that was good enough for him. He saw the human family as one, partly because of his church and spiritual upbringing. Rich, poor, good, bad—all struggled. All were vulnerable. Too much time and sometimes devious ways were employed to cope with life. Through his training in psychology (He had stopped short of a PhD in clinical psychology, intending to return to school someday. But as each year passed, his will and determination to do so had waned. Eventually, he became content with the master's degree he had taken), he had concluded that most people were doing the best they could to make it in life. Human behavior was a little bit on the nasty, ugly side ever since the fall. All sinned and came short of the glory of God, so life was a little unpleasant at times. He recalled Bishop Padduck saying one time that most people couldn't help the way they were. He made a note to say something friendly to Julie on his way out.

Down a hall, a right turn, and there was Marie. She stood at the entrance to Al's office. Beaming, open, friendly face, an attractive, slim brunette.

"Hello, Mr. Maxey, so nice to see you. How's your day going?"

"It's a good one so far. And I am on time." Reese had something of a reputation for tardiness. They both laughed lightly. It amazed Reese how often he was late. He had read somewhere in his studies in psychology something about tardiness being a symptom of psychopathology.

Marie led the way into Al's office, a miniature room of rich, dark wood. An oversized desk and an overstuffed sofa were accommodated by good leather chairs. A little too dark for Reese's taste, but richly, tastefully decorated.

"Reese, how's it going? Good to see you again!" Al's firm grip clasped Reese's hand, mano a mano. "Give me one minute, Reese."

Al Wolf was third in command at FCI. Right under Lou Maez. Together, directed by Lou, they controlled the day-to-day business of FCI. Lou Maez had input and decision-making responsibilities for every enterprise and endeavor FCI engaged, and that encompassed a multitude of businesses worldwide, including their successful TV productions. FCI was one of the largest Fortune 500 companies, and the only one to maintain that status in the Kansas City area after H&R Block, the former Yellow Freight Company, Sprint, Farmland Industries, and Aquila had fallen off the list.

FCI, Inc.—formerly Fountain City, Inc.—had come out of World War II manufacturing, having been founded by Brooks Symington, who had been a major player in manufacturing, military, and behind-the-scenes politics during that era. An entrepreneurial spirit led Symington into a diversity of products manufacturing. Symington had tried greeting cards, following the locally successful Hallmark card's business model, but the Hall family organization had successfully discouraged him. When his sons became college aged, Symington had pushed them into the Ivy League schools. With the right connections in the Ivy League, with the local farmers, factory workers, and political structures of the Midwest, all kinds of business opportunities had opened. And continued to open. Today,

FCI spreads its prowess into multiple business arenas. Symington's offspring and FCI top execs became a part of the superclass, members of the world's elite.

Reese always felt a little in awe, a little intimidated at acquiring this level of interview. He had happened upon some data once that allowed him to guesstimate, probably with a limited degree of accuracy, Al's salary. He had been surprised at the figure.

Comparing that to his own modest company, and yes, his was a company, albeit a company of one, with occasional part-time help, it was probably not an appropriate or healthy thing to do. He had to remind himself that he wasn't doing too badly considering that he worked in a modest-income service industry. The past few years he had contracted to Readscan Global, an East Coast old-line opinion polling/marketing research company that had been successful for as long as Gallup and Roper and others. Publicly, Readscan was not that well-known. But in powerful business circles, it was the go-to research company. Reese conducted market research studies—he interviewed executives in the Midwest, South, Southwest, and West—the markets in Kansas City, St. Louis, Dallas, Chicago, Denver, and some small cap markets in other states. He spent his days gathering information, opinions, and data from executives. A lot of his work was industrial advertising oriented. Publishers needed advertisers to survive; advertisers increasingly—because of increasing global competitiveness—needed feedback on the effectiveness of their ads. Not just the old days' feedback measures of who saw my ad, when, and where, but more of the qualitative data of why; and thoughts surrounding the reading of an ad were needed.

This was true for trade magazines, for government trade magazines, and for professional and business magazines.

And that input was needed from high-ranking decision makers in government, in the trades, in the professions, and especially so in big business.

Reese made his living interviewing in this context and at this level.

Reese had watched the globalization of commerce. More and more overseas companies advertised in American-based media. Over time, he had watched companies adopt and use the ISO logo in their ads, letting prospective customers know that their products or services adhered to international standards. More American companies were advertising addresses overseas.

He had noted the increasing importance of gathering data that measured attitudes and public sentiment. In years past, his work had been primarily of surveys. Basically finding out in quick, short face-to-face interviews whether a particular ad or article had been seen. Just basic ad recognition surveys or ad recall. In recent years more and more qualitative research had been requested. Not only did advertisers want to know if you had ever seen their ad,but also they wanted to know how you felt about it,and how you intended to respond to the ad—or editorial—message.

And a little disturbingly, Reese had become aware of the increase in research that included questions related to religion and spiritual matters.

"Have a seat, Reese, sorry, had to run to the little boys room!" Al gave an apologetic laugh. Reese sat on the soft sofa, against the right wall of Al's classy office. Reese always took note of the picture—or painting?—over the sofa, a woman sitting on a horse, staring straight at you, leaning into her saddle, a slight knowing smile on her lips. Reese wondered who, what, where. He opened his thin attaché; extracted the questionnaire, notepad, and tape recorder; placed them on the coffee table. Al took the right-angled chair.

"What's been going on, Ree?" Al had always been friendly—easy company—the few times he had taken part in Reese's surveys. He dressed his money—an expensive medium gray wool suit, light pink shirt, wine tie. and polished tasseled slip-ons. He always reminded Reese of Tony Curtis, back in the Tony Curtis days.

"Same old same old, you know, running from one end of town to the other, one town to next, back up, do it again."

"I hear you, man—it's called hard work!" They shared a laugh.

"It pays the bills," Reese said good-naturedly.

"That it does," Al said. Al knew the routine. He had brought the latest copy of *Global Week* to the coffee table. *Global Week* had appeared recently and with a lot of fanfare via ads on the Internet,

TV, radio, and its competing magazines *Time* and *Newsweek*. In less than one year it had passed *Newsweek*, *Time*, and *US News* and *World Report* combined in readership. A miracle magazine, everybody seemed to read it. Its coverage of news, investing and money, entertainment, lifestyle, and religion seemed to resonate with the whole planet; and it was published in dozens of languages. Its "Global Opinion" section was becoming highly influential. Reese subscribed and usually enjoyed the articles. It effectively had a way of covering the local stuff and the global news. Reese's field research focused on the controlled-circulation editions, which targeted corporation and government executives, and specifically went free of charge to the executives of large multinational corporations. FCI executives were a part of that readership.

Al opened his copy of *Global Week*.

"OK, Reese, where do you want me to turn?"

Reese opened his own copy to the "Global Opinion" section.

"Right here, Al." Reese pointed. "But first," Reese backtracked, "let's talk about one of the ads in this issue." Reese thumbed to the double truck ad- two-page ad- of a gleaming G8 Gulfstream Jet in flight. A sleek company jet in midair, sailing through perfectly blue skies, a few wisps of perfectly white clouds below. The simple headline read "superclass."

"Did you see this one, Al?"

"You bet. A beauty. Kind of hard to miss."

"When you got to the page, what did you notice first?" Al, sitting with one fist supporting his chin, jacket now off, studied the ad, doing a careful recall.

"I think . . . the picture of the plane drew me into the ad."

"Why? What were your thoughts?"

"Well, I remember trying to recall if we had one of these babies in our fleet—I'm pretty certain we have more than one—now."

"Anything else?"

"Just how, I don't know—how good-looking it is, sleek, it looks sleek, I guess. And yeah, I guess I looked to see if it was a real corporate jet—you know to see if it was owned by a company or somebody like that, or whether it was just generic."

"What else about the ad did you notice?"

Al picked up the magazine, laid it back down, staring at the page.

"The headline, I saw the "superclass" heading."

"And?"

"I guess—I don't know, "superclass," whatever that means, I didn't give it a lot of thought." Al glanced briefly at Reese.

"What about the placement of the ad?" Reese asked next.

"Well, I guess I did notice that it was right next to the "Global Opinion" article. I usually read that section."

"Any conclusions?"

"I'd like to own one of those babies!" They both laughed. Reese flipped a few pages through the magazine,

"Let's see . . . here, the opinion section. Did you read any of this section?" Al turned to the section, flipped a few pages.

"Yeah, . . . I found it quite interesting. Sometimes, you know, they hit and miss, this time was a hit."

"Which item?" Reese asked.

"The articles about world religion and religion in the workplace." Reese made a few notes. For editorials, his questionnaire was designed to make a note of which articles were read, not to probe. The products and services advertised made money; the editorials and opinion stuff didn't, although there were exceptions.

"OK, Al . . . good."

"No questions about the articles?" Al asked.

"Not this time."

"Well, that's too bad, because this was a very interesting article— one world religion, faith in the workplace—that's worthwhile journalism."

Reese only nodded. Al sat back in his seat.

"Reese, you really enjoy your work." Reese wasn't sure whether that was Al's observation or a question.

"Not easy work, but yeah, I do enjoy it. I enjoy interviewing . . . meeting people, doing research."

Al shifted in his chair.

"Do you ever read the "Global Opinion" sections, the articles? I believe you get a copy of the global edition?"

"I read it pretty much every week," Reese answered.

"What did you read in this issue?"

"Gee—." He was accustomed to asking the questions, not answering them. He wondered if Al was being funny, was irritated, or somehow had been offended.

"Well, I read the article on world religion . . . and the article about the growing international superclass and how they're becoming more influential in world politics and—"

"Did you read this?" Al had turned to a section near the front of the magazine by Fahzi Raheed. Reese recalled having scanned through the article. He recalled a sense of unease. Fahzi had come from somewhere in the Middle East, or was it India? He had acquired a good Ivy League education, a PhD. He had eventually emerged as host of a political TV talk show as well as a successful print media journalist. His TV show had matched numbers with *Face the Nation* and *Meet the Press* and other similar shows. After Tim Russert had died of a sudden heart attack, Fahzi had been seriously considered for Tim's replacement.

The article Al was pointing to had to do with Raheed's series of interviews of world leaders and influencers, opinion shapers, celebrities, and the very wealthy. The interviews had come from a recent meeting at Davos, Switzerland, of the world's elites—"the superclass" as one author had been quoted as labeling this crowd that met annually. As he read the article, Reese had formed the image of a low-profile meeting—he hadn't seen a lot about it in the press—of high-profile people. What struck him was the like-mindedness and cooperation among people of often contrasting views. Meeting (and partying) together were the prime minister of Russia, the pope (one of his high-ranking representatives), the US president, the head of the Chinese government, the members of the G20 (expected), leaders of the World Council of Churches, and other world leaders. The article had focused on a growing consensus that the world needed to unite on religious values and issues. The proposal, and consensus, seemed to be that Christianity, Judaism, Islam, and eastern religions could all worship under the same steeple, without any one of the faiths losing its character. A sort of ecumenicalism.

Reese recalled giving the article some thought, and with a sense of unease, he had wondered if the proposal of one world faith was possible. Reese had thought about the implications. The war on terror might fade away—maybe. Religion, oil, and the Jewish state were the context of terrorism as he saw it.

The world had shrunk, flattened out. One little global community of about two hundred nations. It used to be said that economically, metaphorically speaking, when America sneezed, the rest of the world caught pneumonia. Well, American influence seemed to be waning. Whenever any country sneezed, the rest of the world caught, if not pneumonia, at least a cold.

"Yeah, I did read that section—scanned through it."

"What did you think?"

"I guess I thought that the article was timely, appropriate, and covered a serious subject—a shrinking planet of six billion plus people who have yet to learn to get along with each other."

Al nodded.

"Looked to me like the, the—I guess the people at the top think religion might be one of the solutions to a threatened planet." Reese felt a little uncomfortable with his synopsis, wasn't exactly sure why.

"Good take on it," Al said.

"These were good articles, Reese, some of the most important the magazine has ever put out, understanding that it is a young magazine, that still speaks well for it."

Reese nodded, again not sure how to respond.

"In your surveys, Reese, you don't ask too many questions about the articles, all you guys want to know is which products and services are getting attention. Sometimes you should probe the articles. I'd like my two cents to go back to the publisher on what I—what we here at FCI think about this article. Lou and I talked about this."

Reese fumbled with his attaché case. He said, "I have a space for comments on my questionnaire. I'm sure the publisher would be

glad to hear your comments, and especially so, coming from FCI."
Reese turned his tape recorder on again. Al sat forward.

"I think that global unity—nations cooperating with each other
in military matters, in financial matters, social, political, and in
religious matters—is a pressing matter." Al paused.

"You might write your report to say 'we' instead of 'I,' FCI is a
continuing, active partner of new global thought and opinion, and
action."

"Got it, Al. People pay attention when FCI speaks," Reese
said.

Al glanced at his Rolex. Reese gathered his tape recorder,
notepad, and questionnaire and stood up with Al, who extended
his hand.

"It's been nice, Reese—always enjoy these little sessions. Lets us
give our feedback to the people who are trying to sell us—always
appreciate that."

They started toward Marie's outer office; Al asked, "Are you
seeing anyone else here today?"

"Not today. I think I'm back next week. Doing a survey for one
of the industrial facilities magazines if memory serves me right."

"You contract to a New York company, don't you, Reese,
the—"

"Readscan. Readscan Global."

"Readscan. Sure. I should not forget that name." Al chuckled.

"Low profile, but big player in research and stuff," Reese said.

"You like it, don't you?" That was the second time Al had
asked.

"Love it."

"The work or the company?"

"both."

"Tell you what, instead of Marie walking you out, I'll see you
off—I'm going that way." They started toward the elevator.

"Have you ever thought about expanding your business?" Al
asked.

"In what way?"

"Doing what you do for Readscan Global, doing it for more than one company?"

"For who?—I mean Readscan is at the top of . . . of this game. Not many other people out there in this business with their size and importance. They cover the globe. Not sure there is a need . . ." Al did a neutral grunt. Reese went on.

"Well, If—I guess too I like working solo. That's my personality. Readscan lets me do my own thing." They walked farther in silence. They reached the elevator; Al pushed the button, turned to Reese.

"There may be more out there than you think, Reese. Give the idea some thought. When did you say you were here again?"

"I'm pretty certain, almost 100 percent, it's next week. I'm interviewing one of your facilities men—on Wednesday morning . . ."

"Before you leave the building next time you're here, you give me a ring—you've got my number."

"I will do just that, Al."

Reese took the down elevator; Al took three up. As Al got off the elevator, he looked down to the level of the skywalk connecting FCI headquarters to the mall. He saw Reese walking toward the mall. Rapid businessman pace, head held high, confident. A good image Al thought. Reminiscent of serious-minded business people back in the day—yet contemporary. *Just maybe*, he thought. He started down the hall to another set of elevators and took the first one up to the executive lobby. He entered a large room of busy people working in cubicles and exited the other side.

Down another hall and he emerged into a large reception area, on his right, a seating area of soft, cozy sofas and expensive chairs and coffee tables, a waiting area for high-level salespersons hoping to get lucrative deals with FCI. Three of them were seated, two together probably sharing last-minute sales strategy before the sit-down. He'd been there, done that, and he commiserated. The third guy sat alone, reading FCI's copy of the *Wall Street Journal*. Flawless suit, white shirt, gleaming lace-ups. He looked assured, confident for whatever he faced at FCI.

Up three broad semicircle steps, Al approached the receptionist. Pretty and blond.

"Hello, Mr. Wolf." Bright smile, chirpy.

"Hi—is Lou open?"

"There's no one in with him now—but I believe he is expecting you."

"I get any calls, that's where I'll be—unavailable for the next fifteen minutes."

Al smiled at the receptionist, not sure he had seen her before. Possibly a temp. And smart—she knew who he was.

He descended the steps, continued past the waiting area into another hall and to a miniature security desk. Two burly blue-blazered men greeted him.

"Morning."

"Mr. Wolf."

"Morning—I'll be in with Lou next fifteen minutes or so."

"Got it."

A buzzer signaled the electronic opening of the door; Lou started down another hallway. At the end of it, he turned left. Lou's office started at the corner and stretched almost halfway across the building. Al entered. Another dark wood office, but large, huge in fact, beige and dark brown leather furnishings. At the entrance, a large painting, anchored by a small table. Across the expanse of rich beige carpet Lou sat behind a large executive desk flanked by a couple of chairs. To Lou's forward right sat a large sofa and coffee table, accompanied by two comfortable chairs.

Lou stood. Tall, dark hair with just a little more gray than Al's. Distinguished looking. He wore a well-tailored navy suit, white shirt, navy tie. He usually worked in shirtsleeves. With his jacket on, Al made a mental rate he was probably on his way out shortly. He started toward Al.

"Did you meet with Reese?"

"Just finished our interview."

"What do you think?"

"Probably the way to go."

Lou glanced at his Patek Phillipe watch but gestured for Al to take a seat at the sofa coffee table. Lou always took the seat around the coffee table nearest his desk. It always seemed to Al to sit an inch or two above the other seat and above the sofa.

"I've been impressed with him too."

Several years ago, Lou had gotten his first call from Reese requesting an interview, for a *Fortune Magazine* readership study. Lou had not wanted to be bothered, but he had been impressed, and a little intrigued, by Reese's telephone presence and his persistence. He had consented to the interview. He had found it, not boring, but interesting, and he had liked Reese. Since then, two or three times a year he had taken part in Reese's marketing research interviews for other business magazines such as *Forbes*, *Fast Company*, and *Business Week*. And a couple of times for financial and information technology publications. Each time he had been impressed with Reese's professionalism. Every time Lou had subtly tested Reese's knowledge about a particular subject—throwing in innocent-appearing questions of his own research—he had been fascinated by Reese's knowledge base. He seemed to be knowledgeable and coherent on any important business subject—marketing, finance, selling, who was doing what in the world of business and in government and on subjects from aviation to zoology.

"Do you think we could sway him away from his employer?"

Al paused a second, then said thoughtfully, "Well, he does see the company he works for as his employer—but I think he likes the idea of being his own boss. He likes being an independent contractor. I threw the idea of him contracting to more than one company at him."

Lou nodded. He always appreciated the kind of discernment Al brought to the table. He and Al knew they could handle Reese's employer.

"And?"

"My intuition is that he is open to it. I don't see him turning down a good offer. He has good taste."

"When are you seeing him again?"

"I believe he's going to be here next week, visiting with one of our facilities people—Wednesday morning."

"Think maybe the three of us could get together then?—there might be four of us." Lou did not elaborate.

"I think that'll work—I told him to give me a call before he left the building."

"Good, looking forward to it." Lou stood; Al stood, left Lou's office, making a mental note to call his Facilities Department. He should have asked Reese which facilities man he was seeing. Didn't matter, though; he would find out who and make sure he kept the appointment.

As Lou Maez drove out of the executive underground parking lot, he reached for a cell phone he kept in the glove box of the five-series Mercedes. He did not voice dial as he most frequently did while driving. At the first stoplight he came to, he quickly punched in ten digits.

"Brad?—Lou Maez. Got a job for you . . ." He quickly, in partially cryptic words, outlined instructions for Brad's mission.

Reese left the darkness of the multilevel parking lot, hit the brightness of the sunshiny day. He started into the busy traffic, with a growing sense of excitement. Al seemed inspired to ask Reese about expanding his business. Reese felt, thinking back on Al's words, his demeanor, that Al may have had something in mind. He had heard an undertone of genuine, meaningful probe in Al's question. As he thought about it, he was interested, getting more so every block. He headed over to Paseo Boulevard. An old stomping ground, now turned into gentrified town houses and the expansion of Hospital Hill. He had to make several turns and U-turns to find a through street. Long time since he'd been in this part of town, and it had changed dramatically. The old fish market, corner drugstore, corner grocer no longer there. Reese felt a sense of nostalgia. At times he wished for the old days. Simpler days that also seemed nicer.

His next interview was with a small chemical company. Basically, it would be a typical print ad survey designed to get executive

16

opinions, reactions, intents to buy—on a special advertising section in one of that industry's trade magazines. He had reviewed the section in the magazine last night and found it to be not unlike many special ad sections he had surveyed in the past at this company. He knew the interview would go pretty fast. He could picture the conference room he and the purchasing manager had used last time he was here. Quick, down and dirty.

And so it went. Reese thanked the interviewee and started home. He took the slow route home. Back west to Holmes Road and then south.

He flipped on the radio as he drove and heard the last of a song on one of the Christian broadcast stations. It reminded him he had promised Jan, his girlfriend, that he would go to Bible class with her tonight. At the thought, his heart did a double beat. Just the thought of her, lately, and he felt the heart flip-flop. She was a lovely woman. He found himself more frequently thinking about her.

"And you must make your calling and election sure!" The voice from the radio snapped his attention. He had heard that twice today—his mind jumped to the strange man he had met in the parking lot earlier. He had said something like that too. Hearing it a second time, Reese focused on the words. He felt troubled in spirit. He had become more concerned about his church and spiritual life lately. He wasn't getting any younger, and he believed that one day all had to give an account to God as to how they had lived their lives. He had grown up in a Fundamentalist church. He had been baptized by the time he was twelve years old. Since his parents had trouble with the Father, Son, and Holy Ghost, as opposed to being baptized in the name of Jesus, he had been baptized using both expressions—"in the Father, Son, and Holy Ghost all in the name of Jesus." Covered all bases. Looking back on that years later and having studied the scripture for himself, Reese felt comfortable with that. He also had had the experience of speaking in tongues. He recalled that night. Down at the altar, praying and "tarrying," as they called it then, with a sincere heart, he had sought the experience, and he'd had it.

Over the years he had drifted away from the church. But not too far away. As a youngster, he had been preached to by the elders of the church, and by his parents, about having one foot in the world and one foot in the church, and had been told that people like that were of all men, most miserable. They didn't fit in either one. Too good for the world, not good enough to be called a saint. And at times, partying, drinking, skirt chasing in his college years, especially, he had felt like one of them—the "aint's" as his dad referred to them. Those years had robbed his spiritual vitality. At one point, his faith had been shaken severely. During his undergrad years, majoring in psychology, one of his professors had told the class he would prove, before the semester was over, that there was no God. This had shaken Reese some, tore at his faith. His exposure to theories of Darwin, Freud, had challenged him too. The theories made a lot of sense to him.

But there was something about the faith, his church, that just wouldn't let him let go of either. He had never given up church attendance, even when he was free from parental coercion to do so in his adult years. There were periods in his life when getting there once a month was a struggle, periods when his desire to go weakened. There was always the inner struggle. And the guilt over his fleshly weaknesses—primarily wine and women, with the occasional pharmacological strayings. And always, somewhere deeply within was the sense his strayings were against the grain. Whereas some of his friends seemed to party hearty—like it was a natural part of them, like they were supposed to indulge, by spiritual instinct he knew that he wasn't supposed to. The flesh versus the spirit was the battle.

Now he was approaching fifty. He had found himself, in recent years, looking more toward the things of God. He studied the Bible more—on his own. He attended church more. He prayed more.

He was a little nervous about seeing Jan tonight. And for reasons he couldn't explain, he was a little nervous about attending Bible class. He more often attended church these days, but he had been slow about attending midweek services.

He had a quick mental flash of the stranger he had met in the mall. As he drove, Reese revisited the scene in his mind. When he had driven into the parking lot, it had been less than half-empty, being early morning, a little too early today for shoppers. Reese could have parked in FCI's corporate lot, but he had been a little early for his appointment, and he always enjoyed checking the latest fashion on display at Horshak's. As he had turned into a parking stall, he was pretty sure of it now, as he did a mental picture;there had been someone walking his way at the other end of the garage. His mind had been focused on seeing Al today, on the interview. Reese had parked, gathered his portfolio, exited his Santa Fe. And the stranger had been suddenly there, standing at the tail end of his SUV. Reese thought about the size of the multilevel, enclosed parking lot. It was huge. It served the mall patrons on one side of the street and also some of the FCI employees, FCI being on the other side of the street and connected to the mall by the skywalk. The parking garage was so large; the figure Reese had seen walking down the driveway could not have reached his car that soon. And there had not been anyone else in the parking lot. Reese had taken note of how empty the garage had seemed this early in the morning. Often he had been irritatingly aware of how crowded it was on certain days and certain hours of the day—he had formulated parking strategies in the past to make sure he was on time for his FCI interviews.

And when he had led the man to the bookstore, the man had not gone in. And he had a cane he didn't seem to use or need. Could be something for physical pain that only occasionally flared up, though, or it could have just been a prop, a part of his personality, a part of his style.

And those words—your calling and election sure—something about life and trouble and seeking the chosen? Cryptic comments from an encounter with a strange man. Probably nothing else to it. He should be able to dismiss it at that. But he couldn't. He couldn't explain it, but he felt there was purpose behind that encounter. More to come.

He had reached the south end of Kansas City, south of Interstate 435 where he lived. He liked the semi-suburban feel of the location.

He parked in the driveway of his attached two-car garage, ascended the steps to his California bi level. Split level, bi-level, whatever, to the left you went down to the family room; to the right you went up into the living room and space opening just ahead, and beyond that into the dining room with its floor-to-ceiling window looking onto the backyard. Up and straight ahead the saloon-type doors led into the kitchen with its large rectangular window looking onto the backyard. Reese had long ago vacated the family room, since his divorce. Even when he had been married, they had rarely used the room, viewing TV and entertaining in the living room. He had kept all rooms furnished, though. It still felt like home and looked like home: sofas, coffee tables, artwork on the walls. He still maintained his floor-to-ceiling potted indoor tree. He still gave the furniture a quick dusting and Johnson's wax occasionally.

Turning left at the short flight of stairs up, Reese went down the short hallway, passing the guest bath on his left and the third bedroom on his right; in four steps he turned left at the end of the hall into his bedroom. The second bedroom opposite the master bedroom served as his office. He kicked his shoes off, backtracked across the hall to his office. He sat at his desk, looked out the large rectangular window at the empty farmer's field. The field was rural, in a semi-suburban community, and took up several acres; Reese had met the owner once when he moved in. A friendly man— Mr. McClure, or McCormick or something like that. Reese rarely saw him except through his window at spring planting time or at harvesttime.

A couple of bills and a lot of direct mail marketing comprised the postman's delivery today. Reese filed the bills—to be paid later—tossed the marketing stuff, and headed for the kitchen to find something to eat. He heated a bowl of chili. It was a Cajun recipe he had gotten from a Prudhomme book, and he did it well, and he didn't have to say so himself. A couple of his friends loved it. When they were over, they often tried to get him to cook up some.

He threw together a spinach salad, opened a Coke. Chili, salad, and Coke. Not gourmet, but it worked.

After eating, he checked his messages. A couple of his buddies had called—Jon and his cousin Reggie. He also had a call from Jan. He'd get to Jon and Reggie later. He did a quick dish wash and went to his office to call Jan. She answered on the third ring, "Hello." All sweetness and light.

"What's up, baby girl!"

"Oh, hi!" Reese could hear the genuine gladness in her voice. She wasn't good at faking anything.

"Just got in, ate dinner, was thinking about you. In fact been thinking about you all day."

"Really?—All day?"

"All day long, baby girl—honest to god, wouldn't lie."

"Really—well, speaking of god . . ."

"Yes, I am going to Bible class with you tonight, just as I promised, have not changed my mind."

She laughed pleasantly.

"That is so nice to hear, Reese, for real."

Reese knew Jan was a very sensitive and tenderhearted girl. Very honest and transparent in her emotions. He wouldn't be surprised if a tear was welling up even now.

"What time should I pick you up?"

"About seven thirty?"

"Sounds good."

"Be sure and bring your Bible."

"It's right here—on my desk. And I have been reading it. No dust on it." They both laughed, thinking back about a joke they had shared. Reese asked, "How was your day?"

"Per usual. I spent most of it with my client at the food pantry, and then we went shopping at JC Penny's. I'm trying to get her ready for a job interview."

Jan had landed a good social worker job many years ago, and she still loved it. She worked in a small community mental health center that had focus on getting the mental patients employed. Not a lot of stress, but a lot of frustration, but she had learned to live with it and enjoyed her work. Trying to orient a segment of the population that had a weak work ethic to the world and discipline of work was not easy. Reese at times wondered just how she did it and how she could enjoy it. The helping aspect of it, that he liked, and admired her for it. He hoped someday, he could migrate that way. Maybe. But the frustration—she had told him once—the job retention rate of clients she assisted into the workforce was less than 10 percent; for every ten clients she helped into the workforce, nine of them failed to stay employed. She spent days coaching clients to interview properly. Taught them the how-to of dressing. Took them to the bus routes until they learned them well enough to take the bus on their own. Gave them grooming and hygiene classes. And then, started all over again, too frequently with the same individuals. The center she worked at depended heavily on government support and private-sector donations. FCI was one of the locally based corporations that made large contributions to keep it afloat. FCI seemed to be the perfect corporate good citizen Reese happened to reflect. Made him think of Al's comments this morning. He was very much interested in following up on that.

"Is she ready to go to work?"

"She's ready. About as ready as she'll ever be." Reese heard a little doubt in Jan's voice, but he didn't push it. They had learned to respect the confidentiality built into each of their employments. She added, "FCI need any junior execs?" They both laughed.

Reese said, "Well, I'm going to go, take a few minutes to relax, get myself together, catch the news . . . I'll see you at seven thirty."

"Love you."

"Love you." He hung up. He went into the living room, turned on the evening news. As usual, all of the news was bad, excluding the last-three-minute good-humor piece. An earthquake in Japan, typhoon in China. Several car bombings in the Mideast. A subtle threat from Russia, genocide in Africa. Reese thought about the Bible's scriptures on the last days—"wars and rumors of wars . . . earthquakes in diverse places . . . nation against nation."

Once, in reflecting on the condition of the human family, Reese had envisioned man's stay on earth. From Adam and Eve, the family had continually progressed. But what did that really mean— "progress"? It meant that we had learned to make the material world, the elements of nature work for us. We had learned the laws of nature and used our creativity to make things. Things that made work easier for us. We pulled stuff out of the earth, shaped it, manipulated it, mixed it with other stuff pulled out of the earth, and assembled it into useful product. From the use of sticks for leverage and stones for wheels to harnessing animals, to Boeing 747s. And in it all, it seemed to him that there had to be a destiny, that it was all leading to some significant point, that all down here on the ground was not just happenstance without meaning. It wasn't just a natural order of the progress of stronger things of life progressively surviving, evolving into ever-higher but purposeless forms of life. That could not be. Look at what the Bible said about man's heart and spirit and the future of the human race. And look at so-called progress, from the spiritual side. Man's heart—the invisible, inner, spiritual side of the species. No progress at all. Not one case to be made of progress since the report of Cain killing Abel. Turn on the TV, on any given day, listen to the news. Wars, murders, thefts, oppression, drug addiction, political upheaval, corruption in high places. Violence filled the earth, just as in "the days of Lot." And the natural disasters. One slow day, at the end of an early day, Reese had taken the time to visit the downtown library. He had wanted to do some research on some of the things he had been taught from childhood about the period of the last days according to the Bible. His parents had always taught him that things would "wax worse and worse"; they had been quoting from Paul's letter to Timothy. And they had told him that earthquakes in diverse places, and wars, would increase, that it was like a mother nearing the time to deliver a baby. The "birth pangs came more frequently and became more severe." Bishop Padduck's sermon on a particular Sunday had been on this subject in this vein, so on this slow Monday—he had been near the library and a piece of news he was listening to on the radio, about an outbreak of war in Africa, had triggered the idea—the bishop's sermon had come to mind. The bishop's sermon had emphasized the downward spiral of human behavior. "Perilous times shall come, the Bible says, but I tell you perilous times are already here!" Hand cupped behind ear, voice large, hand on hip, leaning back, the audience had stood on their feet, praising the Lord. It had been a good sermon. Reese believed his parents. He believed his pastor; he believed the Bible. But at times, doubt rose; his faith got weak.

Bishop Padduck had ended his sermon in small voice, warning that declension, decline—of a person, of a people, of humanity—happened slowly over time, almost imperceptibly.

So on that slow Monday, Reese found himself at the library. He looked up the recorded history of natural disasters, specifically earthquakes, since the time of Christ's birth. He understood the "last days" meant the time beginning since Christ. He studied the data, covering the number of earthquakes, the intensity of them, where they occurred, when they occurred. And it was true. Over the past two thousand years, numerous earthquakes had occurred. As he moved across the chart, he saw that the frequency of earthquakes had increased. And the intensity of them had too. He next looked at military uprisings. There had always been wars, but they had increased with time too.

The thing that registered with Reese was that we had been able to master our environment, make the material world produce all kinds of luxurious living for us—but we couldn't master our own individual hearts. We couldn't master lust, hatred, murder, deceit, theft, jealousy, and envy.

So with the planet's population increasing every day—now approaching seven billion souls—and with technology and the progress of technology making the planet an even smaller place to live and with Cain's heart making multiples of weapons of mass destruction of all kinds, the earth was becoming an increasingly more dangerous place to live. He had concluded that the scientific data had supported the Bible's messages about the "last days" and "perilous times to come." And more recently global warming had become an additional planetary threat.

Reese dozed lightly. The shout of *Wheel of Fortune* on the TV woke him. He played along for a few minutes, then headed for the shower, took a good soapy wash down, and dressed. He did a quick visual check of his office—out of habit—saw his attaché on the floor and one of the bills he had received in the mail today. Good thing he checked; he was almost forgetting his Bible. He loved order, a tidy desk; he placed his attaché on the desk, arranged a couple of papers, grabbed his Bible. A few minutes later, he was northbound en route to pick up Jan.

She was waiting for him at the doorway of her town house. Jan lived in a nice three-bed, two-story town house off Interstate 435 and Holmes Road. A quiet—despite the interstate traffic—well-treed neighborhood. Reese had been dating her for well more than a year. He had met her at a singles social at church, and he had initially been taken by her looks: thin, five feet seven inches, tannish skin, shiny black hair with just a hint of "ethnic curl," as she laughingly put it. She reminded Reese of Ashley Judd, the actor.

After their first dinner, Reese found he liked her spirit and attitude and definitely intended to see her again. "Pleasant, intelligent, and fine" were the three adjectives that came to mind about her. She was not the most sexually stimulating—at least sexual arousal was not the primary factor between them. And that was more than fine with Reese. He had been looking for years for a good wife. He wanted a wife, a friend, a companion, and love—the kind of love between a man and a woman that God intended. Sex took care of itself. He had, though, at times fantasized; and he suspected that behind that pleasant, decent personality was a passionate, stimulating woman.

They had both recently hinted at marriage in their conversations. Each time, though, they had ended their dialogue in embarrassed laughter. Too cool to show embarrassment, Reese had deftly steered the conversations into other avenues. Both of them had been married before; both former spouses had deceased. Reese's wife had died at a young age, shortly after she had left the church and him. It was amazing, and kind of nice, that they were able still, even at this stage in life, to feel like teenagers in love.

In a simple dress and boots, Jan slid into the SUV. They both smiled at each other, happy to be together.

"I am on time, and I do have my Bible."

Jan patted his knee.

"I am so proud of you," she giggled.

They drove north in I-435, twenty-three minutes later pulled into the parking lot of the church.

The church was only partially filled. This was a seven-thousand-plus-membership church, which qualified it as a mega church, and especially so in a city of Kansas City's population. It was something of a unique church. Approximately 60 percent white, 20 percent black, and 20 percent other flavors. The pastor was a baptized, Holy Ghost—filled man of high integrity. He believed in speaking in tongues, and had done so, although never while preaching, according to the dictates of scripture. Tall, of African descent, elegant, with a Th.D from an accredited school of theology. A man who knew scripture and knew how to rightly divide it. Bishop Padduck was frequently sought out by other pastors and spent large blocks of his time teaching classes, conducting seminars, and writing pastoral letters. He did not care about fame or fortune; he spent his money on tasteful clothes and cars, but not to excess. A lot of his income was cycled back into the church.

In spite of his expanded clergy duties, he was faithful in attendance at his own church. And he found time—he made time—to study and to fast and pray. And he stayed abreast of current trends—from cultural, to artistic to social and political, locally, nationally, and internationally.

After the praise service, Bishop Padduck stood and approached the podium. He always reminded Reese of Harry Belafonte, a good-looking tall man. And he had a bent—unlike a lot of ethnic preachers—toward yuppie clothing: button-down collar shirts, blazer sport coats, slip-on wingtip, or cap toe shoes. Tonight he wore a navy blazer, tan slacks, penny loafers, button down collar shirt.

Reese took a quick casual look around the church. More people had come in, but Reese estimated there were still fewer than two hundred in attendance. As his head swept back, his eye caught two men sitting together just to his rear in the far left section of the church. They sat together on the end seat, with an empty seat between them—together but not gay perhaps was the message. They both had on sport jackets. Not unusual here. One wore a black crew neck shirt, the other, a plain off-white shirt. Hard looks on thin faces, one with a skinhead-type haircut, the other ponytailed. They looked out of place. They quickly broke eye contact. As Reese looked back toward the pulpit, he had the feeling they had been staring at him.

Bishop Padduck began, "You need to make your calling and election sure."

With a start, Reese went full focus on the message. He had a quick flashback to the man with the cane.

"I had another topic in mind for tonight's class, dear saints, but the spirit has led me in another direction. While I was reading the word earlier today, preparing for this class, a silent voice came to me—oh, some of you out there know what I'm talkin' about."

"Preach, Brother!" Brother Broes expected response to the call. A faithful brother long time in the church, he was one of the most responsive during sermons. Reese smiled. But he recognized the serious tone of the Bishop's message.

"Somebody out there is sayin', he's gettin' old, he's hallucinatin'?, hearing voices, but some of you out there know the real deal."

"Come on, Pastor!!"

Another response. Reese had to smile again.

"But some of you need to make your calling and election sure. Simply that, simple as that, that's the message." Padduck's outstretched arm and a finger swept the width of the auditorium. Silence. Reese felt his pulse quicken. In spite of his increased walk with the Lord, he knew he was not quite where he should be. He was beginning to recognize when the spirit was nodding in his direction. Lately, uncomfortably aware of it. Padduck went on.

"Some of you are too spiritually dull of hearing, too insensitive, too carnal to respond to the word. Some of you are too stubborn. Some of you, well, you just don't really believe." Padduck took a few paces across the podium, looking over the audience. A few eyes avoided contact with his.

"The spirit is talking to you who believe—who have been baptized, have even spoken in tongues, supposed to be saved!" Silence.

Reese felt a stab in his right arm. Jan was pointing to her cell phone. The message on the screen read.

"Mom is sick, wants you here now."

Jan whispered, "Let's go."

Reese felt relief. He was glad to be leaving, yet he wanted to hear more at the same time. He stood, killing guilt and self-consciousness as he and Jan started toward the side exit. He looked back just before the exit door closed, and he saw the two men he had noticed earlier walking toward the rear of the church.

He filled his lungs full of the slightly chilled fall night air. It felt good. Jan had a slightly worried look on her face as they drove back toward her town house. She dialed her mother's phone number. Her sister Sylvia was there. Jan listened for a few minutes, flipped her cell phone closed.

"Sounds like just another one of Mom's asthma attacks. Sylvia's there, but . . . she wants me to come over." She looked straight ahead, poker-faced.

Jan's mom lived just a few blocks from her town house. When Reese pulled up in front of her mom's house, Janet leaned over, kissed Reese, and then embraced him. He responded. She got out, still a worried look on her face.

"Love you—I will call you."

Reese drove toward home. He thought about the message Bishop Padduck started that he wished/didn't wish he could have heard. And the words of the stranger with the cane he had met today. To make his calling and election sure. He felt that he was moving in that direction—if he understood what was meant by those words—but he wasn't there yet. That he knew.

He pulled into his driveway a few minutes past nine. He felt good about having taken the step toward a return to attending Bible class. He hadn't attended a midweek service in a long time. As a child, he had to go every Wednesday night. In adulthood he had long ago strayed from that level of faithfulness, although he wasn't quite sure how internally faithful he had been as a child since most of his Bible-class attendance had been by parental decree.

He started up the steps, unlocked his door, started up to the living room.

Something was a little bit off, not quite right. He sensed an alarm go off in his head; his pulse quickened.

He knew his house smells, recognized them without even being conscious of it.

He sniffed again.

What was he picking up? If it wasn't his imagination, it was the smell he got when he occasionally visited a nearby gym. The smell of perspiration, of human sweat. How could that be? He thought of the possibilities. He hadn't broken a sweat all day.

At times, when he opened his window for fresh air, he picked up the smells of his neighborhood. He recognized them. Not too many blocks away was a chemical manufacturing plant, and at times Reese caught the faintly, sweetly sticky smell of whatever runoff came from whatever chemicals they were making. But it was barely an insult to his olfactory sense.

But this—his heart raced a little more—this was the smell of a person. Masculine, Reese would guess. He tried to think what to do. He had not left any lights on, leaving when he had with his mind on Jan and church. He stood still, listening. He could backtrack to his car, then what? Run to the neighbor's house?

Heart beating fast, he walked toward his bedroom, his body tense. He kept a sig-sauer .9 millimeter in the nightstand next to his bed. He tried to make his steps sound normal. As soon as he reached the nightstand, holding his breath, he reached inside. The gun was still there! He hurriedly opened the case and made the loud noise of pulling the slide back, loading a Winchester into the chamber. He called on the name of the Lord under his breath and started back to the entrance to his bedroom, flipping the lights on.

Everything looked in place. He checked the master bedroom bathroom. No one there. Nothing out of place. He checked the hall bathroom and the adjacent room. That left his office.

With the sig held at his thigh (he could have sworn he had left the door wide open before he had left for church), he paused for a second, pushed the door hard, stepped back behind the wall. Nothing. He flipped the light on. Something was not quite right. He couldn't pinpoint what. He'd feel safer if he checked the rest of the house first though.

He entered the kitchen, turned on the light, the sig-sauer now in his waistband. The kitchen and dining room looked OK at first sight. He walked over to the door leading from the kitchen to the backyard. He turned the outdoor floodlights on. A lone possum stopped briefly, then continued to mosey along.

He went down the steps, down to the entryway, another five steps down to the family room. He flipped on the light. Sofa, desk, coffee table—all as they had been. He almost never used this part of the house. At the bottom of the stairs, the door on the left led to the basement where the furnace and water heater were. He mentally bit the bullet—no place to hide after he opened the door—and shoved the door open hard, quickly reached in, and turned the lights on. Nothing out of place. Cobwebs along the ceiling at the rear. Storage shelves with old suitcases, discarded vacuum cleaners, some old tools. He quickly looked under the bottom shelves, feeling kind of silly as he turned out the light and went back upstairs. The sweaty smell was dissipating, but it was still evident. He walked back into his office. But still, something bothered him. He went back to the kitchen.

There, that was it. The back door was unlocked.

It wasn't apparent at first, but moving closer, Reese could see that the door was about a quarter inch or so from being fully closed and locked. Reese pulled the knob. Tight enough fit to keep it from swaying open, but the door opened easy enough without him having to turn the knob. He felt a slight jerk of dismay. But maybe he had left it open. Could have been unlocked for days—he hadn't been in the backyard, hadn't opened this door in several days. He locked the door.

Reese mentally retraced his steps before he had left for church. He had put some order to his desk.

He hurried back to his office. He had left his desk in tidy order, had done so after he picked up his attaché and the bill he had gotten in the mail today.

His attaché was open and sitting at a cocked angle on his desk, and a desk drawer was partially open. Somebody had been here and had left in a hurry. And robbery didn't seem to be the reason for the break-in.

Reese sat down hard. He tried to think of the implications.

Could one of his neighbors have done this? Not likely. He was the only multiethnic person in the neighborhood, which was for the most part made up of law-abiding citizens. Middle class, with a fair degree of success. It was rare that a break-in occurred here. Reese in reality couldn't recall having heard of any since he'd been living here.

He was also the only one out here who was not married. Both personal profiles could make him suspect. But Reese didn't think so. He knew his neighbors pretty well—Cole on his right, James on his left. They got along fine. No tensions. A year or so ago, the three of them had actually spent a weekend together camping and fishing. They were a neighborhood, all comfortable with and trusting each other.

Maybe something or somebody with FCI? He wasn't sure why he had such a thought. In all of his visits to FCI, he had picked up a sense of the culture there. And there was something secretive . . . something wary? . . . something distant about it in spite of the cultured surface friendliness of the people there. They hired only the best—the socially skilled and fit. Reese always left the place feeling that he had been interviewed in spite of the fact that he was the one asking the questions. And on many occasions he had the sense that the interviewee knew the questions before even asked them.

FCI was big and powerful, and well connected. Reese had a couple of friends who worked there. He remembered all of the hoops they had to jump through to get hired, the endless background checks, the personal-life scrutiny—you'd have thought they were applying for director of national intelligence.

Reese thought back to one of his early interviews with an executive of FCI. He'd been waiting in the corporate lobby, watching the come and go of FCI traffic.

Two big men had entered from the corporate parking lot. Had to be at least six feet four to six feet six, 250 lbs or so. They spoke to the receptionist and had looked at Reese. To his surprise, they had come down the steps; and before he could put two and two together, they were standing over him. Friendly—on the surface—and at the same time intimidating, suit jackets unbuttoned.

"Hi, are you Reese?" This from the big blond with an accent, European accent it had sounded to Reese.

"Well . . ." Reese had started to use a phrase he had heard on television so many times, in similar situations. "Who wants to know?" But he had thought better of it.

"Yeah, I'm Reese," he had said instead.

"You're here to see Harold"—stated matter-of-factly.

"That's right."

They both sat, both facing Reese, who sat on the oversize sofa, feeling intimidated, wondering if passersby were looking.

"What do you want to see Harold about?" This from the big no-accent guy.

Reese had been annoyed, and he had felt some anger rising. He had cooled it and said, "Just doing a magazine market research survey—a readership survey."

They had stared coldly at him for a moment.

"A survey."

"A simple survey," Reese had responded.

"Can we see it?" The guy with the accent had looked at him intently.

"No, you cannot." Reese heard his last word expressed a decibel higher. Both men cocked their heads slightly and continued to stare. A little anger had showed on both faces. Reese broke the tension,

"This is a confidential survey. By signed contract, I am prohibited from revealing any information about it to any third parties. I'm not supposed to let anyone know anything about the contents of it. My employer wouldn't appreciate it, neither would the publisher—and

I think FCI would be of the same opinion." had pushed it a little. "I believe Harold cleared it at the corporate level."

"You and Harold—both of you cleared it at the corporate level?"

"Yes."

"OK, Mr. Maxey, we'll speak with our office. Have a good day." They both had had smiles of mission accomplished when they stood and made their exit.

Reese had been a little disturbed by the encounter. He had sat on pins and needles until Harold had come to escort him to an interview room. Harold was polite, a little distant, but he had made no reference to Reese's exchange with the two men. And the interview had gone smoothly.

Still unsettled, rattled, Reese, with his gun in his waistband, turned on his porch light, brought his SUV into the garage. He left the porch light on and the backyard flood lights on and went to bed.

The next two workdays were uneventful. Reese called on a pharmacist for a drug trade magazine and visited two lawyers for two surveys of the *ABA Professional Journal*. Jan called the first night. Her mom was doing well, and she believed that partly her asthma "attack" was just a way of getting to see her daughter.

It was a balmy day, and it was a Saturday. Reese had his cousin Reggie and his old college buddy Jon Darrett over. Time to chill out on the patio. He would do some burgers and dogs. He knew they wanted some of his chili. Next time maybe.

Jonathan was a special agent with the FBI. Reggie was pastor of a small but growing flock. They had taken an old home, a large old home he had bought on the cheap and converted into a church. A lot of money had gone into the project, but it had been much, much cheaper than buying a church.

He threw a few patties of beef on the grill and a few sausage dogs, brought bread to the patio table, condiments, salad makings, prepackaged potato salad.

He found the cooler, filled it with ice and cola, a Pepsi, and several cans of Dr. Pepper. Nothing fancy but food appropriate and satisfying enough for a barbecue on a fall Saturday. Just cool enough for long-sleeve jerseys or a sweater. Reese had always been a sweater guy, and he chose an old cable-knit wool one over jeans and desert boots. His backyard faced the sun from the east—that would help.

They went through the preliminaries of "What's up!" "What's goin' on?" and "Who won the game?" and kicked back on the patio.

All three of them were relatively tall—over six feet. All three had attended the local university of Missouri at Kansas City. Jon had gone on into the service right after college. Four years later, he had come back for a few weeks, then gone on to graduate school at the University of Maryland and then on into the Federal Bureau of Investigation training program. His wife—part Ethiopian and part Italian—had returned with him from overseas and, it was apparent to Reese, had been a strong support in a good marriage.

Jon had worked in the New York field office at the bureau, had transferred around a time or two, and had cycled back to Kansas City to finish a successful government career here.

Reggie had attended college a year behind Reese. They had spent some time partying together during the college years. After college, Reggie had left Reese behind spiritually, having returned to the church, gone on to Bible College, and later taken a masters in theology at a reputable school of theology.

Jon wore a Windbreaker, and Reggie, a fresh-from-the-washer sweatshirt, both in khakis and tennis shoes. They sat triangular around Reese's patio table. A cell phone rang, and all three reached for their phones not exactly sure which had rung.

"How are you!" Reggie's face lit up as he turned slightly away from Reese and Jon.

"Glad to hear from you, wasn't sure if you were going to call . . ."
He listened and talked intermittently.

"Sure . . . that works, right after church. See you then." He turned back to the table, folded his cell phone,

"That was one of my Muslim brothers."

"Muslim brother—sounds like an oxymoron," Jon laughed; Reese smiled and chuckled.

"I mean, he used to be a Muslim—he's coming into the church now, that's what we're meeting about, what he wanted to talk about."

"Coming into the faith—that's good to hear," Reese said.

"Yeah, sometimes it seems like Islam is growing and Christianity is losing members," Jon added.

Reese thought about some of the reports he'd read recently.

"Seems to me the trend is toward unity, though. Every time I pick up a copy of *Global Week* or *Time* or *Newsweek*, there's some kind of article advocating Christians, Jews, and Muslims to unite, you know, get together, make one world of religion."

"That might stop a lot of fighting, make the world a safer place," Jon said.

"That is impossible," Reggie said; he leaned toward Reese and Jon, a more serious look than Reese would have expected on his face.

"Why is it?" Reese asked. He was curious about Reggie's point and suspected he was right.

"Do you believe the Bible?" Reggie looked at Reese.

"Well, sure—you know I do."

"Do you?" Reggie looked at Jon.

"Sure, I am a believer."

"No, I mean do you believe it verbatim—word for word, literal interpretation about the future?"

"Yeah, man, we're all Christians here," Reese threw in. Wanting to impress faithful Reggie that he believed and knew the Bible, he went on, "You know . . . you read Isaiah and you see where he prophesied about the birth of Christ seven hundred years before it happened, and you read Daniel, and you see that when he interpreted Nebuchadnezzar's dream, he saw the future governments of the world, and it has come to pass just as it was written. And"—Reese went on, sitting forward, index finger pointing upward, warming to the subject—"and Daniel predicted, down to the very day when Messiah would ride a colt into the city of Jerusalem—which he did two thousand years ago." He felt a little bit over his head, but he was pleased to see a hint of surprise on Reggie's and Jon's faces. He continued.

"You have enough evidence of past prophecies having come to pass, therefore, anyone should conclude that those predicted of the future that have not yet been fulfilled someday will be fulfilled. You need to know your Bible, though," he added mock condescendingly. All three of them laughed.

Reggie took up.

"And that's why I know that a worldwide religion will not work." He took a sip of his Coke.

"And before the return of the Lord, the Bible says first there will be a great falling away from the church. Paul wrote that to the Thessalonians. So coming into some kind of unity of world religion is contrary to scripture"—Reggie paused for a second—"unless it is the false religion of the Antichrist, the beast, and the false prophet during the great tribulation." He went on, "but you are right about the magazine articles—there are some who would like to see a world religion, they think it's one of the answers to bringing peace to the earth."

"But they don't recognize the prince of peace," Jon threw in.

"And that's the problem," Reggie added. Reese jumped in.

"Isn't it somewhere in the Bible that all the nations of the earth will eventually turn against Israel?"

Reggie nodded. "In the last days—that's one of the prophecies of Zechariah. I think we are getting near that time." Reese and Jon sat attentively, waiting; Reggie went on, "Look at Israel. She sits alone over there in the Middle East. Surrounded by nations—who hate her, who would like to wipe her off the face of the earth, despised by the nations is the way the scripture puts it. The United States has been her powerful friend, to date. This tiny nation, reborn in 1948—her rebirth, and her importance in international politics relative to her size should tell the world there's something unusual about her—is becoming more and more isolated, just as the Bible prophesied."

A natural-born teacher, Reese thought as he watched Reggie's enthusiasm. "American power and influence is declining. Eastern cultures, India, and Arabs and Arab oil—and the unity of Europe and the Euro, that's where it's at—or where world focus is going in the future."

Reese thought about Reggie's comments for a second.

"But Israel is determined to survive, and in her own land."

Reggie nodded affirmatively.

Jon said, "I can see why some would think that bringing Arabs, Islam, and Christianity and Judaism together would reduce violence."

Reggie nodded. "Ain't gonna happen, though."

"But," Jon said, thinking as he talked, "what if each religion could keep its, I don't knew, its title, and at the same time, interact, you know, worship with other religions . . ." Unable to finish the thought in a logical conclusion, he trailed off.

Reggie picked up, "The problem is Mohammed's book said that the infidel—those who don't believe in Allah—is to be destroyed, that the worship of Allah would be global someday. The Bible says that the only way to the one true God is through Christ, and that one day Christ will rule the earth." Reggie shook his head negatively.

"Two mutually exclusive paths to God," Jon said.

They sat silently for a moment, reflecting on their comments, Reese said, "OK, enough religion talk now."

But the image of the man with the cane flashed momentarily, and he wanted to ask Reggie about that. He also wanted to ask Jon some questions about FCI.

"But before we leave the subject," he said, "I want to ask you something, Reggie." He felt awkward. "Uh, nothing, ask you later. It's not that important anyway."

"Aw, come on," Reggie said.

"Well . . . do you believe that you can . . ." He wasn't exactly sure how to phrase the question.

"Is it possible that an encounter with a stranger could, maybe, have some significance . . . some, maybe, supernatural . . . could have something meaningful in a spiritual sense about it?" he finished awkwardly.

"Reggie looked thoughtful for a moment then said, "You mean like meeting an angel or something?"

Something flashed in Reese's head. Maybe that was it.

"Well, I wasn't thinking about angels, but yeah, do you believe that's possible . . . ?"

"Well, I don't know, cous. I know that Paul wrote that some have entertained angels unaware. And there are dozens of scriptures about angels. I mean, they are real, and the Bible is definite about that. And they have visited us on earth. So"—Reggie let it hang there, an inquisitive look on his face—"if the Lord is dealing with you in this manner, you should pay attention to it." He reached for another Coke just as his cell phone rang.

"OK . . . I'll meet her at the hospital." He had a sober look on his face as he closed his cell phone, stood up.

"Gotta run. One of my members was just rushed to the hospital, not sure what the problem is."

Reese saw Reggie to the door. They did a tentative reschedule for another BBQ, and Reese returned to the patio. Jon was well into his hamburger. He wanted to ask Jon about FCI. He wasn't sure how much Jon knew about them, but with what had happened at his house—or with what he suspected had happened—with John being FBI, maybe he would have some advice or some insight.

"Hey, I want to ask you something . . . you know, I've been talking to FCI about doing some work for them . . ." Reese paused for a second. They hadn't actually offered him a job. He was jumping to hope-filled conclusions. Maybe Al actually had something in mind—it could be for another company. Or it could have been just rhetoric—just conversation to prevent awkward silence for two relative strangers walking together en route to separate destinations, conversation to kill silence. But Reese recalled his sense of directed purpose behind Al's questions.

"Working for FCI, that's hip, man. Opportunity there, I'd take it. How long to your retirement?"

A reminder there of his age. Might or might not be a time to job change. But as a contractor, he didn't have any invested savings in *Readscan*.

"Retirement," Reese said, "I haven't thought too much about that. Probably work until I die." He hadn't invested a whole lot of thought or money into the future, not since his divorce. He didn't particularly want to sit around doing nothing, though—not ever.

"I'm not talking about a payroll job. If anything develops, I'll continue to work as a contractor."

"Lot to be said for contract work. You're your own boss, come and go as you please."

"Do you know anything about FCI? They'd probably do a background check on me . . ."

"From what I've heard, they do background checks—extensive investigations—on anybody that does anything with them." They're a somewhat secretive company. They're publicly traded, so we"—Jon coughed—"the public has access to their business, but they . . . operate like a privately held company. I don't know how they get away with some stuff, but they're well connected."

"What do you mean by 'secretive'?"

"I don't know—just scuttlebutt I've heard around the office."

"So they are on your radar."

"Not really."

Reese thought for a moment. "Is it possible, that if they were interested in me working for them, that they would have searched my home without, well, when I wasn't here—you know, as part of a background check on me?"

Jon gave Reese a stare; taking in his question, he said, "That's interesting," still looking at Reese.

"Interesting?"

"Interesting. You know, you triggered something, an incident I hadn't given a second thought until you asked that question."

"What's up?"

"Well, a few months ago, I'm in the office shuffling some paper. And there was some kind of list, or it was some case files, don't recall which, but by accident, they landed on my desk, so I read some of them for a while before I realized they weren't mine. I recall seeing a sheet that had something on it about an employee filing a lawsuit about a burglary, that got my eye because we normally don't investigate routine burglaries. I scanned it—still don't recall all the details—but it had something to do with an employee, or soon-to-be employee, filing a lawsuit, some guy from some Jewish organization had filed a lawsuit charging FCI with invasion of privacy and home burglary. It's kind of fuzzy—it wasn't my case—but it seemed the guy had come up missing. Maybe that's how our office got involved in it."

Jon looked at Reese closer. "You know, it's not anything I could get into, but that case, whatever it was, and your question . . . that is interesting."

"You recall anything else about it?" Reese felt his heart beating a little faster.

"It's real fuzzy, Reese—I wouldn't even remember this much about it if you hadn't asked the question."

"Overall, my impression of FCI is good—if you like that kind of environment. They pay well—extremely well. I had a friend there, and yeah, I do remember him talking about all the scrutiny he had to go through to get employed . . . but you know, I know of a couple of other people who work there, they live well, drive well, live in one of the best neighborhoods of Kansas City . . ."

"OK, dude, appreciate that piece of information."

"Well, we've got to do this again, get a couple more of the homies over here." Jon stood up. "What about the Bullet Hole?"

He had almost forgotten. He and John had membership in a shooters club and frequently target practiced together.

"Say when," Reese said.

"Well, I'll call you sometime in the very near future."

Sounded vague enough for Reese, he said, "Sounds good."

Reese watched Jon cruise his BMW slowly up the street to the stop sign and then accelerate with zip toward home.

That night, before going to bed, Reese double-checked his doors, propped both of them, said prayers, went to bed with intent to get to Sunday school.

On Sunday, Reese's neighbor interrupted his plans to go to church. Cole, who had heavy responsibility for American Airlines in Kansas City, at their overhaul base had an emergency. He had to go to Kansas City International Airport, and his wife and daughter, who were down in Warrensburg, Missouri, had to get home. Some kind of program his daughter had to attend that afternoon.

Reese good-naturedly stood at his front door and told Cole, "No problem, be glad to pick up your wife and daughter." In his head he heard a *Curse it!* go off.

Cole reached into his pocket and offered two one-hundred-dollar bills. Gas had gotten high, but it hadn't got that high.

"You've got to be kiddin', Reese said. Cole looked at the two bills, back at Reese.

"Are they counterfeit?" Reese had to laugh.

"Keep your money, I don't mind giving you a hand, Cole," and he was beginning to feel it. It occurred to him to ask about a possible break-in.

"Hey, have you seen anyone at my place, you know, evening, when I wasn't here?"

"Naw . . . sure haven't . . ." It was the answer Reese expected.

Getting Cole's family back home took up most of the afternoon. Reese wished he'd taken Cole's money.

Monday was uneventful. Reese's occasional, call-when-you-need-me "assistant" Laurie was a part-time student at UMKC who worked out of her apartment near the university campus, had set up two interviews for him at the University of Kansas for Science Magazine with two PhD's.

Reese read through the study—the questionnaire. There were the usual questions on the articles and editorials, a note for him to focus on readers' responses to ad formats, and there was focus on readers' name recognition of the companies and brands advertising chemicals and of those advertising centrifuges.

At the end of the survey, there was the usual section for collecting demographic data. What struck Reese were the new questions about faith and religion and, particularly, the questions that asked if the reader worked in a setting that encouraged time off for physical exercise at work and for religious worship or prayer. That question was followed by "Do you feel that time off for physical exercise in the workplace would be beneficial to the workplace?" followed by "Why, why not?" The same question was posed for time off for religious worship at work followed by "Why or why not?"

On closer reading the instructions and suggestions that came with the survey, Reese noticed, with some disappointment that he was not to ask these questions. They were typed on addendum pages attached to a postage-paid preaddressed envelope. In addition, Reese was authorized to give a one-hundred-dollar incentive to respondents who were willing to complete the written part of the questionnaire and return it.

Reese had tracked, albeit lazily, the occurrence of spiritual and religious-oriented questions. They had increased in the past year. And the breadth of audience—professional, business, government—had expanded.

Church and work, Reese mused. There was something disturbing about that. He made a note to be more cognizant of what was going on in this area of church, state, and business. Before he left for the University of Kansas, he devised a minisurvey of his own; he had some questions about the faith of this survey's readers.

Taking time to devise a survey turned out to be a waste of time today, though. When he arrived at the office of the professor he was to interview, the spotlight was on the six-feet-seven pro basketball player, who was getting all the attention. Back to visit his alma mater, apparently the player and the professor Reese was seeing had some kind of rapport—they were in his office, with three others, all in awe. Reese got rushed, quick-answer responses from the only-half-attentive professor. Reese got the player's autograph—he had never been a fan, though—and drove back to Kansas City.

CHAPTER

2

Reese woke on Wednesday with a sense of anticipation. He was going to FCI today. First for his market research interview with their Facilities Department, but second, he should be meeting with Al Wolf. Exactly what about, he wasn't sure. But he was excited about it anyway. The prospect of getting a career boost at this stage in life was rejuvenating and exciting. This could be a milestone event. This might be a life-changing event.

He showered and shaved. As he shaved, for some reason, his olfactory memory kicked in. The night he thought he had smelled the sweat of another human being in his home. An uninvited guest. For a few minutes, his spirit and excitement deflated. If FCI told him they wanted to hire him, just what would he be getting into? He thought about Jon's story about the home burglary supposedly involving FCI. Reese wished he had the details of that story. He'd never ask Jon to get them. He'd been clear—he couldn't. But even if he could, Reese knew Jon wouldn't do anything unethical.

Wait a minute, he thought. *Get a grip*. All these assumptions he was making. All these internal conclusions he was coming to without real-world proof. Who said FCI had any real interest in him? And if they had, he'd probably already been checked out by them years ago.

He thought about the two big guys who had approached him in their lobby. They'd probably cleared him for . . . for whatever way back then. And had someone really been in his home last week? Wasn't it possible that there was some other explanation for the sweaty smell? For his attaché being open on his desk? Reese laughed to himself; from experience he knew that there could be. With this thought, his mood lifted.

He wanted to keep today's dress appropriate. Workday attire for the interview with Bob Mathias—FCI's facilities exec—but at the same time a little dressier for the session with Al Wolf.

He chose a black two-vent Boss sport coat, button-down collar, white shirt over gray/olive checked dress slacks and well-shined Cole Haan loafers. Reese checked the mirror. A little too dressy on the casual side, not quite dressy enough on the business side. He didn't know exactly what to expect, so this would have to do.

He took 435 into 71 Highway into downtown Kansas City. This time of morning, traffic was fairly light, and thirty-five minutes later, he was in the office of Bob Mathias.

Reese stood up, shook hands with Mathias. The interview had gone well.

"Al Wolf asked me to give him a call before I left."

Mathias looked at Reese a second too long to hide a flicker of surprise, said, "Sure, use my phone there."

Reese dialed Al's extension.

"Al Wolf."

"Reese here, Al—I'm just finishing up with Bob Mathias—"

"Great, Reese. Glad you called—good timing too. You got a few minutes?"

Reese felt his pulse quicken.

"I'm free for the next hour or so."

"Great—come on over to my office."

"On my way now." Reese hung up, looked at Bob. He was glad he'd already shaken hands with him.

"Very much appreciate your help. The people behind the publication [they had talked about the articles and ads in one of the leading facilities management magazines] are always appreciative of what you guys have to say about plant maintenance. When FCI speaks, they listen." Mathias and Reese shared a chuckle.

"Always glad to help, Reese, anytime." Reese thought he detected a heightened level of respect in Mathias's voice.

As Reese treaded the skywalk toward the FCI building and Al's office, he noticed the sky had clouded up. When he had left his house, it had been a typical beautiful fall day in Kansas City. Now a few drops of rain were beginning to fall. In a few weeks they'd be looking at snow.

Reese and Al walked together to Lou Maez's office.

Al was nattily dressed—as usual—this time in simplicity. A charcoal gray suit and tie. He seemed a little nervous and a little preoccupied.

"How'd it go with Bob?"

"Very good interview—Bob knows facilities and plant maintenance. It's obvious he knows how to keep these buildings humming."

"He's a good man. Been with us a long time. We try to hire the best, the crème de la crème."

When they reached Lou Maez's office, Al ushered Reese in and followed. At the entrance, Reese became aware there were two men sitting at the occasional table just inside the door to his right. They were big, and in a side glance Reese thought that he recognized the face of one of them, but he couldn't immediately recall from where. They were both dressed in well-cut but badly rumpled suits. Two oversized duffel bags lay under the table at their feet. One of the men looked up, nodded to Reese. Sandy-haired men with rimless glasses, filling out some sort of paperwork. With an extended glance, Reese saw they were doing crossword puzzles.

"Well, there he is!" Lou's voice boomed goodwill. He met Reese and Al halfway, hand extended, but his voice extended the length of the room as he looked over Reese's shoulder back to the entrance.

"Come on in, Lee, join us." Maez gestured toward the seating area to his right.

As they sat—Reese at the left edge of the sofa facing Maez, Al sitting to his right on the sofa—Reese checked the fourth party out. He sat adjacent to Lou Maez. He had an air of importance about him. Tall, handsome, patrician, intelligent eyes. The lines around his mouth and eyes said seasoning, not hard wear and tear. Slightly curly, steel gray and black hair. Tusseled hair, but stylish. A medium gray suit of superb wool, a subdued tone of shoe polish on John Lobbs, a Patek Phillipe watch. Reese noticed the ties that the three men wore were almost of the same color, a subdued hue of green, which did not seem to clash at all with Lou Maez's chocolate-hued suit.

Reese stole another glance at the fourth man. For some reason his face looked familiar to Reese. He couldn't place it, though. And the name "Lee" didn't ring a bell. Lou got the ball rolling.

"Lee, this is Reese Maxey."

Reese stood with the stranger, extended hands into a shake over the coffee table.

"Very pleasant to meet you, Reese"—an accented, cultivated, confident, controlled, and commanding voice.

"I have heard a lot of good things about you." The man gave a charming yet mano a mano smile. Reese felt nervous.

"Azko Lee Britton, Reese." His nervousness heightened as he detected by Lou's voice that he was expected to know who Azko Lee Britton was.

'Very privileged to meet you . . . I thought I recognized the face." He wasn't lying about that.

Lou started in, "Reese, you've been coming here, calling on us, with your marketing research studies, I don't know, what . . . ten, fifteen years?"

"Somewhere in there." Reese tried to do a mental count back of the years and couldn't.

"A pretty long time," Lou went on.

"I've always enjoyed the visits here," Reese said. "FCI hires some of the most knowledgeable—and influential—people in . . . well, in all of the sectors of industry I call on here. Excellent personnel here."

Lou nodded, seeming to suppress a smile.

"Well, we've appreciated the fact that the publishers, and the advertisers have been interested in what we have to say—on feedback." Lou looked at Al, who nodded.

"We certainly have that," Al added.

"How much do you like what you do for a living?" Lou cocked his head, studied Reese closely.

"I love it, I mean I'm a born researcher. I started doing behavioral research, attitude surveys in undergrad school as independent field projects—didn't have to go to a class, just finish the field project by semester's end, and I always managed to ace it . . . you know, what I do is kind of . . . natural for me."

"Well, that certainly fits what I've seen of you, what Al and a lot of other company staff say about you—we've all observed that you do your job well."

"Well—thank you." It was a little unsettling to know that FCI personnel had been talking about him, but at the same time, he was pleased with Lou's comments.

"So you plan to stay with it?"

"I plan to. I haven't had any reason so far to look elsewhere." Reese was aware that all three men were scrutinizing him. He forced more calmness back into his awareness. Al asked, "Does the routine ever get to you, Reese? Sitting down with executives day after day, asking sometimes the same question over and over again. I imagine that takes its toll?"

"I get tired sometimes. Some weeks are longer than others. But I guess I don't see a lot of tedium in it"

There was a group silence.

Reese went on, "No two days are alike. Each interview is different. Even when the questions are the same."

"Have you noticed any changes in your work over the years?" The question came from Azko Lee Britton. He was staring at Reese, twirling a mont blanc pen with both hands.

Reese thought for a few seconds.

"I guess, the research questions have become a little more . . . maybe detailed. Years ago, advertisers, companies were content just to know that executive readers had noticed their ads. Ad recall and recognition was satisfying enough. More recently, companies want to know more about you—what you think and feel about their name, their products, their image . . . it's a little more in-depth and detailed today." Reese noted a nod from all three men.

"Anything else?" Lee added.

Reese thought more about the question for a second.

"Well, I've noted the increase in questions of a religious nature."

Britton paused his twirl of the Mont Blanc.

"And how do you feel about that, the changes you've noticed?" Lou asked. He was sitting back in his chair, both elbows resting on each armrest.

"It seems a little over the top . . . but then, no one's forcing anyone to answer the questions."

"But you're glad they do," Al threw in, and all four men shared a small laugh.

"You better believe it," Reese said.

Britton asked, "Any opinions on the trend with religious issues showing up in your surveys?"

"I really haven't given it a lot of thought," Reese answered.

"Really?" Lou asked.

"Really."

"That aspect of your research is probably going to continue—even increase." Lee was watching Reese closely.

"So be it. I'm a researcher, an interviewer. I'm paid to conduct research interviews—with important people."

Lee looked thoughtful, then said to Reese, "Religion is going to become more important in the future, Reese. As it is now, religion divides the world, makes groups of people hostile toward one another—makes them kill one another. I—we, the three of us in this room, FCI and the other major entities on the planet are taking steps to make religion work for the global family. Faith, prayer, spiritual issues, you are going to see as hot topics in the news—on

TV, radio, and in the printed press—in the future, Reese. If we structure religion right—or perhaps I should say, if we restructure religion—bring more faiths together, under one steeple, so to speak, that act alone will bring more groups of people who have historically hated one another into a new and more harmonious and loving relationship. The people in this room are going to be major players in that transformation, we want you to be a part of us."

Reese felt his excitement zoom at Lee's last sentence. This interview just might turn into more than he had expected or hoped for. He tried to hide his exhilaration. But he wanted them to know that he was their man. He hoped there were no other candidates for whatever job they had in mind.

"Well, you know I was reading an article a few days ago about the different religions coming together and how that would contribute to world peace. Unity of religions and a more peaceful world. I can see the correlation there. And if there is anything I can do, to contribute to world peace, well, . . . and, not to flatter any of you, but to be part of such a group and purpose . . . that would be far more than I would have hoped for coming to this interview."

Lee continued a thoughtful stare at Reese a second longer, gave Lou an almost imperceptible glance, then stood with another glance at his Patek Philippe.

"Well, I have a plane to catch." Lee paused for a second.

"You know, Reese, we are a dedicated group. We love this planet we live on, and we intend to preserve it. We want dedicated men with us, who feel like we do, who see the world the way we do." Lee extended his hand to Reese; Reese quickly jumped to his feet and shook the firm hand.

"Once you're in, you're in—permanently." He gave Reese a quick smile.

"Nice to see you again, Al." Al jumped to his feet and took Lee's extended hand.

"Good to see you, Lee."

As Lou and Lee walked toward the door, Reese noticed the high-end duffel bags were gone, but the two men had returned and were holding the door open for Lee.

Lou returned to his seat, didn't say anything for a couple of seconds, then said, "You have a degree in psychology . . ."

"Master of arts in counseling psychology, on the clinical side," Reese said.

"How much do you make, Reese?"

Caught a little off guard, Reese had to do some quick mental math.

"Not enough." Laughter all around.

"None of us do," Lou offered.

Reese doubted that.

"You know . . . as a contractor, my income is not static. In a bad week, a show week, I take home"—Reese felt diminished to admit it—"maybe five, six hundred dollars . . ."

Lou showed no reaction to Reese's paltry income. Reese had seen some stats somewhere a few years ago; he didn't recall where he'd seen them, but it had been a published list of some kind that showed local executive salaries. Reese recalled Lou's salary somewhere in the double-digit millions and Al's not far behind it.

"In a more productive week, I'm good three thousand." The reality was the five-hundred-dollar weeks were rare and so were the three-thousand-dollar weeks.

"You are open to expanding your contract work."

"I am open to new opportunity."

"How would you like to work for us—as a contractor?"

Reese felt the exhilaration rising again. To work for FCI as a contractor—he didn't think a lot of people would turn that down. He didn't want to show too much enthusiasm, though. And he didn't want to accept a job while his emotions were overpowering his reasoning capabilities.

"As a contractor."

"As a contractor."

"I think the answer is yes, although I am curious as to what I can do for you—for FCI."

Lou and Al exchanged a brief glance.

"You would report to Al."

Lou had not answered his question, but Reese looked at Al briefly, did a slight shrug of shoulder.

"That works—probably better than Al reporting to me." Whatever that meant, they all did a quick laugh.

"You'll work hard for us, but you'll still be your own boss," Lou said. "Pretty much on your own schedule."

Al hadn't mentioned his current contract work with Readscan. Reese wondered if he had forgotten his obligation there or if they just didn't care and expected Reese to terminate with them. He knew FCI to be an arrogant company.

"You will continue to call on executives, in pretty much the same geographic area you cover now. You will be interviewing executives—just as you do now. The slant of your interviews will change somewhat, but otherwise . . ."

"I'm guessing that I will be more focused or religious issues," Reese said.

"Spiritual issues," Al said.

Lou leaned forward in his seat.

"Religious and, well, not so much religious, but faith and spiritual issues are coming foremost to importance. Partly a function of Islamic fundamentalists, the world can't take too many more attacks like 9/11, can't keep moving in that direction. We've had a wake-up call. When men fought with bow and arrow, sword, knives, sticks, and stones—even gunpowdered cannon, we could take a lot of violence. Not today."

"Ever heard of sky?" Al asked.

"Sky?"

"S-C-I—"

"Can't say that I have," Reese said.

"S-C-I are the initials for 'Spiritual Church International,'" Lou said. "It's referred to simply as 'Sky.'"

"Well, that I do recall," Reese said. "I have seen the name in the papers and in the news magazines a lot lately."

With a little bit of discomfort, he recalled an article he had read not too long ago about S-C-I. He hadn't paid much attention to it, but he recalled the gist of the article having to do something with a worldwide church. Al continued, "You might not have been aware of it, Reese, but the faith-oriented questions you've been asking in your surveys lately—they're indirectly related to Sky and that movement."

Lou was looking intently at Reese.

"I see . . . I'll be ever more conscientious when I administer those questionnaires."

"That part of your research will be increasingly important," Al said.

"As important, maybe more important, than the questions you ask about the advertising and other editorials," Lou added. He continued, "You're pretty comfortable making speeches, aren't you?"

"I've made a few presentations in the part, I've been comfortable with it."

"And it's pretty obvious you aren't intimidated by high-powered executives—we may need you to present some of the religious material to executive groups—chamber of commerce—type meetings, that kind of thing."

"Right down my alley."

"Good. You mix well with a wide variety of people. You're very . . . artic—you talk well."

"And you know the Bible," Al added. There was an awkward silence for a second. Lou kept his eye on Reese.

"Well . . . thank you . . . both of you."

"We need some of your charisma, your persuasive dialogue," Al continued. "You help us promote some of the movement coming out of Davos—you'll hear more about Davos, Switzerland, the Club of Davos, etc., later—and some of the good Sky plans for . . . for the world, Reese, you'll be helping good people save the world, and you'll be amply rewarded."

"You'll make good money, Reese," Al added.

"Your very, very best week at Readscan, add a couple thousands to it, that'll be your worst week with us," Lou said.

"Plus expenses," added Al.

Reese was feeling the exhilaration again.

"I'm your man," Reese said.

Everyone stood. Lou said, "Come in tomorrow for a few minutes, see Al. He'll have a contract drawn up."

At the door to Lou's office, Reese and Lou shook hands.

"Pleasure to have you in the family, Reese. And one other thing—we have a controlling interest in Readscan. Mitch Iverson is a very dear friend of mine—we'll take care of the transition for you." Lou smiled.

All Reese could think to say was "Thank You." Mitch Iverson was the CEO of Readscan.

CHAPTER

3

At about the time Reese was finishing his interview with Al and Lou, a few floors down, a set of elevator doors on the ground floor of FCI opened. Five businessmen exited, nothing unusual about that at FCI. Well-suited men in business attire made up a large part of the population at this location of FCI. A closer look at the exiting party would have revealed, however, something different about these men. They moved a pace or so faster than normal for pedestrians here. The two men leading the party walked almost in lockstep. One long blond hair, almost womanishly swept back, the other six-footer had shiny short-cut black hair, widow's-peaked, professionally cut. Both wore excellent suits, tailored, but a little bulky in the jacket, looking good in spite of the extra space needed.

Behind them strode Azko Lee Britton. Slightly behind him were two more "businessmen." Also suited in well and purposely cut dark business attire, one African American, the other of indeterminate ethnicity.

All of the men seemed to stare straight ahead as they walked. But four sets of eyes were taking in any and everything in and near their path to the exit.

They hit the street, immediately scanning everything within a block of them. The rear door of a shiny black Mercedes Maybach swung open, held open by a sixth man in sunglasses, questionably worn on such a cloudy day. In front of the Maybach, a Hummer idled. To the rear of the Maybach sat a Suburban, driver in place.

As Britton entered the rear of the Maybach, one of his escorts got into the opposite side. The sunglassed man closed the door and slid smoothly into the front seat. The big blond got into the Hummer; the other two men entered the Suburban. As if on signal, the three vehicles left the curb, quickly accelerated into traffic.

Inside the Maybach, Azko Lee Britton relaxed, sat back, closed his eyes for a minute. He reflected on the past twenty-four hours. That he could see productivity in his day was extremely important to him.

He thought about the people he had met on yesterday. The "field rep," the meeting yesterday was in different venue, but it paralleled in purpose the one he had just attended with Lou and Al. The focus of the meeting in Parkville, Maryland, had been a person similar to the Reese he had just met—without quite the looks and charisma, but he'd had a certain social grace and strength about him. He'd work out. He'd do what he was told. At the street level, they were fielding good men. All of them had strength, were well educated, were trained in the behavioral sciences, had business-related experiences—real world experiences—and they were well-informed on the topics and spirit of the times. They were persuasive men. Good articulation. That was of great importance. And they would not come on board looking for a lot of money. Well paid, that they'd be, but not astronomically so.

And they'd stay on board. Once they were in, they wouldn't ask too many questions, even if they found anything questionable, which they shouldn't.

The guy Reese. He seemed to be the most attractive of the men Britton had interviewed. He had a lot of business-world experience under his belt. And he had a charisma of presence. And it was obvious that he had the intellectual ability to carry out the program.

Still, there was something unsettling about him. He couldn't define it. Lou had already confirmed that the guy was churched and a believer. Still, there were believers, and then there were real believers. They needed believers, not fanatics; there was something too real, too honest and sincere, about the guy for Azko's tastes. But on the other hand, he had a lot to offer. And he mused—he had a lot—no, not a lot, but adequate faith in Lou's judgment.

He felt the car speed up, looked out; they just beat the red light, the Suburban right on their tail. They had just crossed the Broadway bridge and were now turning into the lot of the Kansas City downtown airport. He spied the Gulfstream sitting on the tarmac. One of his. He had several.

One more stop on the West Coast and they would head for appointments in South America. Then back to the continent. Hard work, he thought. But he enjoyed every minute of it. He was determined to be one of the men—if not the man—that led the world out of the mess it was in.

A few minutes later, he was napping as the Gulfstream lifted off the tarmac into the cloudy sky.

CHAPTER

4

The next day, in Al's office, Reese found out Lou and Al had fixed things with Readscan International. When he talked to his longtime source of income—Reese spoke to the national field director—it had been arranged for him to stay connected to Readscan, with a kind of "on leave" status. He would, in effect, work for FCI—as a contractor—but would be available to Readscan too, if needed.

Somewhat to Reese's surprise, the field director admonished Reese to learn all he could about the Spiritual Church International, which he referred to too as "Sky." He was told that a lot of media attention would be going in that direction.

"You are going to see a major push toward church in the workplace, Reese—by government and legislation, by corporate America, and by the church." Reese wasn't sure who "the church" referred to. "You are a lucky man, Reese—you are going to become a player in a world-changing movement. Do whatever Lou and Al tell you to. You're going to do well the rest of your life."

Reese and Al sat down to look over the contract.

Reese read it twice to make sure he understood it. He would get a kind of retainer for the duration of the renewable contract. He'd get a healthy check each month, whether he was on assignment or not. In addition, he'd bill for every bit of service he performed on behalf of FCI, plus he'd be paid reimbursement for all his expenses. He was elated.

He was to take the next week or two off, reorient to his new assignment after a few days of rest. He shook hands with Al, drove home on cloud nine.

Over the next few days Reese prepared for his new duties. He searched his home "library" for literature on public speaking and public relations. He found a couple of books he'd picked up at a used bookstore a few years ago.

He found an old copy of Letitia Baldrige's book on executive manners, scanned it with some musing: corporate America had progressed—or regressed, depending on how you looked at it—from mandatory suit and tie to dress casual to bedraggled. Oh well.

On Saturday he called Jon, half-expecting him not to answer his phone, but he did. They spent an afternoon shooting at the bullet hole. Whoever hit the highest number of bull's-eyes would buy dinner for both. When Reese said Dennys, Jon thought he was joking. They did dutch at Macaroni Grill; Jon still owed him one from earlier this year.

He picked up Jan, took her to church on Sunday. Reese was disappointed that Bishop Padduck was not in attendance. He was attending a conference. The two visiting choirs were good though and took up most of the service time—"put on a show" as Jan described it after service. Reese didn't comment. For some reason, he was feeling a little troubled in spirit. He really had wanted to hear the word today.

One good benefit of being an independent contractor, occasionally you got a chance to sleep in. Reese usually scheduled late-morning starts. Frequently if he hadn't set up the week's interviews on Friday, he called his call-me-when-you-need-me assistant, Laurie, and he and she spent Mondays on the phone scheduling appointments.

Sometimes Readscan called early Monday morning with special assignments out of town. Either way, scheduling on Monday usually meant a crowded week.

Reese luxuriated for a few minutes in the shower, trying to make himself enjoy the promising slow pace of this Monday morning. But the urge to get to work was strong.

He put on a lightweight V-neck sweater, khakis, Top-Siders, went to his laptop to look up what he could on the Spiritual Church International.

The organization—a church, really—was intriguing. It was a growing influence internationally, much larger than Reese would have guessed. As far as Reese could trace its origin, it apparently had roots in Europe. It seemed to be focused on de-emphasizing denominations—while embracing all denominations—and it emphasized spirituality and world brotherhood. It sounded like religious Utopia.

He made a quick-scrambled egg, toast, coffee, and orange juice, returned to his office and laptop. As he ate, he thought about the implications of SCI. Maybe. Just maybe all of the religions of the world could work together. Work toward understanding each's approach to God. And if they could come together at worship time, under the same roof, well, he understood the interpersonal healing power of proximity. If all could work together—and as he read on, it seemed worship in the workplace was one of the goals of SCI— and pray together, then they could learn to live together and play together, that certainly would lead to a more peaceful world.

What was really surprising to Reese was the willingness and support of the national business community to allow anything smacking of religion in the workplace. And this, in a nation rife with litigation, prone to sue over the slightest indication of insult or violation of one's rights. And what about separation of church and state issues? Bring a Bible to work and you were liable to lose your job. As Reese read the various supportive news articles, he only found a couple that seemed to object to the goals of SCI. Amazing. Maybe there was hope. And he would become a visible proponent of the emerging movement.

He felt a stir of excitement; there was no telling where this might lead. His career could be just taking off.

And yet—Reese took another sip of coffee—there was something about the whole idea that made him uncomfortable. As if what sounded so good on paper was not quite what it was cracked up to be. And that it should not be.

He knew he should spend more time studying the Bible. He again felt the unease of neglect of his own spiritual life. He knew that this unease was stronger now than it had been years before and that it was growing.

He believed scripture—the Bible—and he believed it was the Word of God. And he had been taught that there was no other way to God—the true God—except through the Son of God, Jesus the Christ. He had been taught well by his parents and by his Sunday school teachers and other ministers in the church.

He also believed that the world was in its last days. As a child he had thought that meant literally a few more days. He wasn't sure how many, but he had thought in terms of days. And that had frightened him. As he grew older, he came to understand that the "last days" meant the last period of God's dealing with man, that the period began when God spoke to the world through his Son, Jesus, two thousand years ago. He saw the world as in a period just before the return of Christ to the earth. The next worldwide event of God's dealing with man would be the return of the Lord.

In the past year or so, he had felt this stirring—this unease and anxiety. The spiritual lessons of his youth seemed to come to mind, increasingly more frequently. He found himself praying more and reading the Bible more often and attending church more. He inwardly had the sense of moving in the right direction but not having arrived yet.

Reese was startled by the telephone.

"How's your day going, Reese?"

It was Al Wolf.

"How are you—going good, Al—getting up-to-date on Sky."

"Great! Good timing because that's exactly what I want to talk about."

"I'm all ears."

"Better yet, let's talk about Sky in my office. Can you come in tomorrow AM, nine o'clock?"

"On time," Reese said.

"See you then."

Reese called Laurie and requested delay in setting up any more interviews. He spent the rest of the day learning all he could about the new worldwide church referred to as "Sky."

The next day Reese showed in Al's office nine o'clock sharp, gave himself a mental pat on the back.

Al greeted Reese with a hearty "Do I have good news for you!"

They sat at Al's coffee table. Reese, casual in sport coat, pressed khakis, button-down open collar shirt, ankle boots, Al in work mode, tie loosened, sleeves rolled up. The attire gave Reese an impression of hard work he hadn't seen in Al before. With a beam on his face he addressed Reese, "You are going to be one of the guest speakers at a regional chamber of commerce luncheon. And you are going on national public radio!" Al had a big grin on his face.

Reese took in Al's message, found himself smiling, broadly.

"Woa—really? Well, if you say so, I'm your man." Only a little uncertainty bled through Reese's voice. He was beginning to pick up Al's apparent excitement, though.

"You are a good public speaker, Reese—articulate, good voice, persuasive, we've got you scheduled at the next Dallas Chamber of Commerce meeting. And you are slated for NPR—the local station—right after that.

"And while you're doing your thing in that part of the country, your counterparts will be doing the same elsewhere. We're hittin' 'em hard, Reese."

"And," Al continued, "Fahzi Raheed will go on *60 Minutes*, and he'll also promote Sky." Al was a beaming.

Reese absorbed Al's message. This "Sky" really was becoming a big thing. This information and his awakening as a result of the research he had done yesterday told Reese that somewhere, powers that be intended to push Sky to make it a worldwide presence that would engage as many as possible into universal religion.

"Well . . . I guess we are going to . . . save the world."

"Before it goes to hell in a handbasket." Al laughed. He pulled out some papers from a folder.

"Here's your play in this, Reese." He scanned a couple of lines, looked at Reese, smiling still but a little more soberly.

"We want you to convey—plant in the minds of the business community—the new order of religion, particularly its emerging role in the workplace. We want to bring about a positive view on businessmen—and woman—of the merging of work ethic and spiritual and religious life. Can you imagine that, Reese, people coming to work to work—and also to exercise, worship, and pray together?"

Reese had trouble framing the scenario, said, "Kind of hard to imagine, really, but with hard work, it can be done."

"You bet—we've got some scripts for you, but we all think that maybe your converting these to your own words is probably the way to go. You and Fahzi, and the others, are going to get the word out. We'll do market research to get feedback on how well the message is being received."

Reese mentally assimilated Al's selling and ego-inflating flattery, "you and Fahzi." Pretty good. Al still had a lot of sales schmooze in him.

"You've got all of the next week to work on your presentations, Reese."

A week later, Reese flew to Dallas.

CHAPTER

5

"Oh my." Azko Lee Britton reached a hand to his wife just in time to break her undignified backward fall into the slush on the sidewalk.

"Why don't they ever shovel the snow here!" Anger pitched her voice higher than it's already naturally high daintiness.

Azko had often wondered that same thing, but he said nothing. He didn't want to get caught in trivial dialogue. Too much of importance on his mind.

This was the place of one of the most important meetings in the world for people who were some of the most important in the world. Negotiating slick spots and chunks of ice and snow was a small price to pay, came with the territory, literally, here.

They were taking a walk on promenade street, heading to the Gentiana Restaurant in Davos, Switzerland. Seeing, and being seen, of course.

"Lee!". Wondered if you had arrived yet—good to see you!"

Lee stopped to acknowledge one of the chiefs at NBC, accompanied by a leading Harvard professor, both having exited the Gentiana just before Azko and his wife arrived.

"Got in last night," Azko said. They exchanged a few pleasantries and promises to do lunch, and Azko with wife went in to dine.

Azko liked to dine at the Gentiana. Cozy authentic in a world-class way with its wood floors and main-floor seating for no more than twenty-five.

He had barely seated his wife and himself before a hand touched his shoulder. He looked up into the tan face of Fahzi Raheed. Name and face had been one of those top of mind since Azko had arrived.

"Well, thinking of the devil!" Azko said. They both laughed. Azko stood.

"You know my wife."

"Yes—how nice—pleasure to see you again, Mrs. Britton." They exchanged a slight handshake. Raheed looked back to Azko.

"What's going on with you?"

"Finishing touches for the meeting. It really is great to see you, Fahzi." Azko meant it. He would be depending on Fahzi for much in the days and months ahead.

Fahzi Raheed was the man to know at *Global Week*. Indian born, from a wealthy family, Fahzi had early on come to America in his youth. Smart and well financed, he had had no trouble getting a good education at Yale and at Harvard. Afterward, he had ascended to galaxy level in the world of journalism. Everybody read his articles, listened to his opinions. In addition to magazine writing, he made frequent guest appearances on the TV talk shows, the news shows, and he frequently hit the speech circuit. He seemed to be favorably received by secular groups and by religious groups. His rating was high across demographic groups.

"If you need my help . . . just ask," Fahzi said.

"I might just that," Azko said. "Free this evening?"

Fahzi shrugged. "Sure."

"Can you come to my suite this evening?"

"I'm easy." Fahzi laughed, hands in pocket and back out again, showing only a little nervousness. He tugged briefly at his cardigan sweater—he was famous for his cardigans. Today he wore a beige brown version. Azko was always slightly amused by his semimonotone voice. It reminded him of some cartoon character whose name he couldn't quite recall.

"I'm at the Zauberberg," Azko said, "on Salzqabastrasse."

"Know it well, Lee."

"About seven," Britton said.

At about 7:00 PM, Mrs. Britton conveniently found a dinner meeting to attend, hosted by the wife of the chief executive of International Monetary Fund.

Azko and Fahzi sat in Lee Azko's suite sipping Barni from Swiss-based Felsenau Brewery.

Azko dressed comfortably in slacks and long-sleeve polo, Fahzi dressed similarly with his signature cardigan.

They shared a small table between them. Comfortable chairs of modern design, leather and flex steel that still permitted a kick-back-and-relax attitude.

For a couple of minutes they enjoyed the view through the bay window facing the balcony: an ascending snow-covered hill dotted with evergreens. The faint lilt of approaching voices caught their ears. Coming out of the hotel, climbing the hill at an angle was a group of five playfully laughing, throwing snowballs in a self-conscious way as they walked.

Azko Lee recognized Brad Pitt and George Clooney. A third face looked familiar, but he couldn't attach a name to it. Taking a sip of his brew and a sideways glance at Lee Fahzi said, "I see Hollywood arrived early this year."

"And a good thing too." Lee nodded. "They've been helpful with philanthropy, and they seem to want to promote the spirituality thing. We need them."

Lee stood, walked to the bay window. He recognized the third face.

"I thought I recognized that face—it's Bono." A question mark still in his tone of voice.

"It is him," Fahzi said.

Lee returned to his seat.

"You know, Fahzi, we need to step up our efforts for world religion."

Fahzi set his glass down, leaned forward, not quite sure what Lee meant. He had a lot of confidence in Britton. He had worked with him on several committees related to social and financial movements in the past, and he had been impressed by his professionalism, his judgment, and his influence.

As a member of the Club of Davos, Azko Lee Britton ranked high. He was elite among the world superclass—sophisticated, rich, and influential. He was chief executive officer of the New World Bank. And now, he headed a committee in the Club of Davos dedicated to bringing about a worldwide church and religion. One of several programs world planners were hammering out to reduce violence in an ever-troubled, increasingly dangerous planet to live on.

In spite of Britton's magnitude, Fahzi always felt a little uncomfortable in his presence. It was not his magnitude that made him uncomfortable—he was accustomed to and comfortable with his circle of famous people—it had more to do with some undefinable spiritual quality.

"Step up—in what way?" Fahzi asked.

Lee sat back, a contemplative look on his face.

"To be honest, I have been surprised—pleasantly surprised— as to how well Sky has been accepted in the church and in the corporations. Especially in the States. They talk God over there, but you try to take religion into the schools or into the workplace and you get the worst kind of backlash."

Fahzi nodded. "With competing religions, active atheists, hypocrites who only tolerate mention of God on Sunday and then only at church, religion in the workplace is still a hard sell."

Lee suppressed a smile at Fahzi's cartoonish voice.

"And yet," Lee took up, "I'm seeing an increase in the number of American companies that are joining Sky. One company I read in one of the business magazines has instituted "Sky breaks"! Employees set aside a few minutes a day to exercise, pray. And they do this in an on-site chapel under the Spiritual Church International banner. "And . . ."—Lee's voice climbed a decibel—"the Sky group at this particular company is composed of Christians, Jews, Muslims,

Hindu, and Buddhists. This is the kind of group we want to promote to the World, Fahzi."

"If you can find enough groups like this, I can write persuasive articles about them, and I can arrange some TV PR for them—on the talk shows and the news shows."

"On the other hand," Lee said, "there are always the jerks—on the very next page of that article was a piece about a business consortium organizing to protest on the grounds of keeping church and state—and work—separate."

"I have been surprised at how little of that kind of protest we've had. The line between church and state is a prominent one in the States. You're not hearing much negative about Sky from legislators and Congress."

"Well, from the Club of Davos to the US Senate, and house, it's not as far a reach as you might imagine." Lee added a wink to his comment, and he and Fahzi smiled.

Lee stood up, walked to the bay windows, turned.

"What if we were to begin reporting of truly spiritual events Sky members were beginning to experience—even supernatural ones?"

Fahzi's eyebrows shot up.

"And," Lee continued, "what if heads of corporations—or even junior execs—were to testify about leaps in productivity—happier, more productive workers, fewer sick call-ins, less downtime . . ."

Lee paced halfway back to his chair, looked at Fahzi—a discerning, penetrating look. With undertones.

Fahzi returned the look, but with internal focus, absorbing the potential message of Lee's words.

Lee took a couple of paces. "And what if these experiences were being had only in groups where there was a mix of Christian, Muslim—especially those two—and other religions represented?"

"I think that would either stretch credulity or get a lot more people and corporations to sign up." Fahzi smiled.

"It would—one or the other," Lee acknowledged. He continued, "But if these . . . events . . . occurred at random locations and were reported by, and happened to, credible employees—workers with some kind of meaningful credentials—good work track records, credentialed execs, respected blue-collar workers, upstanding citizens . . ."

"And if you were to write about this . . . phenomena and PR it under guise on the talk shows . . ."

"Sky membership would, well, Sky rocket." Fahzi chuckled; Lee laughed.

"You bet it would," Lee said.

"You see a need for this kind of"—he almost said deception—"of strategy."

Lee sat again, took another sip of Barni.

"Well, here's the deal." Fahzi again noted Lee's jargon was almost pure American. If it wasn't for the accent, you'd never know he was European.

"Here's the deal, Fahzi, the Christian and the Muslim are the only two world religions that have a universal mission. The Christian, to call all to accept the Son of God—Jesus Christ—as Savior. Because He will rule the world one day. And He will judge all men.

"The Muslim—their mission is to convert the world for Allah. To bring everyone into Islam because eventually the whole world will one day be ruled by Allah.

"Now, how do we bring these two groups together? We don't have to worry too much about the other religious—their goals are a lot about self-improvement, self-actualization, self-perfection.

"But Christians and adherents of Judaism are committed to Christ.

"The Muslim is dedicated to Allah. And therein lies a chief problem. Half of the world population is a member of either the Christian religion or of Islam. And thinking in terms of radical Islam—three hundred million members of the one point three or four billion worldwide membership—will kill masses of people in the name of Allah. That takes a lot of peace from the earth. Just look at the ripple effect of all—the work of nineteen men in less than one hour on 9/11."

Lee picked a pen off the table and began twirling it, briefly lost in thought. Fahzi took a sip of his drink, waited.

"If we can get Muslims and Christians to look at Sky, Fahzi, see that it exceeds all other religions in bringing people together. And if they see some miracles being performed in it—happy faces, healthy lifestyles promoted, good, productive work ethic, we will gather all men under one roof. And if they see miracles performed, I mean some tangible, real-world stuff that can be seen on TV, not some questionable verbal testimony that can't be proved, but events that the whole world can see and hear about, then we will succeed. We will control the souls of men!"

Fahzi was startled to see the enthusiasm Lee had worked himself into. And the strange gleam in his eye. He was ready to go to work on this; after all, he made fame and a small fortune getting the words and ideas of Britton and his circle of friends to America and the rest of the world. Still, he felt uncomfortable, for some reason he couldn't define.

Lee stood again, looked with more calmness at Fahzi.

"Fahzi, if we can get Christians, Muslims, Hindus, Buddhist in the same room together, get them worshipping together, get them focused on prayers answered in this life—answers to prayers for practical, tangible things—and get them doing so under the control of Sky, well, Sky's the limit!"

They shared a laugh and toasted.

Britton had dinner with the head of the International Monetary Fund, the newly elected CEO of IBM, and a leader in the World Council of Churches.

Hot pot Zurich style followed by schokolade kuchen hit the spot. No matter how you cut it, schokolade kuchen was still calorie-loaded chocolate cake. But Lee ate to accommodate the appetites of two of his guests.

He dominated the conversation without appearing to do so, and when he excused himself early, he felt reassured of his stature at Davos, and even more optimistic about the speech he was scheduled to make tomorrow.

He returned to his hotel room and reviewed notes he had made in preparation for his speech.

"Are you coming to bed soon?" He felt the soft touch of his wife as she leaned over the back of his chair and kissed his forehead. He had been so engrossed in the speech preparation he hadn't heard—or seen—her emergence from her bath. He rolled his head back and smiled, admiring her long wavy dark brown hair and her makeup-free pretty face. He detected the fragrance of her new perfume.

"I am going to be up awhile." She smiled, kissed his forehead again, and started to bed. Romance, lovemaking were far from his thoughts tonight. His responsibilities—his task was far more important than a mere wife. He returned to his notes for the next hour.

The dream started shortly after he had fallen asleep. It seemed to be coming toward him. A bright light at first. As it got closer, it seemed to be a light . . . in the form of a man? He started toward the light, to meet it, and then he saw it was actually in human form. But the light seemed to be . . . it . . . flames licked upward from it, surrounded it. It seemed to be a human torch. Walking toward him.

He felt a sudden fear. It came closer. Lee wanted to run but couldn't. He felt paralyzed to the spot. It was coming very close to him now. It looked like a human torch. With red and black eyes. He felt his heart race; the human torch stared malevolently at him as it neared him. And he couldn't move. He felt real terror; it was only inches from him now and coming closer . . . he felt the heat of it.

"Oooohh."

He was suddenly awake, his head being cradled and stroked by his wife's tender hand. With one hand holding him, she reached for two pills on the right stand and placed them one at a time to his lips. She followed with a glass of bottled water.

"It's all right, Lee, just a bad dream."

He slowly pushed the image of the . . . the flame out of his mind. He had been afraid, terrified, really. But it had been only a bad dream. He patted his wife's hand and lay back on his pillow. He trembled. He had been afraid of the human-torch image coming at him in the dream. More terrifying was the fact that he had recognized a kinship with the terrible form. Almost as if he were face-to-face with himself. He shuddered and reached for his wife.

He ordered room service the next morning—boiled eggs, two strips of bacon, toast, juice, and coffee. A simple American breakfast for a change. A slow dresser, his wife had a piece of toast, ate while she dressed.

He wanted to eat alone anyway. He wanted to think about his mission. As he saw it, the world needed people like himself. He was rich. There were just under twelve hundred billionaires on the entire planet, and he was one of them. He could pick up his phone, make a couple of calls, and literally move whole towns of people. He understood finance and how global money worked. He knew the fourth estate, and he understood the power of the press. What they worded, how they worded it, where they worded, and when and to whom they released news shaped public behavior. He had more than a working knowledge of middle-class values—across cultures, nations, ethnicities. And what the middle class valued informed the future.

At least that's how it had been heretofore. He intended to change that.

Unabashedly he admitted to an elite superclass of people. He was one of them. And they were the people who should rule the world.

The whole purpose of the Club of Davos meeting each year was to devise plans to make the planet a better and safer place to live. Because it was not becoming a better or safer place to live. Man's smartness, his ever-increasing knowledge base, made him more capable of harnessing nature into his uses. It amazed Lee that, internally, man's nature, capability, goodness didn't parallel his progress with technology. He was still the same old killer, and therefore, increased knowledge and technical skill made him deadlier; ergo, we have a less-safe planet on which to live.

The Davos people didn't need the violence of the earth—they were not religious, so no religion divided them. They were happy right here. They didn't need some pie in the Sky by-and-by religion, some hope for a future heaven. They had heaven right down here on the ground. Poverty was far removed from them. They didn't need to fight some religious war to convert souls so that they could selfishly find some favor with some god who would let them live forever in some far-off paradise. Davos people knew that you only go around once in life. Heaven was planet earth.

And racial hatred didn't divide them either. And if it did, it was handled well, in nonviolent ways. But when violence had to be used, well, it was done in nonviolent ways. Lee chuckled at the oxymoron.

He pictured a more Utopian world. Everybody pretty much living the same—a flat earth (excluding the Davos types, though). He wanted to see a universal "middle class." Universally, socially, and physically healthy populations. Sharing the same health care systems, the same currency, transcending race and skin color. Sharing the same religion. As he saw it, religion—belief in some kind of god—was engrained in the human family psyche. There seemed to be a need to believe. The Davos Club had launched human behavioral studies for years, across nations—often done in university settings under non-Davos guise—and the conclusion was always that man needs religion.

As chair of the Davos Global Faith Committee, he was responsible for initiatives that would bring about a world church, a worldwide religion that would encompass the major world denominations, bring them under one, well, under one steeple he liked to joke. So far, so good. Progress was even more accelerated than he could have prayed for—if he'd been a praying man, another little chuckle comment he shared with his Davos friends.

If anybody could pull this off, he could. With the help of Davos-minded people.

They really were the elite of the earth. A group of like-minded, well-accomplished human beings, well rounded, of sound judgment.

Lee reflected it took a high degree of human ability to become a member of the Club of Davos. In times past, a lot of the older members had gotten in by dint of family fortunes. Money and wealth inherited, not made by personal character and skill. Not so true today. Most of the Davos people—and Lee knew most of them—had gotten to Davos by sound work habits, natural intelligence, good judgment, foresight, leadership skills, and discipline. They had strength of personality and presence and clarity of vision. People who understood human behavior: who had a strong sense of every culture, who knew how to communicate at the feeling level.

And Lee knew that he was a leader among these elites. He knew he was sometimes described as the "go-to man" at Davos.

This was his comfort zone. All of his work life, his leisure life, and most of his personal interactions were with people who lived and thought like he did. Most of them looked like him.

He had watched Davos evolve from a concept of Klaus's into a body of very rich, very capable, very influential people. A "superclass of elites" was how some authors described them. Lee intended to see their power grow.

They transcended governments, made social and other policy for ineptly governed states. Laws had to exist to keep order in the world. Davos people had a lot to say about those laws, even formed some of them, expanded some of them, extinguished others. And ignored those that were in the way.

The world was ripe for takeover. It was becoming smaller, more manageable, more internationally interconnected. European unification was firming up. The EU now had three ruling bodies—a parliament, a council, and the European commission; and Lee's influence reached high into its ranks, as well as into the European Central Bank and the European Investment Bank. Rumor was that one of his close Davos friends would become Europe's first president of the council.

And in the states, a black man had been elected president for the first time in its 230-plus-year history. Lee already had a block of time scheduled on Obama's calendar. He liked the global orientation of the new president. Davos would orient him slowly, break him in to the ways of the world.

As he put finishing touches on his dress—he cinched the wrinkle in his tie, put a miniature whisk brush to his Canali suit—he thought about his presentation today.

Religion. They were in the early stages of reforming that. The Muslim, Islam. Just the thought disturbed his sense of power and serenity.

Every other religion on the planet—excluding some localized Hindu outbreaks—was content to invite you to their god, or their gods and, if you chose to reject it/them, let you go to hell on your own.

Not the Muslim.

Their most radical were determined to convert the world for Allah, or blow it up. And that, with a nuclear bomb—as soon as they could get their hands on one.

And you had to deal with them. They had all of the oil, or such a significant amount of it. And with the oil—or because of it—they had a lot of money. Barrels of it. And they hated Jews.

Lee had been educated in America, and he had grown up in Europe with a somewhat supportive attitude toward the Jewish state. Some of the vast wealth he had acquired had come indirectly from the mentoring of Jewish "friends."

In spite of his anxiety about things Muslim and things Arabic, as a leader in the Club of Davos, he was keenly aware and sensitive to global attitude shifts and global sentiment. He was increasingly aware that the Arabic nations of the world were increasingly getting more attention and respect. At times he wondered if there was even a future for the Jewish state.

One of the members of his Global Faith Committee this year was Ahmed Al-Nawsoni. With powerful ties to the OIC (Organization of Islamic Conference) and OPEC (Organization of Petroleum Exporting Countries) and the Arab League, he'd get to know Ahmed a little better.

The telephone brought him back to the moment.

"Britton here."

"Your car's at the entrance, Mr. Britton."

Thirty minutes later, Lee emerged from the metal detectors of the Congress Centre. He was escorted by two big guys, walking on either side of him slightly to his rear. He acknowledged several greetings as he made his way to the conference room. Some, catching his entrance out of the corner of their eyes, found excuses to disengage conversations so that they could be found in his path, hoping for esteem-boosting nods from Lee.

"Lee baby!" That from an industry leader in the recording business.

"Hope you are coming to the game this year."

Lee responded with a laugh.

"Wouldn't miss it—just to beat you second time around!"

Lee had beat him last year in a card game at the Bohemian Grove.

"Yeah, sure—we're playin' real cards this year." They both laughed. Lee noticed the heightened level of respect on the faces of the group the man had been talking to.

Lee made his way through the crowd. A well-dressed crowd in Armani, Oxxford, Chanel, and numerous labels and of bespoke attire. Many of the faces had international recognition.

"Hey, Lee, you're not going to preach us a sermon today, are you?" The chairman of Royal Dutch Shell grabbed his hand, gave him a slap on the back.

"And I'm taking confessions right after the sermon," Lee shot back. "We need to talk."

"You got my number."

"Me, you, Al-Nawsoni, make some arrangements, Lee said as he continued his journey. "And no sleeping in the pews!"

When he entered the conference room, an athletic tall dark-haired man approached.

"All secure, Mr. Britton—your chair is center of the dais—you've got the stage solo. We're on either side of you."

"Good." Lee waved off the two men with him, who found strategic seats in the audience.

Sitting on the stage, Lee scanned the crowd. He saw Bill Clinton—here on behalf of his CGI (Clinton Global Initiative) program. He recognized one of the heads of the European Union, chatting energetically with Tony Blair. Tony Blair was also rumored to be in the running for president of the European Council.

He recognized most of the faces. Heads of major US corporations were here—IBM, GM, GE. He saw the admin head of the World Council of Churches sitting near a cardinal who was supposed to be the most effective at the ear of the pope.

The most influential in government, industry, clergy, and academia were at Davos this year. Any enterprise that influenced masses of people had some level of its top-of-the-industry representatives here today: business and industry, government, clergy, media and entertainment, fashion, social service, and nongovernmental organizations (NGOs).

As he reflected on the who's who in attendance, he noted that what used to be a sea of white from this perspective now doubled included black, brown, and Asian ethnicities. Good, Lee thought. In the world to come, there would be no place for exclusion. The planet was too small for any kind of marginalization or isolation based on color of skin or ethnic makeup.

"And, ladies and gentlemen, the president and CEO of the New World Bank, the chair of the Davos Global Faith Committee, Mr. Azko Lee Britton."

Lee stood and walked toward the podium, waited for the enthusiastic applause to die down.

"Thank you, Bill." Lee nodded to today's acting master of ceremonies. He thought better of the corny joke he had planned and went right into his speech.

The first emphasis of his address was to the fact that the world population of nations, the masses, needed Davos. The "Davos Elite" as he put it, and he made *elite* palatable to his audience.

The second point he made was that spiritual life, faith (he made a point of emphasizing *spiritual* and *faith* rather than using the term *religious*) was essential to every living human being. It was inherent the masses needed to believe in a higher power. The urge to worship something or someone could not be crushed. That led to the next point that since the world was shrinking and with the logic that the more people came into contact with one another, the more they needed to share the same values to avoid conflict. So spiritual life—the act of worship—would meld all together into one church, one "religion, if I may," for the sake of peace.

He pointed out that religion was only one of Davos's initiatives, and the responsibility of a world church was his. There were other initiatives underway. He gave his Utopian ideal view of one world, one church, one middle class, one currency, one world-class police force, "without loss of natural freedoms," a world of "diversities of unity." He had run that phrase by his wife a few weeks ago, and she had pinched him on his rear and said, "Go, Lee baby." He quickly killed the smile that almost formed as he recalled the scene.

"Sky will be the first real, true worldwide church. Many denominations worshipping in unity under one banner," he told the crowd. Sky was in its early stages, but it would succeed.

He admonished the crowd to support it fully. Only a Davos group, a group of people "who transcend governments and other earthly organizations could accomplish these goals. Concentration of global wealth and power, of global influence, the accumulation of man's knowledge since the beginning of time, superfast communications and transportation, all of it had its destination at Davos." He ended with "If you can accept it, ladies and gentlemen." His voice rose with supernatural force, persuasiveness, and passion.

"If you can accept it! The world needs the Club of Davos. It is ripe for our leadership and rule. We who own the world's money, who have the superior intellect, who have the power, prestige, and influence—it is we who control this world. We have the duty— no, not just the duty—we have the privilege and the obligation accompanying it to serve the citizens of planet earth!"

As he walked back to his seat, the roar of the audience went up like that of a rock concert. Lee stood for a few seconds, bowed to the crowd. He basked in the adulation and adoration. His message had resonated at Davos.

But this meeting was not over.

When the master of ceremonies opened the floor for follow-up comments, two attendees, sitting near each other, stood. By their demeanor, the crowd sensed some unpleasantness coming.

Occasionally, a high-ranking member in the Club of Davos followed the main speaker of the day. But usually not.

By Davos house rules, the MC was obligated to invite the two men to the stage.

As they made their way to the stage, they seemed almost reluctant to engage the room. As if they were going to address the crowd with some terrible memo.

Lee gauged them as they approached, keeping a slight but tight smile.

Rev. Ehud Brochman led the way to the podium. Pastor and general superintendent of the Worldwide Church of the Bible, Rev. James Patterson, followed him. They ascended the stage and walked to the podium.

Of medium height, thick, wavy gray/black hair, wearing brown*rimmed glasses, dark suit, Brochman began, "Ladies and gentlemen." Rev. Patterson stood just to the right and rear of Brochman—a tall man, brown of face, wavy black hair, neatly dressed in a medium gray suit, white shirt, blue tie, hands folded behind him, he made for a distinguished look. He looked passively at the sea of faces in front of him. He had seen many of the faces for years in magazines, newspapers, on TV.

"Ladies and gentlemen"—Brochman sounded just like he did on his Christian Jew TV and radio shows—"I wish to thank the Davos group for this opportunity. I will be brief."

"I sincerely beg you"—he gave a slight twist of face toward Lee's chair—"to please give more thought to the global-faith initiative. "I—we"—he gave an arm gesture toward Rev. Patterson—" have concerns about the logic of such a monumental undertaking."

There was dead silence in the room.

"I ask you this question: how can all of the religions of the world come together when they don't share the same beliefs, the same god? Do you really believe that a Muslim is going to worship with a Jew or a Christian?" He paused, let his questions sink in. The room remained silent.

"One believes that the world will be conquered by Muslims for the worldwide rule of Allah. The other believes that Christ will rule one day." Ehud paused, to silence. But they were listening.

"The two religions cannot dwell together—cannot worship together. They are mutually exclusive pathways to our creator."

"I know that there are good and noble intentions behind this movement"—Brochman coughed—"but I am afraid that we need to face reality. I have seen the press coverage of Sky. And I have read the glowing reports in the business magazines of how it is waking, how it is spreading, bringing people into harmony in the workplace. To be blunt and honest, I am very skeptical. I wonder if true believes in Islam are truly—from their hearts—worshipping with Christians, and vice versa. And if I am right in my skepticism, we will see the Fatahs and the jihads continue. And unless I do see this—the impossible—I will air against universal religion. My TV and radio show will protest this initiative. And so will the Worldwide Church of the Bible."

Brochman stepped aside to let Patterson have the podium. With an orator's voice, Patterson addressed the still-silent, hostile audience, "We have to concur with Rev. Brochman. We have taken a close look at this faith initiative and see no way for it to become theologically or spiritually viable.

"We love our Muslim friends—I have several friends of that religion, in fact. Live together, love one another, work together, play together. We embrace that kind of goodwill and fellowship." He paused.

"But two religions—any two, pick any two—don't easily blend. And when it comes to anything as serious as worship—reverencing God—the object of the worship has to be one. One in the biblical sense. The issue here is spirituality, not religion. And we're talking about genuine faith. And spirituality that leads to real eternal life. And the way to that eternal life is through the one and only Son of God—Jesus of Nazareth. There can be no compromise."

He stepped back from the podium. The two men exited the stage; heads held high, they traced their steps to their seats, avoiding eye contact with members of the audience. To relieve the tension, the room emitted a smattering of perfunctory applause.

Brochman and Patterson gathered belongings at their seats and left the conference room.

As the two men were exiting, Lee's computer-like database brain recalled who these men were: Rev. Ehud Brochman was a Christian Jew who hosted a TV program and a radio show. Both programs were for the encouragement of Jews to accept Christ as having been the Messiah the Jewish nation had looked for, and now as their Christian savior. He existed on donations and on the sale of his books. A bell rang—a disturbing one. One of Brochman's donors was Barak Zonman, of New York. Zonman was somewhat of a mystery—to a lot of people. For example, it was known—known and not talked about much—that he had ties to the Israeli Mossad, the American CIA, and the former Russian KGB.

By the late 1990s, he had become a very wealthy businessman. He had amassed hundreds of millions through stocks and multiple business enterprises. In a couple of cases, he had taken military technology and converted it to consumer electronics and into products for use around the home. His fortunes continued as did his under-the-radar power and influence. Rumor had it that Zonman had become something of a closet Christian.

Lee knew everybody on the planet worth knowing. He knew them as well as he cared to. Zonman was one exception. For some reason, the desire to know him was not there. In fact, his intuition was to avoid him. And for someone of Zonman's stature, that would normally be counterintuitive for Lee.

He knew what he needed to know about Rev. James Patterson. Simply, he was becoming a face not be marginalized. The church he headed was growing internationally in scope. And rapidly so. Pentecostals, Baptists, and a handful of other denominations coming together. True believers who took the Bible at its word and believed in a working and power of the spirit supernaturally.

Lee mused. How had they gotten into Davos?

He doubted that either of them took home one million dollars in the course of a year, including gifts and other nontaxables that preachers were good at getting naive congregants to give them. And they were true believers—old-fashioned, praying and hollering types who believed every word of the Bible.

Lee looked at the MC, who was about to dismiss the audience—even he was probably worth quadruple the net worth of Brochman and Patterson combined. He would check the official list of the membership of the Club of Davos. He didn't expect he'd find their names on it.

Both of them had stepped on his program today. They were too prominent to ignore. He would have to deal with both of them. And soon.

CHAPTER

6

Blochman and Patterson returned to the hotel they had taken in Davos—the Best Western Bahnhof—Terminus, which was not far from the Congress Centre.

After changing into comfortable clothes—slacks, shawl collar sweater for Patterson, plain long-sleeve wool shirt and slacks for Brochman, they retired to Brochman's room to review the day's noteworthy events and to order room service.

They sat on the sofa looking at the TV, sound turned down below audible level.

"There was a chill in the room, but I think they were listening," Patterson said.

"Listening but not hearing, I'm afraid" Brochman took a sip of hotel complimentary coffee, squinching face muscles at the same time.

"I think you're just about right, Brother 'Hude.'"

A long time ago, Patterson had formed the habit of converting Brochman's first name—Ehud—into *Hude*. Brochman never resented it. He rather enjoyed their close friendship. After all, Patterson had been instrumental in converting him into Christianity.

"You know, the more I live the Christian faith, and the more I learn about God, the more I see that you really do have to believe in Jesus the Messiah. And you need to know scripture—and believe it with the heart."

"Otherwise, you'll modify and manipulate it, water it down, mix it, contaminate it for your own purposes," Patterson added.

"That's what Sky is doing."

"Pretty soon God becomes nebulous," Brochman said.

"And you begin to believe that there is more than one way to God," Patterson said, shaking his head slowly.

"I wonder how many people in that entire audience actually believes in God—in the one true God."

"I wouldn't be surprised if there weren't any," Patterson said. "Many are called, but few are chosen. I—"

The knock at the door surprised both men, each looking at the other for explanation. Brochman stood, went to the door.

"Food service."

Brochman looked back at Patterson.

"Did you order dinner?"

Patterson shook his head. Brochman opened the door.

Two beefy dark-haired young men stared at him. Both were dressed in kitchen-staff whites. Brochman spied a large kitchen-type cart behind the two men. He said, "Did we order room service?"

One of the men smiled.

"Oh no, sir, this is compliments of the house."

The two men pushed the cart into the room.

"Kind of unusual, isn't it?" Brochman followed behind them. "Not that we don't appreciate it."

"We don't understand how they decide to treat which guests—we just deliver. Frequently the hotel does this. It might be some kind of information on your credit card, something maybe to do with marketing. We don't know, but for you—you enjoy." He was the older of the two. He nodded a greeting to Patterson, who acknowledged with a smile.

Brochman smelled the food, which had a nice American buffet aroma to it. He reached into his pocket.

"Well, we thank you, thank you much."

He handed two five-dollar bills to the speaker and closed the door behind them.

"What the heck," Patterson said, standing with his hands on his hips staring at the mobile table, top portion now uncovered by Brochman. "That's the biggest food service cart I think I've ever seen."

Brochman was carrying the metal-covered plates to the sofa and coffee table seating area. Rotisserie chicken, baked potatoes in foil, mixed vegetables, bottled water.

"Nothing fancy, but it sure looks and smells good—good American food."

Patterson seasoned his baked potatoes as Brochman took a forkful of chicken.

"Not bad—not bad at all. Reminds me of a buffet we had in the neighborhood many, many years ago. My favorite restaurant—when I wasn't eating kosher." He gave a stifled chuckle.

"Baked potato . . . reminds me when I was eating kosher," Patterson said.

Both men laughed.

Brochman choked and coughed.

"Wasn't that funny," Patterson said. He looked at Brochman, who had suddenly jumped to his feet, holding his throat.

"You OK?" Patterson stood up. Brochman sat down, eyes bulging a little.

"I'm . . . OK . . ."

He stood up again, started toward the bathroom.

Patterson sat back down. A worried look on his face. He took another bite of baked potato; Brochman was right, not half-bad. He forked a piece of chicken breast. Even better. He chewed and churned food for several minutes.

"Hude—you all right in there!?"

Patterson didn't get an answer.

He put his knife and fork down and went to the bathroom door.

He knocked on the door. No response. He started to pull the bathroom doorknob—it was locked.

He suddenly felt weak and dizzy. He felt a searing tear at his neck, a kind of hot choking sensation; he staggered back a few paces.

"Hude! What's going . . . on?!"

Maybe he'd better call for medical help; he turned, but his strength was gone—and he was too dizzy. He went down on one knee, then the second knee. He couldn't breathe; he rolled onto his back.

The last thing he saw before oblivion were the two faces that had brought him his last meal—staring down at him, impassively.

The two men worked with precision and efficiency.

"Took him a little longer than usual," said the older man.

"*Ein grosser mann,*" said the younger as he helped lift the body off at the floor.

The two men made a few fold adjustments and placed the body in a compartment under the white sheet hidden part of the cart.

"Get the bathroom." The younger man pulled a key, inserted it, opened the bathroom door. Brochman lay on his side, head cocked at an odd angle against the bathroom wall.

"Give me a hand." They lifted Brochman, placed his body next to Patterson's. Both arranged the sheets, started the outsized cart down the hotel hallway. As they were leaving, two men nodded and entered the room. They "cleared" Brochman's room and quickly entered Patterson's. Following their learned routine, they repeated the procedures of Brochman's room, wheeled a tall container on wheels down the hall, to an elevator and to the rear dock of the Best Western, where an unmaked white van idled.

The rear doors opened, and the upright cart joined the large food cart. The younger man got in last, pulled the doors shut; he sat on the floor, lit a cigarette, inhaled, and said, "*Weitergehen!*"

The van pulled from the dock, took the highway that led out of Davos, Switzerland.

CHAPTER

7

Reese looked up. Service was over. He stood, Jan at his side.

It had been a great service. Bishop Padduck had preached with sincerity and with the spirit. The subject had been on how to get closer to God. That was accomplished by a sincere heart and faith. And of much importance was getting to know God. And that was done by reading the Bible. And even with that, the spirit had to give you illumination. Reese thought about a theology professor he had heard of who knew the Bible backward and forward and still didn't see the light, wasn't even convinced there was a God. You needed the spirit, not just the letter.

Reese had continued in his renewed faith. He was praying more frequently. He studied the Bible—not just read it—as time permitted.

A lot of the word he knew from childhood: "Thou shalt not steal,"—the ten commandments; "For God so loved the world . . ."; "Whatsoever a man sows, that he shall reap"; "Trust in the Lord with all of your heart . . ."; "The Lord is my shepherd . . ." All such commonly quoted scriptures were familiar to him.

But now he was beginning to connect the dots, so to speak. And yet, he knew he had a long way to go. And he was a little bit ashamed of that fact. Because he had come from a godly family line. His parents were devout Christians and had steered him right; even though he had balked at times and had in time wandered, he hadn't fallen from his faith—the faith—but he had wandered, been disobedient too many times.

Reese wanted to talk to Bishop Padduck sometime, one-on-one. He had sought it out, and the bishop's secretary had promised to get him on this very busy preacher's calendar.

"Let's go to the Plaza III," Jan said. She was in a good mood, feeling "chipper" as she sometimes, tongue in cheek, put it.

She and Reese shook hands and chatted with several members they knew, and then Reese drove toward Kansas City's upscale country club plaza. The Plaza III was a pricey steak house, but Reese could afford it this Sunday. Another beautiful fall day in KC.

Jan stuck an Andrea Crouch CD in the SUV player and hummed along.

Reese reflected on the past few weeks. Things had gone well with FCI.

His speeches for FCI and Sky were well received. The venue was usually at a chamber of commerce—type meeting where he was one of the guest speakers. On a couple of occasions he had been the guest speaker.

On NPR radio he had been the locally featured guest. The tape was supposed to air again to a wider audience sometime in the near future. He had outlined the unity purpose of Sky and had some data from his research that showed improved productivity at several local manufacturing plants that had incorporated Sky into daily routine for employers. The Q and A had gone quite well.

The surveys he had conducted as follow-up to his work had continued to reveal positive regard for the worldwide church.

One academician in another part of the country, skeptical of Sky, had conducted a survey about resistance to Sky because it was still a challenging project. He had concluded in a news article that one thing that bothered many was the fact that "many felt that Sky was adding incredulity to the Bible and the Koran . . . If there were some credible new prophet on the scene, performing miracles, or if there were new writings of scripture or of the Koran, that were found to be credible, that dated back to the writing of either books, that supported unity of all faiths, then Sky could become a credible religion."

The article had incensed several top people at FCI and Azko Lee Britton and Fahzi Raheed, Reese had been told by Al. Supposedly, Raheed was formulating radio and TV shows to counter negative reports about Sky.

"You know, I was just thinking, I have made speeches to just about all of the major cities' chambers of commerce."

Jan turned the CD down,

"I know," she said in a flat voice. Flat and a little sad, Reese thought uncomfortably.

He blinkered for a right turn and started westbound on Eastwood trafficway.

"OK, what's up, baby girl—what's the problem?" Some of his annoyance reflected in his voice.

"Oh . . . nothing . . . not really. I should congratulate you on your success."

"Not really," Reese mimicked flatly.

"Well . . . OK . . . I've been reading about sky, keeping up with what they're doing . . . keeping up with the movement—"

"Movement. OK. I see it as positive, as getting people to think more about God and getting them more into healthy things like exercise at work, more productivity . . . it brings people together. They work together, pray together, play together, get to know one another instead of hating one another. I don't see—"

"It's a little more serious than that, Reese." Jan's tone of voice had turned a little sharper, a little more serious. She turned the CD off and continued, "You're promoting a spiritual thing, you know? . . . You're dealing with the souls of men and women, the eternal part of them. They need spiritual awakening, but in the context of the one who created them—and in the context of the one they will have to answer to one day . . . you know, Reese? . . ."

Her tone of voice told Reese that she felt strongly about it—kind of an I-hate-to-preach-to-you-but-you-really-do, seriously-need-to-hear-this voice. He knew that she did not want to spoil the day. She added, "People just need to be led to Christ, Reese. All the rest of it—homelife, work life—takes care of itself after that."

Reese sped up, passed slower-moving traffic. He liked his Santa Fe SUV, just wished he had bought the 3.3-liter engine. He said, "I don't know . . . I just think you're a little too negative about sky."

She didn't respond. Reese thought back. One evening at dinner, just before thanksgiving, this issue had come up. They went back and forth—pro-Sky Reese versus anti—or more like just skeptical-of-Sky Jan. A chill had settled in, ruining the evening. Neither he nor she wanted anything to spoil a beautiful Sunday. Reese said, "Well, maybe you have a point. Maybe it . . . maybe I need to give it more thought."

Jan brightened a little.

"We can talk about it another day. We've both heard one sermon today."

They drove on in silence the rest of the way to dinner.

CHAPTER

The next day Reese was awakened by the telephone. Still fogged by sleep, he looked at the clock, 8:14 AM. Too early, especially on Monday. He reached for the receiver.

"Hello—Reese?"

Reese recognized Al's voice.

"Are you there?—"

"Here, Al, sorry, you know, it's Monday morn."

"Listen, Reese, got some good news for you. We're going to make some changes in your field assignment. I think you'll be excited about it."

Al had a positive vibe in his voice. Reese was wide-awake now. Al went on, "Can you come in—today?"

"Sure, Al—I don't have anything on my plate today, just some loose end paperwork here. What time?"

"Nine thirty or so?"

"See you, nine forty-five."

Reese clicked off. Weeks of making promotional speeches, of doing research, while he was far from being sick and tired of it, it would be kind of rejuvenating to have a little change in the routine.

Reese showered, shaved, dressed in a suit, open collar shirt, and slip-ons and headed for FCI Inc.

They sat in Al's office, on the sofa at the coffee table. Al's medium blue suit radiated wealth; he poured Reese a cup of coffee, refilled his own cup.

"As I was saying, Reese, you've done an excellent job for us—you're doing great, guy."

Al stared at Reese for a second as if he was actually a little surprised Reese was doing as well as he had stated.

"How would you like a promotion?"

"A promotion . . . well, I'm a contractor, not exactly on your payroll, and in that context, I'd say yeah, I would like a promotion." He laughed, and Al joined with a chuckle. He wanted to remind them periodically that he contracted to the company—he was not owned by them.

Several times, at night, he had awakened with the strong feeling that something was not quite right. Kind of a free-floating nighttime anxiety. Recently the feeling had been strong, right after a dream about FCI, the details of which he couldn't remember.

Al was nodding, smiling.

"How would you like to conduct a couple of interviews on national TV, interviewing converts of Sky?" Al had a big smile on his face.

"Really?" Reese was caught off guard.

"On *Global Week*."

Global Week now had its own weekly TV magazine show that rivaled *60 Minutes*.

"Really?" Reese said again, absorbing the scenario—a smile spreading across his face.

"Really," Al said.

Reese had watched several episodes of *Global Week*. It had been as good as any show he had seen on *60 minutes*. The format was similar at times. Oftentimes it became creative. Frequently there were interviews, and frequently the interviewer and the interviewee were both guests. It had kind of a boutique, ad hoc flavor to it and a more global perspective.

"Is this really a possibility?"

"It's pretty much a fait accompli—we're just waiting to hear you say it's a go."

"Well, I think it would be a good vehicle for Sky, would help promote the cause. Although I have to know the purpose, the intent of the show."

Al nodded again.

"Generally speaking, the episodes you'll host will be for the purpose of informing the public—and promoting Sky's agenda."

"Another thing." Al sat forward, clasped his hands, looking a little more intensely at Reese.

"How would you feel about relocating—to Dallas?"

Reese had lived in his current home about a decade and a half. He had tried the eastern seaboard for a while—he had lots of family there. For a change of pace he had tried Los Angeles and found it to be too cold peoplewise and too smoggy. He had liked the climate though and perhaps would have stayed if he could have found affordable housing in the kind of neighborhood he wanted to live in.

Over the past few months he had made several trips to Dallas to make presentations. On one trip he had gotten there a day early just so he could explore the metroplex of Dallas-Fort Worth. Excluding the traffic, he had liked what he had seen.

Reese slowly nodded.

"Dallas . . . yeah, that's a city I would be open to . . ."

"Good. We would be willing to help you with a move if you decide to relocate. Of course, an option is to keep your home here and lease a place there—commute. We own some properties there— we could give you some assistance with a lease."

"Why don't I go down there, look around, see how it's rolling down there?"

"Sounds like good thinking," Al said, smiling. "You take a look, do some thinking about it." He sat back.

"Meanwhile, let me give you a heads-up on Sky and the TV show. This next phase is a most important one." Al looked at Reese, again in his most serious, businesslike mode.

"You know, when people come together, for religious purposes in a workplace setting, that really is something. When they take time out from work to . . . to love one another." Al choked and coughed; he recovered, continued, "When they greet each other, kissing, hugging, embracing, meditating together, that is amazing: Christians, Jews, Muslims, Buddhist—name it, that truly is amazing, Reese."

Reese nodded, affirming Al's words.

"At that level, Reese, we are doing something spiritual."

Reese nodded again, not sure where Al was going with it.

"I don't know if you've heard it too, Reese, but we've been getting reports that some of the converts to Sky—those who've taken it seriously—are having amazing supernatural experiences."

Reese had seen an article or two with headlines that hinted of this, but he hadn't bothered reading the articles to any depth.

"I think I saw a headline in that context recently," he said.

Al went on, "In one case, one employee had a vision while she was in meditation in one of the Sky sessions. She saw in this vision the solution to a mechanical problem the fleet manager of her company had been wrestling with for months. I mean, this lady has no training in automobile technology, didn't know beans about a car. But she told the fleet manager about her vision, told him how to solve the problem. Bottom line—she got a raise, a promotion, a five-thousand-dollar bonus." Al sat back, let this sink in.

"Amazing—as you've said," Reese said.

"In another case, a Muslim guy, meditating with a Christian young lady and a Hindu. He heard a voice tell him to go to a certain bank—a bank he had never heard of—and collect unclaimed funds. He looked up the name of the bank—it did exist—he went there, bottom line, turned out, a deceased uncle had left him six figures."

"Has any of this been verified—or is it just verbal reports?" Reese asked.

"We've looked into it, Reese—it's hard to believe, but it's all checked out as reported."

Reese wondered who the *we* was but said nothing, except another "Amazing."

"And this somehow relates to what I will be doing on *Global Week*, I suspect."

Al nodded.

"We want audible reports, credibly interviewed, all credible people on this show. And you will be interviewing executives sometimes—we're doing two episodes, but there will probably be more to follow."

Another forty-five minutes of chat, of Q and A, tentative plans and ideas about the new assignment, and Reese departed for home.

On his way out, Reese saw the face of the man he had met in Lou's office—Lee—in a newspaper stack on the table near the entrance to Al's office. Reese took a copy for later reading, headed back to his home and office.

Later that day, at home, Reese, with a cup of coffee, kicked back, feet on his desk, opened the paper.

The newspaper was out of Europe—*European-American News*. Reese saw that the picture of Lee was attached to an article related to the recent Davos meeting. The caption read, "Azko Lee Britton calls for world spiritual unity." The article gave a synopsis of the unprecedented and unique push for world unity of religion, emphasizing the need for the spiritual development of the human family. The article equated spiritual and religious development and unity of the nations with political and commercial unity and peace.

When he had finished the article, it dawned on Reese just how important his new "job" was. He found it a little disturbing that the secular world was pushing for spiritual development and unity more than some churches. But then, these secular people probably had more power than many church organizations. Still . . . He was about to fold the newspaper and push the disturbing thought from mind when his eye caught a headline that said "Police still searching for missing Davos attendees." He would have let it go at that, but he saw the subcaption: "Religious protesters still missing."

Reese sat up, paper fully extended across his desk. Somewhere it clicked in his mind that he had heard—kind of out of one ear—that the head of the Worldwide Church of the Bible and the talk show host Rev. Brochmann were missing. He hadn't paid much attention to the reports.

The gist of the article was that Patterson and Brochman had stood up at a Davos meeting, right after Britton's speech, and flatly told Britton and all attending that particular meeting, with knowledge that the press was in attendance, that trying to unify the religions of the world was an impossible task. That most religions, especially the major ones, were mutually exclusive face-to-face.

And then they had suddenly disappeared. Records showed they had checked into the Best Western Motel. But then, nothing. No luggage, not even a fingerprint identified as one of theirs had been found in either of their rooms.

For a second, Reese wondered if there was a connection between their disappearances and their protest. He thought about his impression of Azko Lee Britton when he was being interviewed. He had low-keyed it in Lou's office, but somehow, Reese had felt the power of the man. He had seen the intelligence and mental activity of him in his eyes. And there had been something just a little subtly sinister about him that Reese couldn't define, even behind the pleasantness, the smile, the sophisticated manner of speaking.

And the two men with him. Polished, refined, probably well educated was the impression he had gotten in the seconds he had to head-to-toe them. Well-dressed hit men would be Reese's guess.

And the night he thought someone had come to his home and searched it.

But these people were trying to bring peace. They were in the business of promoting it and developing international character and spiritual unity. But he thought about Bishop Padduck and Azko Lee Britton. It was difficult seeing them having anything spiritually in common.

The phone rang, and Reese answered on the beginning of the second ring—relieved to escape the direction his thoughts were leading him.

"Hello, my dear."

"Good timing," Reese answered, both his voice and hers lightening his mood.

"Excuse me, good timing?"

"Well yeah, I was just thinking about you—well, not just thinking about you, but getting ready to."

Jan stifled a giggle. "Getting ready to think about me"—a hint of mockery in her voice.

"Well—you know, I was going to call you."

"Am I calling at a bad time?"

"No—glad to hear from you."

"What are you doing?"

"Waking—preparing for an assignment."

"Well, I was thinking about you—past tense, just wanted to hear your voice, see what's going on . . ."

"The day's going well. Real good, in fact . . . something I need to tell you, though." Reese waited out the silence for a second.

"Really . . . well, talk to me."

"I may be spending a lot of time in Dallas for the foreseeable future." Reese waited out another silence.

"What's going on in Dallas?"

"I am going to do some TV work for FCI . . . and for Sky . . . and they have studios there."

"Oh . . . I see."

Reese detected disappointment—with a question mark.

"They want me to find a place there—take a short-term lease, do some promotional work, and some TV work."

He didn't want to push his excitement about the on-air programs, knowing her reservations about Sky.

"I'll be in Kansas City periodically, though. And . . . don't you have relatives in Dallas?"

"I sure do." Reese could almost see her face brighten. "I have an aunt there—and I love to travel, as you know."

They both released small laughter.

"And you are going to be on TV?"

"Interviewing Sky people."

"When?"

"Soon—the very near future. There are a lot of Fortune 500 companies there, and we—FCI, that is—has studios there, so . . ."

"I am going to be interviewing some corporate execs too."

"That is interesting, Reese." Reese heard pride in her voice.

"I take that as a compliment."

"And rightly so—congratulations, my dear."

"Thank you. Between your trips to Dallas and my trips to Kansas City, hope I'll have time for work." They both laughed.

"You are going to need help packing—probably."

"Will appreciate all the help you can give me."

"Just call me girl Friday."

"And girl Saturday through Thursday."

"I think I said call this girl on Friday??—And don't call me a girl." She giggled.

"I wish I had you over here now."

"Really? . . . and what would you do with me—now?" Jan's voice had lowered in volume and grown sultry.

"It's what I would do . . . for you."

"More like what I'd do for you."

"Well, you know what, Mr. Maxey, I'm going to tell you about that one of these days when we're ma—when we're in rocking chairs." They shared the laugh, made a few near-future tentative plans. Reese hung up feeling good again.

CHAPTER

9

A few days later, Reese flew into DFW International Airport in Dallas.

He rented a car, found a motel near the airport, off Highway 183.

Dallas was a big city. The "metroplex," as the greater Dallas-Fort Worth City and surrounding suburbs were called, comprised more than six million citizens, spread over more than sixty townships.

Reese spent two days looking at properties for lease. FCI's real estate looked good—suburban, clean apartments—but for some reason he wanted to see more. He liked Dallas. He entertained the idea of a permanent move here. There was more city here. More nice places to live. More diversity. More of everything, it seemed.

On the second day of his hunt, he found an apartment, off 360 Highway not far away from the airport. The 360 Highway and nearby Highway 121 ran somewhat north-south, although as he traveled around the city, it seemed no true north-south, east-west grid existed, unlike Kansas City, which was pretty easy to map around. And 360 and 121 led to 635 east and west, and farther south to I-30 and I-20 east and west. The apartment he chose seemed to be well located with proximity to major traffic routes.

It was a well-treed, semisecluded suburban area. Ground floor, two-bedroom apartment with all expected amenities. Reese signed the lease and flew back to Kansas City.

Over the weekend Jan helped him pack. He would rent furniture in Dallas. He drove back to Dallas, shopped for groceries at Albertsons. Found some home-office pieces at Big Lots, Officemax, and a locally based furniture company. He jogged the neighborhood, checking out the citizens and the ambience of the surroundings. A few more trips to Grapevine Mills and Northeast Mall for more home goods.

By the weekend he felt like he had a second home. On the phone with Jan he told her he was beginning to feel like a "Dallasite." She said a "Dallasonian"; they both laughed not knowing which noun was the correct one.

Sunday night, and Reese felt a little apprehensive. He was expecting a call from Al Monday. Before that night he ran a search for a local church.

CHAPTER

10

"How do you like the Big D, big guy?"

Al's voice resonated on its most positive note. Kind of early, Reese thought, but said, ""Hey, guy, what's up!?" His Monday-morning voice didn't quite match Al's. "Big D's just fine, and beats that three feet of snow you guys got last night."

"Three-tenths of an inch—or something like that—not three feet—what kinda TV reportin' ya'll git down 'ere,' Reese?" Al laughed.

"Three inches, three feet—I wont have to deal with any of it anymore." Reese returned the laugh.

"Well, you're right, climate down there—hard to beat, although gets pretty hot in the summertime, I hear."

"Well, you know, I'm still a Kansas Citian too, so . . ."

"You bet you are, Reese—listen, I'm calling—wanted to touch base with you. What you're doing down there, you know, it's not just 'down there,' what you're doing—will be doing—well, I can't put into words how important it is." Al paused.

"I understand that," Reese said, gravity in his voice. "Understand just how important, this . . . this work is."

"Do you really?" Al asked, almost under his breath, a genuine question mark in his tone. He went on, "Well, good news, Reese, your first assignment is coming up, right there in your own backyard."

"I'm ready to go to work."

"You are going to be a celebrity." Al laughed. "This week you'll be going on air, on *Global Week*—the TV magazine show. You are going to interview some of the Exxon Mobil people, on the air."

Al paused, let this news sink in.

Reese was feeling an adrenaline flow.

"Sounds good, sounds pretty exciting, in fact."

"You bet it is, Reese. I am going to have Marie send you the particulars, and some other stuff we have that might help you along. Sky is really making headway, all over the country, overseas too. Marie's going to send you some script stuff too. We want you to pretty much stick to the script—to a large degree. Know what I mean?"

"I think . . . I think I do," Reese said.

"You think you do?"

"Well, you know, when I'm probing, I'm pretty focused and maybe a little intense, I like to drill in—"

"We have a good questionnaire guideline for you, Reese—we'd like you to stick to script. You can tweak a little bit—but not much. Can you handle that?"

"Sure, Al. I'm sure what Marie sends will be fine."

"It'll be great. Anyway, you'll want to go to our studios there. The people you're interviewing will meet you there. I'll send you the address and everything else you need overnight, FedEx."

"Do I get to rehearse with the interviewees?"

"No. Not necessary. We've got a good script, and I know you know how to interview, and ad-lib when and if necessary. Everything's all ready to go. Head to the Sky, break a leg, big guy." Al clicked off.

The next morning Reese met the FedEx delivery at the door, took the package to the second bedroom, which was now his office.

Desk, chair, a comfortable futon, bookcase he had found at very reasonable discounted prices by careful shopping.

He spent the next day and a half leisurely reviewing the script and some of the information on the guests he would be interviewing. Marie and Al had sent the most recent copies of *US News*, *Time*, *Newsweek*, *Global Week* that covered the sky phenomenon. On the cover of *Global Week* was a picture of the new pastor of Spiritual Church International—Ferdinand Chezlewski.

He stood, sleeves rolled up, tieless shirt, khakis, and tennis shoes, looking upward, arms uplifted, hands spread to the sky. The caption read, "Heads, hands, hearts to the sky as America embraces global spiritual unity."

All of the magazines carried similar articles, all with the same photo shown on the cover of *Global Week*.

As he read the articles, Reese was uncomfortably aware he was not quite feeling the excitement the words he was reading were extolling. The captions of a couple of articles troubled him: "The corporation, is it an extension of deity?" read one. Another: "Multinational corporations helping workers meet spiritual needs." One article titled "All Under One Sky" gave a partial history of the new pastor of SCI. Supposedly he had tried Pentecostalism, Judaism, Islam, Buddhism, and Hinduism—all to no purpose. When Chezlewski saw the light—melded all of the various beliefs into one, supposedly by visions and dreams—he found salvation, "the achievement," as he put it.

As Reese read it, Sky was to be the religion to end religion, to lead man to true spirituality. It wanted to incorporate all faiths—to be a church made up of all churches, of people coming together to worship under one roof. Global brotherhood. At the same time, melding work and worship. Bringing loyalty back to employment, restoring "hard work" ethics.

That part Reese felt comfortable about.

The aspect of it, purportedly leading to spiritual enhancement and to God, world spiritual unity—he was uncomfortable with. A spiritual movement coming from the wealthy and privileged of the world, supported by the political and commercial world—Reese didn't want to admit it, but that scared him just a little. And he wasn't fully sure why. He could see the good of sky. The work ethic, diversity of people, races in the workplace who needed to relate better to one another—all of these would show improved by the implementation of sky principles. He liked the idea of being a part of a worldwide movement. And he liked the idea of being a part of that movement on TV. And on TV where he was the featured guest interviewer. And he liked the money FCI was paying him as an independent contractor.

He studied the questionnaire, mentally did a guesstimate at time per question. He would have—or take—some leeway with the questions. Looked like a good hour-long TV show.

He prayed that night before going to bed. His spiritual life was still an issue. He started into sleep, with a vague sense that the implications of Sky were contrary to his inner urgings.

CHAPTER

11

They sat in a semicircle facing Reese in the studio. Reese felt composed and ready. Dressed in an Armani suit, in a button-down collar, pale lavender shirt, penny loafer slip-ons, he made some last-minute notes, portfolio open in his lap. The lights came on, focusing him and his guests against a dark background.

He surreptitiously studied his guests. Everyday people. In observing people, Reese had a tendency to see resemblances in terms of Hollywood and other famous people.

Jerome Jackson sat in a sport coat and dress trousers, white shirt, conservative tie. He reminded Reese of Phillip Michael Thomas, of the old *Miami Vice* TV series. Jerome worked at the locally headquartered office of Exxon Mobil as assistant manager of housekeeping.

Next to Jackson and on his left sat Pete Rogdon. He reminded Reese of Karl Rove, with a little more height and slightly less bulk. Dressed in a conservative suit and tie, he was a regional sales manager for the giant oil company.

Next, on Rogdon's left was Ali Al-Jassem, a supervisor in the Security Department of the headquarters location. Sharp featured, dark skinned, somewhat piercing dark eyes.

Molly Reed sat in the end seat. She reminded Reese of Doris Day: clean, wholesome, wearing a knee-length dress. When Reese's and Molly's eyes met, she smiled brightly. Bright, a little bubbly on the surface. But a latent anxiety bled through.

"Aaaand, action!" Reese expected the "on air" light or a verbal "on air" and was caught off guard for a second. He faced the camera.

"Good evening, ladies and gentlemen." He felt composed but a little nervous, but was pleased at the sound of his voice.

"By now you have probably come to recognize the initials S-C-I, and you probably refer to it by its acronym, "Sky."

Reese introduced Sky, gave a little of its history to the viewing audience.

"Is Sky real? Does it have substance? Is it a viable church? Is there really a supernatural quality to it?

"Well, we have guests today on this show who will answer yes to all of the above. In fact, you will probably be amazed at some of the testimonies you hear over the next hour."

Reese turned to his guests.

"I want to express our sincere appreciation to each of you for your willingness to share your experiences with the rest of the world." Reese smiled at the guests.

"If you will, please introduce yourselves."

After the introductions Reese said, "OK—we've all agreed that a question-and-answer format might serve our viewers best. Our field research—our surveys—have told us that the American public is most concerned with the spiritual aspect of Sky, to be more exact, they want to know what Sky has personally done for each of you. And a little troubling to some have been the reports of the supernatural aspects of some of your experiences. Maybe today, we can shed some light on those topics. Let's start on the left here—Jerome, first up!"

Jerome fidgeted for a second until he found a comfortable position.

"Jerome, tell me—tell our viewing audience about prayer, prayer in the setting of Sky meetings. When you pray, to whom are you praying?"

"Well, in our Sky sessions, at work, we all pray. We all pray to God, of course. And when I return to work, I'm all fired up and excited about getting back to work."

"You feel . . . rejuvenated," Reese said.

"Re . . . yes, that too."

Reese heard a snicker behind the camera, and he quashed his own smile.

"But who do you pray to?"

"Well . . . we—"

"Well, Reese," Pete Rogdon jumped into the interview.

"We are encouraged to draw others in, to convert others, and by others, I mean the whole world, to join this wonderful movement—this world church. Do that, and you don't have to ask who God is."

"Amen, brother"—from Molly as Jerome and Ali nodded vigorously. Reese looked down at his notes, looked up, continued.

"We've gotten reports, and recently the media has published the same, that there have been some . . . supernatural . . . events . . . associated with Sky?"

"Yes." Molly and Ali nodded.

"Will you share some of that with us?"

Pete spoke up, "I think that one of the most—no, not one of the most, the most relevant messages we're getting at a spiritual level in Sky is that God wants us all—all of us on this earth, to work together in peace, love, and harmony. The spiritual level of religion is the most important one. And—hear this, Reese"—Rogdon turned briefly to the camera—"and the rest of the world out there—the Christian and Islam unity seems to be the most important thing. I think the experiences that Molly and Ali had illustrate this most vividly . . . if you have time for them to tell their story . . ." Rogdon looked at Molly and Pete.

"Sure, we have the time," Reese said.

He looked at Molly, Ali.

"Molly, Ali, do you care to tell your story?"

Molly spoke up, "I am glad to share this, like Pete said, it's probably why God brought us here." Enthusiasm bubbled.

"And what I'm hearing—and reading—it's the kind of experience other sky members are having, all over the world. It's really exciting.

"Well . . . I started at Exxon Mobil in a janitorial job, very entry level, you know?" I had a lot of debt—lots a bills. I drive a 1991 Chevy, beat-up old thing—well, it looks pretty nice to be that old, I mean mechanically beat-up.

"Well . . . about my second week at work, one of the Sky members asked me to join him for a Sky session. At first, I thought, I, well, maybe . . . not!"

A few chuckles.

"Then, you know, I'm thinking, he's kind of cute, why not?

"That first session—it was held sometime around the lunch hour—I went to the session. I did some exercises, running in place or something like that. We all held hands, we hugged, we kissed—I never did get to kiss that guy who invited me, though—"

Ali, Pete, Jerome laughed.

"So," Molly went on, "we all pretty soon were meditating and praying—this was after we had all shared little, I guess you'd call them 'testimonies,' little pep talks about how good Sky was, how good it was to be together—anyway, that afternoon, when I went back to work, I mean, I just felt so good about working, about Exxon Mobil, about everything.

"So . . . I started going to all the sessions. Every day. One day, well, let me back up a little, talk about my car."

Molly looked at Ali; they both shook their heads vertically with shared knowing smiles on their faces. Molly looked back at Reese.

"My car, every day, I mean ev-e-ry day!—it would jackass on me. At least once a day, every day, it made a point of not starting."

Jerome, Pete, Ali laughed.

"It had developed a reputation for not starting. Even Jerome there—he's had his turn at helping me get it started before I leave work for home."

Jerome was nodding, smiling.

Rogdon jumped in, "I was coming in for a sales meeting one day, four, five of us in the lobby waiting to sign in. All of a sudden,

we hear this loud"—Rogdon cupped his hands around his mouth—
"one of you guys in here give me a jump!—scared the heck out of
everybody in the lobby!"

Molly, Ali, and Jerome laughed.

Molly went on, "I mean, everybody at Exxon Mobil has had
their turn at jump-starting my car.

Anyway, I could not afford a new car. And I couldn't afford
to get it fixed. I couldn't even afford a new battery. And it wasn't
because I wasn't getting paid enough—I mean, come on, Exxon pays
all of their employees a good salary. I . . . I just had so many bills, so
much debt that had piled up . . ."

"Anyway, so one day"—Molly changed to a more sober face; she
looked dead into the camera—"I want everybody out there to hear
me, and take it seriously," she looked back at Reese.

"Mr. Maxey . . . I was in a Sky session one day, I don't know,
maybe six, seven, eight months ago, I was in deep meditation, never
will forget it, I had gone to my favorite corner in the Sky room to
meditate and pray. I heard . . . in my mind, just as clear as your voice
is to me now, Mr. Maxey, I heard a voice. It said, 'I want you and
the Muslim to unite in spirit and worship. Seek him out. The two
of you, go and pray over your car together.' And then, the image of
Ali came to me, just as clear as day, just as clear as I see him now,
sittin' here."

The room was silent.

Molly continued, "You know, I had a cousin once, she had what
the old folks used to call a nervous breakdown, and she was always
hallucinating and all . . . and the first thing that came to my mind
was, well, you know . . . I thought, finally, I've lost my mind."

Reese heard a low snicker from Jerome.

"But you know," Molly continued, "I went to Ali that evening
just before time to go home. I asked him to go with me to my
car—told him it probably wouldn't start. He looked at me a little
strangelike, but he seemed glad to help me. I was real nervous because
I was going to ask him to join in prayer over it, to heal it. Can you
imagine how much nerve—or maybe it was faith?—it took for me to

ask him. And I felt like a for-real lunatic. But I did it—I asked him to pray with me for my car—it's healing. Sure enough . . ."

Molly began tearing up.

"Maybe Ali should finish this story . . ." She looked at Ali, biting her lip, a tear falling.

Ali, a trace of a tear in one eye, looked at Molly. He wiped the tear away, cleared his throat, began, "About a week before I met Molly, I was meditating in a Sky session, and I too heard a voice. It said to me, 'A Kafir—that means unbeliever, in Islam—will seek you out. Join her and help her. Do not reject anything she asks of you.' I was shocked. I have been a Muslim all of my life, and I had never had any kind of experience like that. So the day Molly asked me to help her, I guess I was prepared for it. And when she asked me to pray for her car, well, I just didn't think it weird at all. And it turned out, we didn't even need the jumper cables. We held hands and we prayed together. When we finished, I got into Molly's car, turned the ignition switch. It started right away."

Molly, shaking her head slowly, a gleam in her eyes said, "It's been running ever since. Hasn't failed to start one time since then."

All four went silent, meditatively so, Jerome and Pete slowly nodding.

Reese felt uncomfortable. Surely they were lying. Or was it possible something was going on here?

"That is quite a story," he heard himself say. He looked at Rogdon.

"And, Pete, I understand you also have had some mystical experiences? Some events that, uh, transcend the normal . . ."

"That I have, and I'll be glad to share one of them.

"I was visiting one of our branch offices not too long ago. Got there about the Skybreak time. Because of a mix-up in scheduling, I saw I was going to have to wait an hour or so before I could meet with the manager I was there to visit. So I'm sitting in her office, and this guy—one of our employees there—pokes his head in, says, 'Join me for a Sky session?' Well, you know, my mind is on business, but I think, why not? Long story short, I end up in a prayer session with the guy who invited me. He is a Muslim, by the way. He tells me,

'You have a tenfold blessing in your safety deposit box because you have honored me and the church of Sky,' Well, you know"—Rogdon guffawed laughter—"I'm thinking, so now we're hiring from the looney bin."

Molly, Jerome, and Ali laughed.

"Anyway, a few days later, I'm going to my safety deposit box. Now, I have kind of a personal policy of keeping anywhere from a thousand to twenty-five-hundred-or-so cash in my SD box. Every time I go there, I make a little note of the balance, keep it tucked in my wallet. So I'm going there, I sign in, get the key, me and the teller unlock it, before I leave, crossed my mind what the Sky session guy had said, I take a look—in my wallet, I checked my little scratch paper that I keep record on, and it indicated fourteen hundred and, seventy, dollars and change. I found a little packet in my box, get this—one hundred-and-fifty-hundred-dollar bills!"

"Wow." Molly's smile spread across her face, beaming.

"Go, Sky!" Jerome had a fist balled up, raised high.

Ali and Rogdon did a high five, sat back down.

"Amazing," Reese said, feeling that he should somehow express some appreciation for the story. His discomfort level had accelerated.

"Truly amazing." He leaned back in his chair, stared at the ceiling for a moment; bringing his gaze back down to the group, he said, "So what message, what do you want our viewers to take away from all of this?"

Molly spoke up, "I would say this, Mr. Maxey, keeping it simple, if you want to be happy, you know, find your spiritual self, join others who are looking for the same thing . . . if you want to be happy at home, at work—join Sky."

"That certainly—"

"Let me add something else too. You know, I was taking prescription drugs, for depression and for anxiety. Well, I don't take them anymore, not since that—well, I stopped taking them sometime around the time Ali and me had that prayer. So my advice to everybody out there—wake up and join up!"

Reese sat at the desk in the small office the studio had set aside for his use and completed some paperwork—feedback notes for Al and others regarding his take on the show.

He should have been elated about a successful show and his first TV appearance on an international broadcast.

Instead, he was depressed. And a little perturbed. He was almost persuaded by Molly and Pete Rogdon's testimony. And that bothered him. Surely there had to be some conspiracy somewhere in all of this? But suppose there wasn't. Suppose each one of them had told the truth, related the facts just as they had experienced them? That was most disturbing to him.

He had grown up in a Fundamentalist church (Fundamentalist had a different connotation those days), one where the faithful of the church believed in a literal interpretation of the Bible. People who believed that nothing was impossible for God. Who believed that there was heaven, and there was a hell, and there was a judgment day coming. And who lived like they believed, and not just out of fear, but also because they loved God.

And they too believed in miracles. He had a friend he had grown up with in the church—Shelly—Shelly had walked faithfully with the Lord. When Reese had been backslidden, worldly focused, out partying, down at the local club, Shelly had been at church, even in his youthful years. Later, Shelly had come down with "incurable" cancer. A rally of prayer had gone up for him among the saints. Within a year the doctors could find no evidence of the cancer and had no explanation for how Shelly had been "cured." A miracle. A real miracle.

But these prayers had gone up to one God, the God of Abraham, Isaac, and Jacob and through His only begotten Son—Jesus. And God had heard the prayers of the saints.

And now, today, he had heard of prayer answered, miracles performed by people who he wasn't even sure knew the same God he did. It was almost enough to shake his faith. He wished he had a way of proving—preferably for sake of his own faith—of disproving what he had heard today.

There was no way of proving or disproving Rogdon's story. He certainly couldn't get to his safety deposit box, and if he could, it wouldn't prove anything either way.

Molly had said that she had to have her car started every day. And then, she has this vision and lo and behold, car problems end. Fantastic.

He suddenly had an idea. He hurried down the hall leading to the parking lot. He had some more questions for Molly, off air.

When he got to the parking lot, he looked around, afraid that the group might have departed already.

He saw Pete and Molly; apparently they had been talking. They were just leaving each other, Molly en route to her car.

Reese did a slow jog to catch up with her. He timed his pace over the freshly white-striped parking lot. Molly had parked in the farthest row from the studio even though there were many vacant parking spaces closer to the studio entrance. Molly's car sat alone in the last parking space.

He was about twenty-five feet away when Molly heard his approach; she turned.

"Oh, Mr. Maxey!"

"Hi again," Reese said, smiling widely. He took note of the Chevy she was driving. Calling on his previous memory, in a previous life as a field rep for GM, 1991 was about right. A big boat of a car, probably a 5.0-liter-gas-guzzling engine. A big brown caprice. As he recalled, it was a nice, soft ride. Not something you rocked to brag about, but Molly apparently was proud of it. It looked freshly washed and waxed.

"That was a real story you gave us, Molly, just wanted to thank you again."

"I really enjoyed it, Mr. Maxey. I just hope the viewing audience will come on board with us. And if you need me again, all you have to do is call—I'm glad to share, my story." She gave Reese a bright smile.

"You never know, the opportunity to do that might come around again."

Reese looked at Molly's car.

So this is the beast resurrected from the dead."

"Or at least raised from her deathbed." Molly laughed.

"1991—'hum'—looks pretty good."

"I try and take care of it—keep it clean, looking good. This old can't afford not to." She give a little laugh.

"You haven't had any trouble at all since?—"

"Not since my—our prayer over it—thanks to Sky."

Did he detect a note of insincerity, of nervousness, of lack of conviction in her voice?

"Did you buy it new?"

"New to me." Molly laughed, but there was definitely something tight and tense about her voice.

"How long have you had it?"

"Oh, let's see, maybe six, seven years, didn't have any trouble with it until about a year ago when it started stopping on me."

"And you had to have it jumped—every day?"

"Every day. Triple A dropped me. Between several good neighbors and my electric starter—and my coworkers—I was able to keep her going. Had her checked a couple of times, battery always checked good because I kept new batteries. Mechanics, never could pinpoint what was wrong with it, so I started carrying jumper cables. Had the hood up every day . . ."

This didn't fully add up, Reese thought. He had been a service rep for GM years ago, and he knew, on cars this old, in spite of computer technology, diagnosis of an electrical problem could be challenging. Still—

"Did you ever think about just overhauling the engine, or just finding an old rebuilt engine—"

Molly blinked rapidly, dropped her purse. Reese bent over to pick it up. He corrected himself, "On the other hand, that wouldn't have made a lot of sense—you can sometimes buy a used car cheaper than replacing an engine—"

"And I couldn't afford either one," Molly said. She was backstepping to her car, had the driver's-side door open.

Reese said, looking at the car, "Boy oh boy, that sure brings back memories—my old GM days. I wouldn't mind looking at the en—"

"Mr. Maxey, I have just got to run." She looked at her watch.

"Oh my!—I have got to get outta here."

"Didn't mean to keep you. Again, appreciate the interview, Molly."

As she pulled into the driveway, Reese watched her leave, waving bye. He made a careful note of the car's vanity license plate number.

That night Reese spent time reading the Bible, and in prayer. His call to God, to the Lord, was to strengthen his faith. He prayed more earnestly than he had in recent petitions to God.

Later, picking up the Bible, thumbing through it; his eye was drawn to the book of John, chapter 14. It seemed to him that the words leaped off the page and highlighted themselves.

"I am the way, and the truth, and the life. No one comes to the Father but through me."

He read verse 9; here Jesus addressed his disciple Philip's request to be shown the father.

"Jesus said to him, 'Have I been with you so long, and yet you have not known me, Philip? He who has seen me has seen the Father; so how can you say 'show us the Father'?"

The verses stirred and lifted Reese's spirit. His melancholy left him. He felt the rejuvenation of his faith.

Before he drifted off to slumber, he thought over the day's events—Molly's and Pete's "testimonies." He thought about his years at GM. As a service rep he had spent a lot of time looking at and diagnosing mechanical problems of GM automobiles. And back then, they had had a lot of them. Part of his job had been that of field warranty administrator. When there were questions about whose fault a failed part on an auto was—GM's, because of faulty workmanship, or a customer's, due to lack of maintenance or care of the car—Reese had to make the call. He had spent a long time in training for the responsibility, looking at and studying failed parts to determine cause of failure; learning locations of serial numbers, parts build dates; and learning how to interpret serial numbers. This part of the training had been primarily for keeping dealers honest with warranty claims. When looking at warranty parts that GM was paying for, occasionally a dishonest mechanic would throw in an old, say starter, motor. Reese's training enabled him to look at the serial number on the starter motor and determine if it matched the serial number and build date of the car the starter motor had supposedly been taken off. When it didn't, Reese charged the repair order back to the dealer. The warranty service reps over time saved GM a lot of money, although fraud was the exception. Most dealers had played fair ball, served their customers and GM well. Always paranoid, and skeptical, Reese had, over time, found this fact a pleasant surprise.

Molly (and Pete too)—something just didn't add up. But suppose it did? What were the implications if they had been telling the truth? Could there be some explanation for the "miraculous" stuff they had experienced, something going on that even they were not aware of?

And what were the implications for his faith? From what he had learned of Sky, they were not leaning in the direction of the scriptures he had read. He needed to know the truth.

He couldn't validate Pete Rogdon, but maybe he could Molly.

Was it his imagination, or did Molly become a little tense and anxious when he wanted to take a closer look at her car? He didn't know her well enough, but it seemed to him he had seen a look of fear in her eyes behind the banter. And the sudden rush to leave when he had started to say he wanted to look at the engine.

The healing of a car. He would have laughed if the implications for him were not so serious. As ridiculous as Pete's and Molly's stories were, there would be tens of thousands of viewers swayed, to some degree, by them.

Before falling asleep, he decided he would find a way to get a closer look at Molly's car.

Al called the next morning, wanting to know how the taping went and congratulating Reese on his "celebrityhood," which they both shared a joke about.

He didn't have a lot to do until time to prep for the next show.

In the afternoon he stopped at the cleaners, picked up his freshly laundered, pressed garments. He had owned two homes, had never bought a washer and dryer. He wondered how much money he could have saved over the years if he had.

Instead of heading back to his apartment, Reese mentally rehearsed the plan he had formulated last night and started north on 360 Highway, into 121 highway and then east on 114.

He turned on Satellite radio, pushed back the sunroof cover, felt the heat of the bright sun. A nice day in Dallas.

He drove in the slow lane, or the slower lane—nobody drove slow in Dallas. He ran through scenarios he had imagined. And alternative actions if his plan failed.

He drove casually down Las Colinas Boulevard passing the Exxon Mobil headquarters. It was a huge complex. Even this late in the year a large number of groundskeepers were out working the shrubbery.

As he scoped the complex layout—and the security—it was obvious that just driving into the parking lot to inspect an employee's car was out of the question. Reese looked at his watch. He had a little time, he guessed. He wasn't sure when Molly got off. Today might turn out to be just an exploratory trip. But being new to Dallas, it wouldn't be a wasted day; he still took time, periodically, to explore the geography of the Dallas-Fort Worth metroplex.

He took a random turn away from the Exxon Mobil buildings. A few blocks away he happened upon the Neiman-Marcus Building. For some reason it seemed fitting to Reese that the two big companies had offices near one another.

He cruised past Exxon Mobil again. A few people working the grounds, but no sign of workers leaving for home. He didn't want to draw attention to himself. As big and powerful and as geopolitically relevant and sensitive in today's tense world Exxon Mobil was, their security was probably extreme. He didn't want to risk more than three slow-cruise passes. He was about to leave the area when he saw a stream of traffic exiting the parking lot. He pulled over, as if waiting for someone.

He saw the big brown Chevy emerge from the parking lot. When he was able to merge with the traffic, he was three cars behind Molly. He was certain it was Molly. Couldn't be more than one of those big brown beats in a company the size of Exxon Mobil.

He wanted to confirm that though. At the light, he switched lanes, his SUV still the third car back from the car that was neck and neck with Molly's. He did an eye-straining scope of the Chevy's license plate. He recognized the "Molly 91".

While waiting for the light, Reese reached for his old slouch hat, as he referred to it. He always kept it in the car.

Molly took off with traffic, driving only slightly above speed limit. Reese had to work at staying three to five cars behind her. He didn't want to lose her, yet he didn't want to get so close that she might recognize him. He didn't think he had seen him in his SUV anytime at the studio, still—he didn't want her to detect him following her.

She was pretty much retracing his route. She headed south on 360 Highway, signaled for exit at westbound Harwood. Reese slowed a little, waited one car making the same exit, and headed west on Harwood.

He followed a little less than a quarter mile behind the Chevy. The light caught Molly at Euless-Main Street. Reese suddenly slowed. He didn't want to end up right behind her or right next to her. On the left the median just before the light was split to allow traffic to turn left into the strip mall and the Kroger parking lot. Reese did a quick signal light, swerved over into the left lane, down into the Kroger parking lot. He continued on past the grocery store to the end of the lot, turned right across the lot and up onto north-south Euless-Main traffic. He exited north to the corner in the far-left-turn lane. He saw Molly's car continuing west on Harwood.

When the light changed, he had to accelerate above speed limit to get within a safe distance of the Chevy. At Industrial Boulevard Molly turned into the Quick Trip. Reese followed a minute later.

His eyes scanned the parking lot; she was at the farthest gas pump, North end of the lot. He parked at a pump at the south end of the lot sat and waited.

After filling up, Molly got into northbound traffic on Industrial. Reese waited a few seconds and then followed.

At Cheek-Sparger Road, the Chevy signaled left, drove a block, and turned left up into the vast Wal-Mart Super Center parking lot. Reese relaxed some at the Cheek-Sparger and Industrial red light. He knew her destination now.

A few moments later, he was in the Wal-Mart lot, driving slowly, hat brim pulled down, sunglasses on; he scanned the cars parked.

He spotted the space she had taken and drove slowly past it, circled around the lot, and back pulled into a space five cars from the big brown Chevy.

He sat and thought.

Security was probably tight here. Just a few days ago a man at another Wal-Mart parking lot—could have been this one, Reese wasn't sure, he'd paid less-than-half attention to the TV report—had been caught by the store security camera flashing female customers. It hadn't taken more than a few minutes before the police had arrived. Cameras were everywhere these days.

He exited the SUV, started toward the store entrance. At Molly's car, he cut to the right, as if taking a short cut, continued up the inclined parking lot. He had seen enough; the door lock was up, in the unlocked position.

Just inside the store, Reese saw Molly—ironically she was wearing a female version of the kind of slouch hat he was wearing—pushing a cart toward the back of the store.

He grabbed a snicker at the nearest checkout aisle, paid, quickly exited the store, headed back toward Molly's car.

The lot was beginning to fill with shoppers making quick stops on their way home from work; Reese joined the shopper's pace. When he got to Molly's car, he took a quick look back at both entrances of the store. He didn't expect her this soon, but he couldn't take the chance.

He opened the driver's door, popped the hood latch. He went to the front of the car, raised the hood.

Looked like a brand-new engine. Confused, he looked a little closer. There was some dirt, a little oil around the crankcase. She took good care of her car. Maybe she had recently washed the engine or had it cleaned.

No, it was too shiny, too like new.

He looked back to the store entrances—no Molly.

His heart beating fast, he dropped to the ground, crawled under the car on his back. He wasn't sure how he'd explain his actions if security showed up, or worse maybe, if Molly did. He'd tell them something they'd believe—and do so without lying.

He pulled the penlight on his key chain out, found some numbers off the block, scrawled on his hand. He couldn't tell if the starter motor was new. He slid forward, stood up. He noticed the battery had a date mark six months back.

He closed the hood, looked at the emerging foot traffic from the store. He didn't see the flop hat among the heads leaving the store.

He opened the passenger-side door and opened the glove box. A bunch of stuff in there. Papers, Kleenex, a map, coupons, and some loose change. He opened a couple of the loose papers, a paid-bill receipt, a couple of fliers.

And then he found it.

It was a copy of a repair order for a 1991 Chevrolet from "Vickery's Remanufactured Engines and Repair."

Reese checked the date and read the details: "1991 Chevy Engine short block assy—5.0 liter," "replace starter mtr, repl battery, install new mich trs." The repair order was dated six months ago. Where it said "total due" was a "N/C." In parenthesis was a hand scrawled "N/C, see SM." The "N/C" would be no charge, and the "SM" would be service manager.

Reese tore off a piece of paper, recorded Vickery's telephone number. He returned the repair order. His eye fell on empty prescription bottles. One was for Xanax, the other for generic Chlorazepate. Both were dated refilled in the past month. So much for Molly's story about not needing mood-altering prescriptions anymore.

He looked up; his heart skipped a beat. Molly was making her way back to her car, pushing a cart. He bent low, closed the door of the car. Partially bent over, he started toward his SUV. He was in the SUV, heading for the access road by the time Molly started unloading her cart.

On the way home Reese picked up a subway turkey and ham, chips, and Coke. At home he spread a table on the coffee table and mulled over his new discovery.

So it appeared there was nothing to the Sky miracles, at least at first blush it appeared that way. It was possible that Molly had lied independently. Make that Molly and Ali. He wondered how Molly had gotten to the spotlight. How had she been chosen to go on the *Global Week* show?

Some of Molly's story was verifiable—just ask the local Exxon Mobil Corporate office staff about her now-famous car problems. That part was too verifiable to be lied about. The conspiracy was in the part about "healing" the car. The fact that Ali had testified about a vision was suspect too, particularly in light of its fulfillment being Molly.

Reese felt relieved by the conclusions he was coming to because it troubled him to think that the newly forming Sky movement had found answers that he and all of his background world of church as he knew it had not. That a Sky member could lay hands on a car and "cure" it of all it's mechanical problems, that was a little hard to take. His parents and other saints he knew, spent nights on their knees fasting and praying, seeking the Lord for such miracles. And they had found their prayers answered through normal everyday events and people.

But Jan had been right, there were masses of people who would believe the message of his TV show. Souls of men were at stake. And more and more souls were being drawn to the message of Sky. These "miracles" would just accelerate that draw.

Molly had not paid for any of the repairs to her car. Reese calculated the costs would have been anywhere from three thousand dollars to five thousand dollars. Relatively serious money for anyone modestly paid, and with beaucoup bills to boot.

He had transferred the numbers and other information he had improvisedly written on his hand to paper and filed it.

He took a few bites of food, turned the volume of the TV up. He perked up a bit. Bill Moyers on public TV. He didn't watch the show that often, but in the background was a picture related to one of the topics being covered tonight by the guest. The picture showed the newly elected president in pose with Sky church pastor Ferdinand Chezlewski, Azko Lee Britton and the prime minister of Israel. Reese realized he had just missed Bill Moyers's guest.

The phone rang as he finished eating. He answered Jon's call glad to hear from his friend. Twenty minutes of guy chat—convincing his buddy that Dallas was at least as nice a city to live in as Kansas City (he didn't want to say better than)—some up to dates and Reese hung up.

Before going to bed that night, he made a note to look into the details of Molly's miracle repair order. If there was any kind of miracle in all of her story, it was that she could have gotten that much work done on her car without paying for it.

On Sunday, a bright, clear, slightly chilled day, Reese attended one of the churches he had found on the Internet. He sat near the back, looked around the audience. Middle class, mostly white, but with a few black and brown faces. Conservatively dressed. He did a second scan of the six hundred to seven hundred present. He concluded, middle class, but a little more upmarket. He had noticed quite a few BMWs, Mercedes, Audis, SUVs in the parking lot. The pastor that came to the rostrum reminded Reese of the late Dr. Jas Kennedy. Tall, slim, with an intelligent, school-of-theology look about him, wearing a blue and gold robe.

"Ladies and gentlemen, brothers and sisters," he continued in a very authoritarian voice, "unity of faith, or I should say unity of faiths, is the call of the day. Christian, Muslim, Jew, Hindu,

Buddhist, Unitarian, and all others—you are welcome here. We are all servants of God and children of God. Love one another by unity of faith. Prepare your hearts, for that is what I want to talk about today. First, let us all stand and take a moment to greet those who are sitting near you."

Reese rose with the crowd. The lady in front of him turned. Sixtyish, stately, in expensive blue dress, heavy makeup, glistening earrings, and matching neck jewelry. Wrinkling face, but well camouflaged with skillfully applied makeup. A rigid face. She held her hand out and beamed a bright smile at Reese. Her clasp was ladylike. It lingered a second larger than normal, Reese thought, with the pressure of a lingering index finger. And a wink. "Good morning, welcome home!" Reese returned a "Good morning." Her husband had the look of a retired executive: tall, heavyset, aging, in good-fabric sport shirt with an artsy design and tan dress slacks. He gave Reese a limp hand, a "Mornin'" and a cold eye and quickly turned around to shake hands (both of them) with the man in suit and tie in front of him. Reese said "Good morning" to the young college preppie—looking man behind him, and to a short heavyset lady to his left, who gave him a warm smile and handshake.

The choir sang next. "America the Beautiful," followed by the "Battle Hymn of the Republic." The mood of the crowd lifted, converting stiffness into self-conscious and contrived casualness.

Reese turned his attention to the sermon. The pastor spoke on,

"And so, my brothers and sisters, I urge you to embrace all religions as equal before God. He loves us all. I admonish you: Love your neighbor as you love yourself. Do unto others as you would have them do unto you. Be tolerant, be accepting. We want peace in this world of ours. Who better to bring peace to the world than the church?" Both arms and hands spread before him, he let the question linger. "Think, my people. Whether you believe that Christ literally came out of the grave or not, that is not important. The important thing is that His message lives on. His command lives on, love one another!" His voice rose several decibels. "It's not a wish, it's a command!" "That is the way to peace. Peace within.

Peace at home. Peace at work. Peace between nations." He paused, folded his notes.

Reese did not hear one amen. The church was quiet. Not in hostility or resistance to the message, but it seemed to Reese there was just an air of neutrality in the place. Sunday service. Go out to recreate. Go back home—relax and prepare for Monday's grind or for Monday's monotony for those who were retired or who did not need to work. A dead church receiving a lethal message. "Whether you believed Christ came out of the grave or not was not important." Reese almost couldn't believe he'd heard right. Back to the yellow pages and the Internet, under "churches."

As he walked to his car, walking quickly past the mostly silent, exiting attendees, Reese had a disturbing thought. He wondered if the message today had been in line with the church's long-standing philosophy (and that's how he saw it—a philosophy, certainly not Holy Spirit inspired), or whether he had heard words inspired by Sky. If this so-called church was being influenced by Sky, he felt partially responsible. He felt guilty. As he drove home, he once again had that now-familiar anxiety; he was beginning to wonder if he was moving in the right direction in his vocation.

Later that evening at home, at broadcast time, he tuned into *Global Week on Air*. Seeing himself on TV made him uncomfortable. But, he was proud, and he had to admit that he couldn't find any flaws in his presentation. Not in his personal appearance or dress, nor in his verbal delivery.

When the cameras focused on Molly, Reese sat forward and gave her close inspection. She was saying, "Mr. Maxey, I was in a Sky session one day, I don't know, maybe six, seven, eight months ago, I was in deep meditation, never will forget it . . ."

Molly looked good on camera. On the surface she appeared as sincere as the preacher this morning.

"Well, you know . . . I thought, finally, I've lost my mind . . ."

Reese zoomed in on Molly. Her right foot was on toe, heel lifting up and down spasmodically. Could be just habit, could be just spotlight nervousness—although Molly hadn't impressed him as one to shy away from the spotlight, but just the opposite. From his training in psychology, Reese knew that when the tongue was lying, other parts of the body betrayed the lie, usually. In the case of psychopathic personalities, that was not always the case. But usually, the direction of eye roll, a tic, galvanic skin response (if you could measure it), or some indication of the lie surfaced.

In Molly's case, not enough evidence. He thought about the repair order for Molly's car.

He went to his file drawer, pulled the sheet he had scrawled on. "Vickery's Remanufactured Engines and Repair," 1-800-555-4949.

He finished watching the broadcast, pleased with the production.

He'd call Vickery's tomorrow.

CHAPTER

12

He made a trip to the nearby Kroger's on Monday. He had previously shopped Albertsons, and he liked the store although the prices looked a little high. Kroger had been a major part of the Kansas City grocery business back in the day but with union troubles, it had, along with A&P and Safeway, deserted the city. Just out of nostalgia, Reese chose Kroger.

He picked up some fruit, a couple of TV dinners, salad makings, orange juice, and Coca-Cola. As he stood waiting for the cashier to finish, she said, "Are you from around here?"

"Well, I'm from Kansas City, but I live here now."

"I've seen you somewhere before." She stopped sacking for a second and gave him a closer look. "Yeah, I'm sure."

Reese noted the beauty of her smile. He wondered if she had seen *Global Week* last night. She didn't seem like that demographic, though.

"Maybe you've seen me around the neighborhood." A possibility.

"Naw, I think I've seen you on . . . TV?"

"On what show?" Reese asked.

"I don't know, are you a newsman for CBS or NBC or?—"

Reese interrupted, laughed. "Maybe you've seen me around the area here." He laughed again, took his change, and exited the store.

He was not looking for celebrityhood. Not his personality, not his ambition. Success at low profile had always been his goal.

He put his safari-type hat and sunglasses on. Not the most inconspicuous look around here, but it did permit anonymity. He was not the baseball cap type. He caught his reflection in the store glass. Looked like something he'd seen in *GQ*, not bad, didn't look as strange as he'd imagined.

His cell phone rang as he headed west toward 360 Highway and his apartment. The number had been blocked.

"Yes?" he answered the anonymous caller. He was surprised to hear Al's voice.

"Hey, Hollywood, tell me something good!"

"Something good."

"I didn't say 'say something good,' I said 'tell me something good.'"

"The sun shines, the world goes round, it never gets as cold in Dallas as it does in Kansas City—"

"But you don't live in Dallas—not yet at least—you're just there temporarily—"

"But I'm thinking about moving here."

"Are you, really?"

"I am."

"Well, might be good for you. Our offer to help you relocate is still on the table. Reason I called though, I want to congratulate you on an excellent show. Your opening night was a hit, guy."

"Thank you, glad to hear that, Al, I did the best I could."

"You tell *60 Minutes* if they call, we've got your contract." Al laughed.

"I'm your man."

In a little more serious tone, Al continued, "Listen, can you attend a Regional Chamber of Commerce meeting this week?"

Reese mentally searched his calendar,

"Don't have anything on my plate—sure, sure I can be there, if it's this side of Timbuktu."

"It is. Meeting's at the Gaylord in Dallas—the one in Grapevine, I believe. This is going to be a pretty important meeting, people from Midwest, South, East and West Coasts, and a few of them—heavyweights. All but a handful Fortune 500."

"What role do I play?"

"Mainly, just show up and present Sky stuff to 'em."

Reese felt a tug of anxiety.

"They've slotted you five minutes to get your message over."

"And when is this?" Reese struggled to keep his voice upbeat.

"In just a few days—I'll send the particulars to you—FedEx, or I might just fax you—you faxed up yet?"

"Sure am."

"You'll enjoy the Gaylord—ever been there?"

"Passed by it—"

"Humungous place, I mean, huge!—Don't get lost in it." Al laughed.

Reese unloaded his groceries. He left his fax machine on. He called Laurie, his call-me-when-you-need-me assistant in Kansas City, mainly just to touch base with her.

Next he called Jan. Leaving out any mention of Sky, they had a pleasant conversation. So very nice to have her, to be in this relationship, he thought as he hung up.

He heard the fax ring, heard the whir of the machine, watched as the pages from Al slid slowly onto the out tray.

When the machine finished its duty, Reese studied the papers it had spit out. There were some big-name companies on the list of attendees coming to the meeting at the Gaylord. And there were a few big-name individuals—names in the business news frequently.

The agenda showed him speaking on "church, spiritual, and social issues in the workplace" near the end of the program.

He felt some tiny bit of relief. This was going to be a PR/reinforcement speech for Sky, not a hard sell. Maybe not so bad.

127

He was recognizing a growing internal need to soft sell the spiritual side of Sky and to emphasize the social and workplace benefits of diverse people working together. Comradeship while working. Why couldn't that be the goal? Looking at the suggested script, though . . . well, he could modify it some. In time maybe he'd have the influence to steer all of this to two goals: exercising in the workplace and morale building among people of diverse religions, cultural and racial backgrounds. That would serve the purpose and do so without getting in the way of God's work—the real God.

He suddenly had a fearful thought—suppose Molly had lied but the other miracles being reported were for real?

He took a legal pad to his desk and began a rough draft of his upcoming presentation.

CHAPTER

13

Reese pocketed his house and other keys, left the SUV key in the ignition, motor running, thanked the valet, and took the ticket.

The Gaylord was a monstrosity of a hotel. One thousand five hundred guest rooms, four hundred thousand square feet of meeting space.

He found the Texas room where the meeting was to be held.

He had decided to wear suit and tie and chose on the conservative side.

He made his way to the meeting room two minutes before the doors were closed.

His seat was at a round table that seated six comfortably.

The place was abuzz with conversation, the tinkle of glasses and plates being served.

Reese looked around; the lighting had been slightly dimmed to give the right atmosphere for the sixty or seventy or so guests. In a day of dress/casual, Reese noted all, excluding a half dozen, wore suit and tie or the female equivalent.

On his right sat two men, Ford Motor Company execs by their place cards,—Andy and Fred. On his left were two ladies, attractive, well dressed—they somehow impressed Reese as social service types.

More like social-service-and-business-in-tandem types. One of them caught Reese's eye.

"Hi—Shelia."

Reese took the hand offered.

"Nice to meet you—I'm Reese Maxey." He'd never gotten comfortable with first-name-only introductions.

"And I'm Stacy." Reese partially stood, reached across the table a little awkwardly to shake the outstretched hand.

Introductions all around followed.

"Oh—I think I saw your name on the program." Shelia had a pleasant, open voice.

"Yeah, that's me . . . gettin' my five cents—five minutes, I guess it is, of fame."

Light giggles from Shelia and Stacy, tight smiles from Andy and Fred. Stacy said, "What do you do?"

A little more mature voice, pleasant smile. Reese wondered if she had read the program. He wasn't sure how it described him, if at all.

"I'm a contractor—I'm in industrial marketing research and executive interviewing."

Reese could tell by the expressions around the table, and the silence, that they weren't sure exactly what he did for a living. He reflected quickly with self-condemnation that lately he was a promoter—of a questionably viable universal church that was stealing men's souls.

"You've probably heard of Sky?"

"Sure have," Shelia threw in as Stacy nodded, Andy said, "You bet!"

Stacy said, "Are you a part of that?"

"I do some PR work for Sky."

"That's wonderful!" Shelia said, "Do you know Randy"—she turned to Stacy—"what's the guy's name, we met—"

"Randall—Randy . . . Connors."

Reese had seen the name on a memo in Al's office.

"I know of him—I know the name. I believe he's one of my counterparts—out east."

"We met him a few weeks ago at a meeting in New York—wonderful guy. So you go around converting people to Sky, getting them to join . . ."

Fred jumped in, "You also host a TV show, think I saw you on *Global Week*, not long ago . . . ?"

"Oh—yeah." Sheila, nodding her head up and down, pulled her napkin away from her mouth.

"I thought you looked familiar!—You did the show that the, that Molly somebody—she had prayed, her car was healed, something like that. And this guy had a vision." Reese wondered if Shelia was always this hyperactive.

"Guilty," he said and picked at a piece of his chicken breast.

"You did a great job with that show," Fred said. "Mike Wallace, look out!"

Reese thought Mike Wallace had retired.

"Well, I'll take that compliment since Mike Wallace is retired."

Table of small laughter. Fred chewing his food smiled and said, "That goes for Chris Wallace too."

Table of big laughter.

They ate in silence for a minute. Reese said, "What's going on over at Ford Motor Company?—I used to be with GM myself."

"Everything's cool at Ford," Andy said. "We've got a Sky program working at several of our plants, and man, I tell you, productivity has shot waaay up!"

Reese took a few more bites of chicken and green beans. He noticed the "EAP" identifiers on Shelia's and Stacy's name tags.

"You are part of an employee assistance program?"

"Sure are"—Shelia did a hasty napkin wipe of her mouth—"with H-H-A, Human Health Agency. We go into the big corporations and provide social services—mostly counseling," Stacy added.

"And we are getting oriented to Sky. So much emphasis is on spirituality these days, and with the world moving in that direction, well, we've been real busy—lately we've been prescribing Sky as a part of therapy."

Andy asked, "What's your take on that, Reese?"

"On what?"

"Well, maybe kind of a dumb question but on second thought, since you're PR for Sky, just overall, what's your take on the big worldwide push toward spirituality?" Andy looked like he was almost sorry he had asked the question.

Reese finished a sip of his tea.

"Well, I'm convinced that we have become too materially oriented. There is a spiritual void out there. And . . . I'm convinced that there is a need for unity, for comradeship—for lack of a better word—in the workplace. We need to rebuild our work ethic, we've lost a lot of product quality to other countries that have integrity in the workplace. We've become a much more diverse nation. People who are look-alike are more comfortable with one another, there's more interaction between like-image people. If you're comfortable with the person you work with, you work . . . better . . . together.

"Problem is we no longer all look alike. America is not as homogenous as it once was—not in the workplace. So there is a need to—a need for . . . programs that bring diverse people, diverse in cultural background, in race, in religion—to bring them together in the workplace so that they become comfortable with one another. If they're comfortable with each other, they'll work together better—more productively—employees and employers both benefit. Everybody ends up happy."

Shelia said, "And the spiritual side, I guess. Church at work—so-called church, at work, well, that speaks to a spiritual component."

Stacy said, "You know, Reese, I'm really impressed with what you and, and Randy and all the others of you are doing. I mean, a business executive out promoting things that are spiritual, I mean, well, it's so humane. How cool is that!"

Fred laughed. "You tryin' to say we business types are not human?"

"No, no—nothing like that. It's just that when you, well, I just picture business types as so material and money oriented—"

Fred said, "I'd like to ask you something, Reese, why do you think we've lost a lot of our market to overseas?"

"Well . . . I do believe the American auto industry failed to listen to Demming—Big Mistake—but the Japanese did.

"He," Andy threw in, "brought in that whole philosophy had a lot to do with continuous improvement in manufacturing, quality circles, stuff like that."

"Right."

Fred said, "And he kind of spoke to spiritual issues, I believe . . . ?"

"I'm not an authority, on Deeming, but I believe he did advocate individual development of workers," Reese said.

Fred said, "Well, I think what has happened over the past thirty, forty years or so, we in the business world did wake up to the fact that it is not so lame to bring our inner selves to work. Back in the '40s, '50s, and before, you'd have been laughed all the way home to talk about anything that related to spirituality or psychology at work.

Today, we've gotten smart enough to know it takes the whole person—mind, spirit, and body to make work. Productive work, at least."

"Heavy," said Andy.

All laughed.

"That's exactly right," said Reese. "Carl Rogers, Maslow—their concept of self-actualization—you don't hear the term much these days, but their concept is still valid. You need the whole person, and the person who is whole—who is doing what he or she was cut out to do—that's who's needed in the workplace."

"Spiritual development is a part of becoming whole," Stacy said. "People who have the same worship of God and who work together, well . . . makes for a nice little cozy world—I guess."

Reese said, "Theoretically," and took a spoonful of ice cream.

Fred chuckled, "Do I detect a little 'Ye of little faith there?'"

Reese wiped his mouth.

"Well, I believe that if you can change the heart of a person, modify their belief system, their perspective, you can change their feelings and their external behavior, and that includes their productivity at work."

Wiping his mouth, looking at the tabletop, and as if talking to no one in particular, Fred said, "Regeneration, born again, and the Prince of Peace—"

"And the golden rule and Ephesians 6 five and six and this wouldn't be our dinner-table conversation," Reese cut in. He and Fred exchanged brief nods and a wink.

He heard the loud tinkle of spoon against glass, looked up to see the MC of today's program at the dais. A corporate type in button-down collar pale blue shirt, tie and gray suit. He reminded Reese of Kevin Klein.

"Listen up, ladies and gentlemen!" The noise of the noon luncheon grew dimmer as the MC waited. "Thank you all for coming today, I know some of you had to leave all that ice and snow back East and come hear to moderate-clime Texas." laughter.

As he made introduction, Reese gleaned just as Al's fax had indicated, the luncheon and meeting to follow was a general get-together of business execs to discuss various issues related to globalization. Reese's part was mainly just a few words confined to encouragement of represented companies toward Sky groups, to get them to increase local membership, to quote a few statistics that validated production benefits for those companies that were participating in Sky. Representatives from finance, banking, manufacturing, construction, IT, and food service were scheduled on the agenda. There wouldn't be any breakout sessions, but there would be a period for questions and answers after the last speaker. Reese detected a lively group, a lot of enthusiasm for the topics at hand.

When it came his turn to speak, Reese was more nervous than usual, and not sure why. The MC was saying,

"OK, guys and gals, I hope you took in all the points Frank just made about Industrial Design Build and Construction. This next guy you're going to hear from, you might have seen this past Sunday night on *Global Week on Air*. I watched the show, and I can say he did an excellent job with the new Sky series. Give a big welcome for Mr. Reese Maxey."

The applause was appropriate in volume and duration, Reese noted as he made his way to the dais.

"I want to thank the US Chamber of Commerce and the Consortium in attendance for this opportunity," Reese began.

His goal was to make the points that (1) in the production side of life—the workplace—the whole man is needed, mind, body, and soul. "Evidence based research has proved that." (2) Divisions in the workplace meant alienation, hostility, low productivity, and sometimes violence. Hence, Muslim, Buddhist, Hindu, Christian, Jew, and any other if they could find time to worship together ("and they're not going to do so on Sunday"), (3) "All of this melded together in Sky in the workplace." (4) "To present some evidence-based cases."

He ended with "Some of you probably knew Alexander Furniture Company or read the piece in *Fortune* about them. "They've had a long history of falling short of production goals. Sky sessions were introduced, with a 90 percent plus of employees' participation. Within thirty days they saw improvement. At the end of the quarter, they were ahead of production goals by just under 20 percent. First time they'd even met production goals in more than a decade. And this was tracked by scientific-based research, by the way, so"—he glanced at his watch—"to keep within my five minutes up here, I'll end by simply asking you to seriously consider the Spiritual Church International as part of your creative capitalism."

Reese heard a decent level of applause as he returned to his table, feeling pretty good about his presentation.

"And now, people"—the MC had returned to duty—"the floor is open to all for any questions you might have of our speakers."

"I'd like to ask Mr. Maxey about that evidence-based part about Alexander Furniture."

Deep voice, Southern twist, from table at the far wall. "I'd like a few details."

Reese stood. "Well, the—one of the issues of *Fortune* magazine—I believe it was one of the February issues, has the full story. In a nutshell, plant managers tracked employee productivity of a sample of Sky members before and after Sky membership. And did the same with those few employees who were not members. Productivity went up double digit for Sky members. The non-Sky members showed some increase too, but it was small, something like 2 percent, 3 percent as I recall, and evidence suggested that 2, 3 percent was a rub-off from the increased productivity of Sky members."

Reese was about to sit down when a guest, two tables in front of Reese, near the podium stood up.

"I'd like to ask Mr. Maxey about the spiritual side of Sky."

The MC said, "The floor's yours, Mr. Zonman."

Reese detected the respect in the MCs voice. He looked at the guest a little closer. Neatly and conservatively dressed, he reminded Reese a lot of New York mayor Bloomburg.

"Mr. Maxey, when it comes to religion and faiths, is it not true that Christians and Muslims both believe in one God?"

Reese felt his heart do a quick flip.

"Well yes, that is true."

"Two distinct gods."

"Well, I believe they both—they both attempt to worship the same God . . . the God of Abraham." The room seemed to have gotten more quiet.

"But I believe one faith says that no man comes to the Father—God, except through me."

"Is that a question?" Reese heard a smothering of laughter.

"I believe it's a quote, Mr. Maxey." Zonman had a small smile on his face as he watched Reese.

"I believe you're right," Reese said.

"And," Zonman continued, "if 'except through me' is to be taken literally, well, we have something of a problem when it comes to people worshipping together, and praying to God—the One true God. Would you not agree? Is that not an issue?"

Reese glanced at the MC, no help there.

"I'm not trying to put you on the spot, Mr. Maxey. I am just seriously wondering how two faiths—people who don't have exactly the same concept of God, of who God is, can come together and worship Him." If Allah is God, and there is no other god beside him, then Jesus Christ couldn't be the Son of God, and in fact God too. In fact, Muslims see Jesus as only one of many great prophets."

Reese said, "Well, I wish I could discuss with you how Sky overcomes that issue, but we don't have the time now. Maybe we can meet in private sometime, and well, I'll show you the light."

Reese gave a smile he wasn't feeling. The room relaxed with polite laughter.

Zonman gave a small nod of his head and sat down, a slight smile on his face.

At the end of the luncheon, Reese saw Zonman coming his way. He extended his hand; Reese shook it. Neither man felt any animosity.

Up close Reese saw that Zonman bore a world-weary, savvy demeanor. A world-class savvy, a little hardness there, yet something gentle underneath. At a distance he looked like Mayor Bloomberg. Up close, his demeanor reminded Reese of Robert Mitchum and Gene Hackman, both. The eyes projected a good IQ. For some odd reason, Reese felt a kindred spirit.

"You gave a very fine presentation, Mr. Maxey."

"Well, I appreciate that—Mr. Zonman." A lot of execs in the room today. Reese recalled the singular respect he had detected in the MC's voice when he had addressed Zonman.

"My questions were deliberate, with a purpose. I was not trying to put you on the spot."

"Your questions were very appropriate," Reese said truthfully.

In fact, Reese thought, Zonman had raised questions that he had been pushing to the back of his mind.

"I must say I believe they were," Zonman said. "If Muslims and Christians believed in one God, in one source of reference as the Word of God—the Bible—then the world would be a better place to live, a safer place to live. And yes, the products and services producers of the world would reap the rewards of having that kind of believer working for them. But that is a world to come. It's not the world we live in today."

"Meanwhile, we can certainly work toward it," Reese said.

"If the approach is right."

"We brought people of different races together—that's what affirmative action was about—and we brought people of diverse gender, sexual orientation, different age categories, we brought them together and made the workplace a better place."

Zonman was nodding as Reese talked.

"But, Mr. Maxey, Sky goes past integrating people socially and vocationally. It tampers with the spiritual side of mankind. Trying to worship God at work. What about those Christian sects who still keep the Sabbath? What about unbelievers who don't know God? Pretty soon they will equate the factory, or the office, with God, I mean Sky proposes to bring man to God, to unify the planet via religion, and more than mere religion, quote, unquote, but to unify mankind at a spiritual level, the realm where man meets God.

"The Bible tells you how to meet God—in this life—and prepare for dwelling with him through eternity. Any other approach is—I hate to be this blunt about it, but I feel strongly about this—any other approach extrabiblical is wrong."

The words were a little harsh, but the look in Zonman's eye was kind.

"No pun intended, Mr. Maxey, Sky did not come from heaven— it came out of the Club of Davos."

"Mr. Zonman"—a young executive type appeared at Zonman's side—"your car is at the side entrance."

"Mr. Maxey, it has been a pleasure meeting you."

He reached into his jacket breast pocket and extracted a leather business card case and handed it to Reese,

"If you are ever in the New York area, give me a call—for some reason I feel our paths are going to cross again."

He stuck his hand out; Reese took it, both men giving appreciative, warm handshakes.

"And, Mr. Maxey . . . if you ever need my help . . ."

Reese watched as Zonman exited, shaking hands with several attendees, escorted to his car by two military-looking fit men in business suits.

As Reese drove home from the luncheon, he was troubled by the questions Zonman had raised. Reese felt a small sense of anger rising. Had Zonman been posing serious questions, or had he simply been trying to show off, show some authority and knowledge in the meeting, and just enjoying putting the speaker on the spot? But, most of the speakers had had one or two questions asked of them about their topics.

In meeting Zonman face-to-face, Reese had detected a look of genuineness in the man; Reese's impression was of a man of substance and sincerity. Not a man who needed to reaffirm or prove his power. And not one who would be so shallow or mean-spirited. The genuine article was Reese's impression. A for-real dude. So his questions were asked from a sincere heart. Or rather, the questions he asked were to a make point. And for some odd reason, Reese felt the questions Zonman asked were more for Reese's benefit. And Reese was very much troubled by the thought.

For something to distract his thoughts, he switched to his intention to buy a watch. He was an admirer of good clothing and good watches. The challenge for him was to find clothing and watches on the upper end at lower prices. He liked styles that were always in and on the conservative side but with a hint of not hip, but a little bit of flair. He probably spent more time at the malls than most guys, but then, with the advent of the metrosexual male, he felt more at ease shopping these days. He had discarded the *Esquire* magazine issue in which he had seen the watch he has considering. But the local library likely would have it.

He recalled a visit to a library—in Euless.

He drove down 360 Highway, took the 183 west exit to Ector Street, then north a few blocks. As he recalled, it was behind the police and fire stations.

He went to the magazine section, found the issue of *Esquire* with the special advertising section on watches. He would concentrate his shopping on Rolex—a little too rich for his blood, though—and Omega and Tag Heuer. He found the ad section.

He browsed for a while and gave a little more attention to a couple of models by Omega. He made a note of the specs and the model numbers. He liked the look of one in particular.

As he returned the magazine to its place in the rack, Zonman once again popped into his head. It occurred to him that he might find some information on Zonman before he left the library.

Zonman. Barak Zonman. Yes, he was sure he had heard the name, or more likely seen the name in print at times. He went to the reference desk.

"Excuse me, I'm trying to find some information on a business executive—A Barak Zonman."

"The library lady looked up—she looked scholarly. Brown hair, short, white plain blouse, rimless glasses. She reminded Reese of one of his old sociology professors during his undergrad years at the University of Missouri.

"Do you have a library card?"

"Sure don't," Reese said regretfully.

She turned to her computer. "Did you say Barak Zonman?"

"That's right."

She tapped a few keys, lightning fast. She watched the changes on the screen.

"There was a piece on him in *Forbes* magazine a few months ago."

She gave Reese the issue date. "That issue is probably still on the shelf. If you'll wait a few minutes, I think I can find it."

"Reese thanked her. When she returned, she had a magazine in hand. "Found it," she said with a friendly smile.

"Thanks very much." Reese took the issue to a nearby vacant table.

The article was a list of profiles of the one hundred most interesting personalities in business. Reese read with interest. A couple of the names in the section were people who had attended today's luncheon. The last profile was Zonman, with, as the others, just a snapshot of the man, less than a half page.

Zonman's qualifications for making this list included his mystery: not a lot was known about him. At least not a lot was published about him, Reese guessed. He was head of a holding company whose name Reese recognized by name. Reese scanned the list of companies under the umbrella of the holding company. Reese recognized several names including one he used to call on as a market researcher in the Kansas City area. He recalled one of his early visits there, about fifteen years ago.

B&C Tool company. The engineer he was interviewing that day had invited him back to the plant building after the interview. He had shown Reese the process of designing a plastic bottle on a Silicon Graphics CAD Computer. Reese had been fascinated. He had recalled his drafting class many years earlier in junior high school. Back then, design had been done tediously, using compass, straightedges, slide rules, pen, pencils, graph paper.

Reese had called on B&C Tool numerous times over the years. He had not been aware that B&C Tool—Boyd Christopher, its publicly visible president—had a higher level of ownership.

Zonman owned a lot of companies like B&C Tool.

The last paragraph of the profile struck Reese as especially interesting. It indicated Zonman was something of a "mystery man" with strong ties to the intelligence communities of several nations, including the United States' and Israel's.

As he finished the profile, Reese had the image of a wealthy businessman, well connected to leaders in industry and government. He kept a low profile. For some reason, the word *chosen* popped into Reese's head.

Reese returned the magazine to the reference desk and headed for home. He was glad that he had met Zonman. But as he drove toward his apartment, he couldn't push Zonman's questions out of his mind. They continued at the back of his mind, played through his TV watching that night and on into his slumber. He needed to talk to someone. He made a resolution to try to get an appointment, not just try, but get and confirm an appointment with Bishop Padduck.

With commitment to do so, he drifted easily into sleep.

CHAPTER

14

"Hey, big guy!"

Reese had slept well and soundly. Al's voice on the phone was a booming wake-upper.

"What's up, big Al," Reese tried to boom back.

"Just want to make sure you're ready for tomorrow. I'm going to be out of the office tomorrow, thought I'd call you before I leave, see if you need anything."

"Think I'm ready to go."

"You'll do well—you did well last week, and that was your first show. I think Marie sent you everything you needed, but I'm going to fax it to you again. Stick to the script, Reese."

"It'll be a good show, you'll be happy with it." Reese was wide-awake now.

"I'm sure."

Reese paused a second then said, "You're out tomorrow. Taking a little vacation time?"

"A few days in the Ozarks."

Reese tried to picture Al in the Ozarks and smiled to himself.

"Doing what?" he asked.

"Boating, fishing—ice fishing," he finished with a laugh. "Nah, me and the wife, maybe some boating, but mostly away from the rat race here, in a cabin by the lake, relaxing and watching TV, and we're going to some group function—my wife's plans for Friday night, rest of the time catch a couple of Vegas shows over in Branson."

"Must be nice," Reese said.

"You need to marry that social worker you're dating—life's more interesting with a partner. This world's made for couples. Reese, listen, gotta run, but I'll fax this stuff to you right away, later."

"Later," Reese said, clicked off.

Reese thought for a second; a vague troubling feeling lingered. And then it dawned on him "that social worker you are dating." Reese did a flashback. Employers were delicate and inhibited these days about asking their employees about sexual matters, private romance, etc. Reese didn't recall ever mentioning anything about Jan to Al.

He heard the fax ring and padded to his office to receive the transmission. Before leaving the room, he thought about his promise to himself to call Bishop Padduck.

He went to his briefcase, got out the little calendar/phone directory he kept. He rarely used his cell phone to store numbers. He looked up the church number, picked up the telephone receiver. Second thought, he reached for his cell phone. Reese felt nervous. He wasn't sure why. He pushed himself to dial.

On the third ring a voice answered, "Bishop Padduck." Reese was caught off guard by the bishop's voice; he had expected a receptionist's voice. It occurred to him that he had gotten the number he had just dialed from Jan.

"Bishop Padduck, this is Reese Maxey." Reese felt his palm moisten.

"Who—oh yes, brother Maxey! How are you?! The warmth in Padduck's voice relaxed Reese a bit.

"Doin' pretty good, Bishop. I don't know whether Jan mentioned it to you, but I'm temporarily in Dallas working on a project."

"Well, I thought maybe you were away. Wasn't sure, but I did see you on TV last week."

Reese tensed.

"That show is a part of my work here," he said.

"I thought maybe that was the case." The warm voice had cooled, Reese thought.

"You know, Pastor, I—I guess I need to talk to you."

"Yes."

"And that's why I'm calling. Thought maybe I could get an appointment with you—don't know exactly when I'll be in Kansas City, but I expect in the very near future. I . . . uh, just wanted to talk . . ."

"That would be good, brother Maxey. In fact, I will tell my secretary to give you priority when you call—whenever you call. Looking forward to it, in fact."

Reese felt relief flow.

"I very much appreciate that, Bishop."

"We are helpers of one another, brother Maxey, looking forward to our meeting. Just give me a call when it's convenient."

Reese said good-bye. Sat down, stared at his desk a few minutes. He felt relief; he felt rejuvenated, like a too-heavy backpack had been lifted from his shoulders.

He took a look at the papers Al had faxed. He'd do the TV show. And if any more phony, supernatural hocus-pocus came up, he'd investigate it thoroughly, on his own time. And he'd document it. How he'd use it, or even if he'd use it later, was yet to be seen. If nothing else, the disproof of the false way of Sky would strengthen his resolve in his own faith.

CHAPTER

15

Reese arrived at the TV studio early. He parked where Molly had parked last show. He wanted to see his guests as they arrived. Do a pop psychology personality preshow assessment. He'd know a little about his guests just by their individual gaits, the way they walked into the studio—individually and as a group. And he wanted to see what kind of cars they drove just in case he needed to follow one or more of them, and at the same time he would prevent them seeing his SUV from his vantage point.

He had picked up a pair of inexpensive binoculars in the sports department of Wal-Mart.

He felt a little sneaky, a little predatory, and a little silly. He wondered if stalkers felt this sense of guilt. But he reminded himself of why he was doing this. Put in perspective, a worldwide movement was perhaps fostering a religion of deception. Influencing gullible souls. As Zonman had put it, tampering with men's souls. And Reese was becoming a catalyst for this evil. Did he have enough information at this point to categorize Sky as evil? Maybe Molly and Al were just big liars, needing to suck up to their employers for whatever reason. But that still left a more important aspect of Sky at issue for Reese. As he saw it too many people were beginning to take this seriously, believing that they had found God, the real God. In one editorial last week in *Global Week*, a reader had said she had resigned from her job to become a missionary for Sky. She had merged Buddhism, Christianity, and Islam in her life. Just how she had "merged" them wasn't clear, but she had said the melding had come in a vision of a symbol. The symbol was of a circle around what looked like an arrow. To Reese it had looked like the old '60s hippie symbol of an encircled, broken cross.

He had been waiting twenty minutes. He was beginning to feel a little ridiculous.

He was considering going on into the studio to finish last-minute prep when he saw a black late-model BMW 5 Series enter the parking lot.

The car pulled into a space near the studio entrance.

Reese saw four people exit the luxury car.

The driver, in a crew neck sweater and dress pants, exited the car, exchanged a few words with his passengers who were exiting the other three doors, and walked ahead of them.

He walked confidently, like a leader, Reese thought. That was probably Ed Caulfield. Ed had executive-level responsibilities related to marketing for the Southwest and Western states Wal-Mart stores.

The man following Ed was of medium height of Mideastern skin tone, receding shiny black hair. That would be Ed Al-Harbi. He had flown in from the West Valley City, Utah store to be on the show.

The two ladies following would be Pia Robinson, a local Wal-Mart pharmacist, and Rosie Hernandez, a stocker at a local Wal-Mart.

Reese started toward the entrance to the studio. He took a deliberate route past the black BMW and recorded the license plate number.

The five of them sat in the semicircled spotlighted area of the last show. Today's show would be a live broadcast. After the introductions and welcome, Reese faced his guests.

"Welcome to *Global Week on Air*."

"Glad to be here," Ed Caulfield said, apparently speaking for the group.

"Each of you has had a unique and noteworthy experience as a member of Sky. That is why you have been chosen to participate in this broadcast," Reese began. As he set up the introductory part of the show, he tried to read the personas facing him.

Ed Caulfield looked confident and a little polished for Wal-Mart. Handsome, hair brushed straight back, purple blue crew neck sweater, over a pale lavender shirt, rich fabric, neatly creased slacks over well-polished tasseled loafers. He looked confident. His eyes were constantly moving. Searching yet rejecting being searched.

Ed Al-Harbi looked Mideastern. Olive skin, shiny black hair. Constant smile on his face. He wore a jacket and slacks, bulky casual/dress shoes. Again, shifty eyes, searching but not wanting to draw attention.

Pia looked professional and dressed the same.

Rosie was dressed in a pants suit. She seemed friendly and open to Reese.

"Let's start with you, Rosie. Tell us the noteworthy experiences you've had as a member of Sky."

Rosie beamed a big smile,

"Ees like, for one, I needed to lose weight. But I could never make it . . . I could never stay on a diet. I tried many, many times.

"But when I start to go to Sky, well, you know, look a' me now!"

Ending on a high, loud note with a laugh, Reese and his guests joined her laugh; Pia and Ed Caulfield applauded good-naturedly.

Rosie continued, "And you know . . . Sky, it help my . . . my attitude, and it help my work. My . . . my perform—how you say—"

"Performance," Reese said.

"Si—yes, my job performance. And I get raise. Uno, dos, tres"— she raised three fingers—"three times."

Reese nodded.

"So Sky has helped you in improving your health and improving your attitude about your job, and has improved your job performance."

"Yes! And it is fun to do too!"

Rosie had an excited look on her face.

Reese looked at Pia. "And you, Pia, what has Sky meant to you?"

Pia sat forward slightly, hands folded in her lap, a tiny lady voice. "Oh, I have to concur with Rosie. Sky is fun, and I have found that the exercises, the meditations, those things we get into in Sky sessions at work carry over to after hours. I exercise regularly now. I find much less stress at work. I'm less short-tempered at work and at home."

"Have your coworkers, your friends, family noticed these changes?" Reese asked.

"Oh yes! You bet. My husband mentioned that the other day— last time I asked him to take the trash out!" Laughter all around.

Ed leaned forward, looked at Pia, and said:

"So, Pia, you're not still beating your husband, I take it."

The behind-camera crew, Reese, and guests all laughed.

"Only when he needs it," Pia shot back, more laughter.

"And with all your exercise he's probably too scared to fight back anymore," Reese threw in. Another round of laughter. When the laughter settled, Reese turned to look at the two Eds and said, "From my notes, Ed . . . and Ed,—two Eds here today—I understand you two have quite a testimony to share with us."

"Well, I think it's a story worth sharing," Ed Caulfield said.

Ed Al-Harbi nodded and said, "Oh yes," under his breath.

"And as I understand it," Reese continued, "it has something to do with an automobile again, coincidently."

"A car stolen and recovered," Caulfield said.

"A miraculous car recovery, not a car healing," Reese said. Two Eds, Pia, and Rosie chuckled.

"A miraculous car recovery," Caulfield said, nodding in affirmation.

"Can you tell us a little bit about it." The two Eds looked at each other. Caulfield said, "I think it's appropriate for Ed to start this."

Al-Harbi shifted. "Well, I work at the West Valley City store—"

"That's West Valley City, Utah," Reese clarified.

"Yes."

"That's about what, one thousand air miles from Dallas?" Reese said.

"That's right."

"I work as an assistant manager. I joined Sky about six months ago. So one day I'm doing meditation with my Sky sisters and brothers, and I get this flash, kind of like a vision." Reese noticed Al-Harbi's seat position had shifted again toward Ed Caulfield sitting next to him.

As he talked, Al-Harbi made only fleeting eye contacts with Reese.

"I'm almost in a trance."

"Reese said, "Again, was this a vision, a dream, or an image that came to your mind's eye?"

Al-Harbi's eyes rolled upward, rightward as he entertained Reese's question.

"In my mind's eye."

"Go on," Reese said.

"In my mind's eye, I see this car—a black BMW." Al-Harbi scratched his nose.

"And I wonder why. Just this BMW. What does it mean? . . . So I forget about it. Next day, same thing. This time it is clearer. I see the license plate number—some letters and then zero, one, three." Al-Harbi had folded his arms, leaned back tight into his chair.

"Then I see, like a big neon sign, in bright light some letters—"

"This is still a part of your vision—your mind's eye?" Reese asked.

"This is the second vision, the second time these letters form in my mind's eye, one at a time—C-a-l-l-o-w-a-y-C-e-m-e-t-e-r-y-R-o-a-d-F-o-r-t-W-o-r-t-h—I remembered them after I got home too."

And then I heard a voice, it said 'Stolen car, help your brother.'"
Al-Harbi, looked closer and a little longer at Reese, like he's looking for validation, Reese thought. He returned a poker face.

"And then what?" Reese asked.

Ed Caulfield jumped in, "Well, he writes this stuff he got in this vision down, on a piece of paper, and he calls the Forth Worth Police Department and gives them this information."

"Did they believe this guy?"

Caulfield's laugh sounded a little strained to Reese.

"They were suspicious at first," Caulfield continued. "They did a missing car search—but, backing up a little here."

Caulfield paused, shifted his seat, with a little lean toward Al-Harbi.

"About a week before Ed had this vision. I was visiting one of the DFW stores. Parked in my usual space. I come back, after my meeting, no car!"

Caulfield, shifted, sat forward, right hand holding his left wrist.

"I mean, was I mad! I called the police, gave them a report, all the details on the car. They did a data base search, came across Ed's story. Did an investigation on Ed too!"

"Thorough investigation," Al-Harbi said, looking at Caulfield. They both did a little chuckle.

"And," Caulfield continued, "believe it or not," they found a street called Calloway Cemetery Road, right off 157 Highway, somewhere up near Arlington, Forth Worth, and voila! And that was where they found my BMW! Except for tires missing and my logic 7 Sound System, the car was otherwise in one good running piece." Caulfield sat back.

"Eventually, the insurance company replaced my tires and stereo system.

"When I heard the story of how they found it, heard about Ed and his vision, well, let's just say that I'm a more faithful Sky member now."

And Ed went on, "I also want to add, I too exercise more, I feel better at work, and I've dropped a few pounds . . . and no"—Caulfield looked at Pia—"I don't beat my wife anymore either."

The room exploded with laughter, guests, behind camera, and Reese politely joined in. Caulfield looked into the camera.

"Just a little humor there, honey."

Reese waited until all laughter had subsided,

"Well, quite some story there. I should say stories there." He nodded smilingly at the rest of the group.

"Now, we're going to put a little twist on today's format. We're going to open up to our audience across the country and accept some on-air questions. Are you all ready and willing for that?" Reese looked at each guest.

Rosie was nodding enthusiastically. Pia shifted nervously but looked excited about answering questions on live TV.

"Sure," Caulfield said.

"Of course," Al-Harbi followed.

Both Eds held fixed smiles.

Reese fielded a handful of telephone calls. All of them innocuous questions.

"We have James from Tulsa on line one—go ahead, James."

"I'd like to ask if any of your guests are Christian?"

Pia spoke up, "I was raised that way—"

"What I want to know is how you integrated your Christianity with s—"

There was a sudden silence.

"Are you there, James?'

James didn't respond.

"Are you still with us, James?"

"I guess we lost James. We apologize for that, James. Try back and we'll give you priority. I think what James was going to ask was how—"

"Go to the next caller, Reese." Reese heard the director's voice behind camera. Reese started to push James's question, thought better, and took the next call.

At the end of the taping, Reese shook hands with each of his guests. When he got to Ed Caulfield, he said, "Just exactly where did they find your car, Ed?"

"Somewhere off Highway 157, where Calloway Cemetery Road intersects it. Don't know where it is but that's my recollection from the police report, It's just a, something a little better than a dirt road, real isolated, runs just a few blocks."

"You were lucky to get it back at all."

"The power of Sky!" Ed laughed.

"Appreciate your coming on the show."

"Anytime, Reese."

Reese exchanged a few words with the camera crew and the TV show director and hurried to his office. He wrote down the location of where Ed's car had been recovered and started to his apartment. Tomorrow he'd take a cruise down Calloway Cemetery Road.

CHAPTER

16

Midmorning next day, Reese slipped into a leather jacket, V-neck sweater, khakis, and ankle boots. He grabbed his tape recorder and portfolio and followed his map quest to Calloway Cemetery Road.

As he turned south off 183 onto Euless-Main, he entered a residential subdivision of modest homes—small but well-manicured lawns holding two-car-garage houses for the lower middle class. He drove three, four minutes. The road suddenly narrowed into woods and dirt road. Trees were heavy on both sides of the road. A few hundred yards and the road veered right almost a ninety-degree angle; on either side were more trees but interspersed with small industrial buildings, old but still in use.

In a few minutes he had come to 157 Highway. He made a U-turn that took several forward and backups to retrace his tracks. He looked closer at his surroundings as he drove back. Where would anyone leave a stolen car? As he made the ninety-degree turn back onto the road leading to Euless-Main Street, he noticed tracks veering into the grass on his left. Tire tracks that didn't belong on that terrain.

Reese looked at the small houses just beyond the grassy section between the trees; he could see a couple of the neat little houses he'd passed. From two of the backyards, the site of a truck pulling off site the road could have been seen. Maybe. The two at this end of the block. He started forward, then noticed on his right a small run-down trailer home, set well back from the road up the hill. If anyone lived there, they would have had a good view of anything happening downhill on this road. Looked vacant, though. Reese drove on to where civilization began and parked across the street from the two end homes, took his attaché, checked his tape recorder, knocked and rang the bell of the first home first door. An upper-middle-aged man came to the door. Balding, in house slippers corduroys, and sweatshirt.

"What can I do for you?" Reese noticed the chain held the door only partially open.

"Hi, hate to bother you, I'm with FCI—"

"Not buying anything today," the man stated to back his face out of the opening to close the door.

"Not selling anything."

"What do you want?"

"Just wondered if you saw anything of a car that was stolen. A BMW, black BMW—I think the police found it a few yards from your backyard," Reese said, hoping he would be confirmed right; Reese held up a fifty-dollar bill. The man looked at it, studied Reese's face, relaxed a little.

"A stolen car? Naw, first I've heard of it. Pretty quiet neighborhood around here not much like that goin' on here."

Reese said, "Are you sure?"

"Positive." He looked at the fifty-dollar bill again.

"Sure wish I could help you," he said, eyeing the money.

Disappointed, Reese said, "Well, . . . thanks anyway."

At the next house, a senior citizen, a little old lady, blue hair and all came to the door. Friendly and open. She stepped out on the porch. Reese introduced himself, stated his purpose for his visit.

"Somebody stole your car?"

"Not my car. I'm doing some research, an investigation on a car that was stolen a few weeks ago. Police recovered it. I think they found it not far back of your house."

"I didn't see it. Didn't even hear anything about it, that doesn't happen too often around here."

Reese thanked her, started toward his car. Maybe he could figure some way to get a copy of the police report.

"Did you check with that couple up on the hill, in the trailer home up there?"

"Didn't look like anybody lived there."

"They stay to themselves, but they see everything goes on 'round here."

"Really?" Well, thanks a lot, I'll give them a visit."

Reese got into his SUV, turned right, and drove up the hill toward the trailer home. Decaying old wood served as a porch to the trailer. The sloping front yard looked like a junkyard. Old wagon wheel, two sawhorse stands, water barrels on the side of the trailer, an rickety old swing set, long rusted. A couple of old tires.

On the first knock, Reese heard nothing. He knocked louder the second time. Maybe he'd come back later today. The door suddenly opened, startling him. Reese swore he was looking at Jed Clampett. Hat, coat, mustache, and all. And about three inches taller than Reese.

"What can I do for you, young fella!" Intelligent eyes, distrusting eyes. Behind him stood a tall very thin lady in an apron, gray hair rolled in a bun. "I'm Reese Maxey. Reese extended his hand. The man scrutinized Reese's face for a few seconds, visually searched him head to toe, then extended his hand.

"I'm Jed."

Reese blinked a couple of times, not sure if he wasn't being put on.

"I'm with FCI"—not wanting to have to explain *FCI*—"I'm conducting an investigation on a car that was stolen not too long ago. I think the police found it near here." Reese held his breath, heart beating a little faster in hope.

"That black BMW?"

Reese felt the flow of relief.

"That's the one."

"What you want to know about it?"

155

"Let the man come in, Jed." The lady in the apron had a soft country twang.

Reese sat down. Cluttered but clean trailer home. And comfortable. Reese sat in an old wingback chair as Jed and his wife, Reese guessed, sat on a large sofa.

"That was a strange piece of work," Jed said.

"How's that?"

"Dangdest thing. The people—three, four men as I recall, I guess it was six men altogether, they drove it up on the grass down there, where the tracks are."

"I saw that, didn't look right to me either," Reese said.

"Thing is, they drove the BMW over there. Two men get out, took the wheels off it, took something from inside it—probably the radio. Thing is, car right behind them when they drove up was a Lincoln town car. Big shiny thing."

"Looked suspicious," Reese prompted.

"Well, they kept looking around, you know, like people do when they're doing something they don't want anybody to see them doin'. One of them pointed up here. And then two of them started up here, knocked on the door."

"Scared me to death," Jed's wife said, the soft country twang pleasant.

"How's that?" Reese asked.

"Didn't look right," Jed said, "didn't look right at all, they looked nervous. They had on suits too. Looked like gangsters."

"Or government men," Mrs. "Clampett" added.

"We didn't answer the door. We just sat real still-like, didn't move. One of them tried the door, but we keep it locked."

"One of them peeked right through where that blind is broken over there"—Jed's wife's voice reflected anxiety—"thought sure he saw me, but I guess he didn't."

"It was what they said that made us know we were doin' the right thing not lettin' them in," Jed continued.

"One of them said he didn't think anybody lived here, and the other one said he was glad because he didn't want to have to waste anybody today. We didn't know if he was jokin' or what, but we wasn't goin' to the door.

"Right after the Lincoln town car left, a big shiny black Hummer pulled up over there and picked up the others. It was just strange, the whole thing was strange.

A few days later when the police came, they didn't ask anybody any questions. Just picked up the car on a truck, took off. Took 'em less 'n fifteen minutes. Real strange. But I guess cars get stolen, ever' day, and the police got their hands full with more important stuff, in the insurance companies—BMW ain't no money to them."

Reese thought over the scenario he had just heard. An upmarket car like a BMW gets stolen, it's usually gone forever, and if you do find it, usually nothing but the frame left.

"Would you be willing to tell me what you just did—let me put it on tape?" Reese wasn't sure how he'd use the information—or that he ever would use it—but you never know.

"We don't want no trouble—"

Reese held up the fifty-dollar bill.

"Those men in the suits—with the car—looked kind of scary to me, but heck, I'm not the fearful type, why not."

He quickly folded the fifty into his pocket, looked at Reese.

"I keep a little snub nose on me, and we got a couple of twelve gauges, anyway . . . sure, let's git 'er done."

Driving home, Reese thought over the story he had just heard. Sounded like a theft by professional car thieves or professional criminals. The theft sounded like there was more to it than just absconding with an upscale car for ill gain.

This was the second time a shadow had been cast on Sky's miracle testimonies. He still had that copy of the repair order from Vickery's Repair Shop for Molly's car. He should look into that, see why there was no charge for Molly's car repairs. His heart beat a little faster as he stepped down on the accelerator.

When he got home, he went to his file cabinet. There it was. "Vickery's Remanufactured Engines and Repair." Reese's heart beat faster, nerves a little ragged. He picked up the telephone and dialed.

"Vickery's Repair." The voice was young, upper teen or early twenties. Reese steadied his breathing.

"Hi, this is Reese Maxey with FCI."

"Yes?"

"I need to get a copy of a repair order—"

"Not many people here today—kinda busy."

"Wont take long," Reese said. "In fact, I think I have the repair order number. It's for a remanufactured engine"—Reese fumbled and rustled papers—"on a 1991 Chevy, 5.0 liter engine, just a little more than six months ago."

"I think I remember that one—we don't get too many of those, brown caprice?"

"That's it," Reese said.

"You say you have the RO number?" Reese gave it to the speaker on the other end.

"And we need some of the accounting papers—billing, invoice, etc. I just need to update some stuff here."

"Well—I . . . don't know—"

"Tell you what, if you have it on a computer, you can e-mail it to me, or you can fax it to me. Let me give you my e-mail address and my fax number."

"Well, OK . . . give it to me. Can I send this to you now—I'm real busy."

"You can send it soon as we hang up."

"What did you say your name was?"

"Reese Maxey."

"OK, I need to do this real quick, got other things to do around here."

The phone went dead. Reese sat down to wait for the transmission; he'd check e-mail a little later if necessary.

He heard the fax whir. A few minutes later, several pages had spilled into the reception tray. Reese picked them up.

His heart did a flip-flop.

There were two reference numbers on a Vickery letterhead statement. One number referenced the RO number of a 1991 Chevy. The other number referenced a RO number on another repair order, which was for a 2005 BMW. The license number matched Ed Caulfield's BMW plate. A whole lot of work besides replacing tires and a radio had been done on the car. He read the "remove and replace engine, "service transmission," new leather seats, new sound system, battery, starter motor, "install GPS system." And there was a "miscell. repairs."

Reese looked at the total statement charge for both cars. Just under one hundred thousand dollars.

Couldn't have cost that much. He looked at the billed addressee.

He sat down hard.

The statement had been sent to FCI Inc. In Kansas City, Missouri.

Reese sat back, stared at the ceiling of his apartment office.

His thoughts did not come quickly. He couldn't grasp what he had just discovered meant. He couldn't pull it together.

He thought back, remembering a visit with Al when he had told him about the "miracles" some Sky members were experiencing and that he—Reese Maxey—would be taking that phenomenon to TV. He thought about the look and tone of voice Al had displayed at the time. He had always been a little slow, a little naive to the subtle ways of the world, probably partly due to his sheltered church upbringing. Maybe. At the time he had been more focused on the fact that he would be on TV.

Or maybe there had been nothing subtly meaningful in Al's voice. Reese wasn't sure what to think. Maybe this whole scenario was just a bunch of coincidences.

Could it be that FCI—his employer, his contract—was supporting a religious conspiracy, worldwide in scope? If so, what were the implications for him, a man who had too much fear of God, to play at church and things spiritual?

On one hand, he felt relief in knowing there was nothing credible about the new religion.

At the same time, his sense of guilt and culpability was increasing.

He also felt a little bit used. What did Al and Lou really think of him? Maybe they thought he was a more hip than he actually was—that he understood this game.

He needed to talk to someone.

He felt a wave of relief as he reached for the telephone and dialed Bishop Padduck's number.

CHAPTER

17

Reese sat a little uncomfortably in front of Bishop Padduck, who seemed very relaxed, which helped some. Dressed in sweatshirt, gym pants, and tennis shoes, Padduck showed trim and fit, even at his age. Reese smiled to himself. For some reason it was comforting to see the pastor in athletic clothes—and a little amusing.

"Did you have a good trip?"

"Smooth all the way, Dallas to KC." Reese noticed occasional flakes of snow through the window. They sat in the pastor's study. A comfortable room, rectangular in shape, comfortably carpeted, walls filled with books surrounding Padduck's sufficient-sized desk.

Reese saw the snow coming a little heavier. He was glad he had worn his leather jacket. Made him cold just thinking about Missouri weather. He had quickly acclimated to Texas. His crew neck sweater, jeans, and ankle boots seemed appropriate now.

"I've been a pastor for a long time, almost four decades now. In my early days, I'd pray, seek the Lord for something or someone, but when the answer came, I didn't always recognize it. I didn't always know the voice of the Master when I heard it, didn't recognize the visions, the dreams . . . I had this dream a few nights ago . . ."

Padduck learned back in his chair, looked up at the ceiling for a second, then back at Reese.

"And in it, I saw several of my saints—members of my flock, this church, that is. They were all running. Each one of them was being chased by something. In the shape of a man. You were one of them running, brother Maxey."

Padduck, hands on desk, arms straight in front of him, looked at Reese with a serious but friendly smile.

"Really?" Reese felt his already-tight muscles tense even more.

"You were running. I didn't see your face in the dream, but I knew it was you. You know how that happens in a dream?"

Reese felt a little sweaty and too tense to trust his voice. He nodded.

"You were running but not like you were in a hurry, more like a leisurely jog. And this—this creature behind you it looked like a man—was trying to catch you. I had a sense it was trying to catch you to do you harm.

"And then a strange thing happened—another figure, in the shape of a man, but with a rod or something like a rod—more like a cane, I guess—"

Reese flinched. The man with the cane he had encountered in the FCI shopping center garage mentally flashed.

"He walked—he wasn't running, but he was gaining on the image that was after you—he walked up close to this figure, stuck his cane out, and tripped the image behind you."

Padduck paused,

"End of dream." He smiled at Reese.

"Sounds like a good ending."

"For those who trust in God, it always is—without fail."

"You think that maybe this dream had—meaning?"

"As I was saying, brother Maxey, four decades of pastoring, of praying and seeking the Lord as a shepherd, not as a hireling—I love the people in my care—I've learned to recognize the promptings, the leading of the spirit. Not all of the time, mind you, but enough to know when to take note."

Reese nodded soberly, his mind still picturing the man with the cane.

"I've watched you on *Global Week*, brother Maxey—"

"I've only done two shows."

"And you've done them well, you're good at what you do."

"Appreciate the compliment."

"How do you feel about what you're doing?"

"Reese shifted his seat. That's one of the things I want to talk to you about."

"I thought it might be. I'm glad to hear that."

"To be honest, Bishop, I'm feeling a little guilty about the TV show."

"A little condemned about the message of Sky," Padduck added.

Reese nodded. "Yes."

Padduck nodded, waited for Reese to continue.

"You probably understand why," Reese said, wanting to hear Padduck's take on the issue.

"Well"—Padduck leaned forward, hands clasped, forearms, elbows resting on his desk—"I am glad to hear that you have a conscious about it, and that the spirit is dealing with you about it."

Padduck paused, looked away briefly.

"I'm going to be very direct and blunt about my take on you and your work for S-C-I. It is a serious matter, brother Maxey."

Padduck gave Reese a hard, probing look. "Able to take it?" Padduck smiled gently.

"I need to hear—the truth," Reese said.

"I can only give you my opinion. But I think I speak—as you said it—the truth, and in line with the spirit."

I do not believe that Christianity can be blended with any other religion—not real Christianity."

Reese nodded, a sinking feeling rising. Padduck continued, "Christianity is Christ based, hence the name. It holds certain premises, conditions, requirements that prevent a true mixture of it with any other religion. Prayer is effective and effected by a righteous man, or when two or more are gathered. Are you following me?" Padduck asked with a smile.

"I'm with you."

"When people come together to pray, if they're not praying to the one God—or ever if they are, or trying to, if it's not prayer in the name of Jesus—no man comes to the Father except by me."

Reese nodded, being familiar with the scripture.

"Then short of that there is no effective prayer. No reaching God."

Padduck paused, looked down at his desktop for a second, looked up.

"I watched the two—*Global Week* shows you hosted. And I've been reading the current news about all the benefits, the good that Sky does. And the miracles."

Reese sat still.

"I'll be honest, brother Maxey, I am a man of faith, but I have a lot of trouble believing what I've seen on your show, and in *Time*, *Newsweek*, and some of the so-called Christian magazines about Sky."

Reese said, "Well, you know, Bishop, some of the surveys on the benefits of Sky membership have shown that employees interact better, they develop better attitudes about their work and their employers, they become more positive about the people they work with. And there have been some health benefits too—a lot of them have lost weight and—"

"You can get the same results with secular counseling, social sensitivity training, and exercise programs," Padduck said.

Reese nodded in agreement, wondering why he was sitting here defending Sky.

"Have you ever had a supernatural experience in your walk with the Lord, brother Maxey?"

Reese's mind flew back to a revival meeting he had once attended twenty to twenty-five years ago. A visiting evangelist had preached his heart out, and several people had gone to the altar one Sunday.

At the end of the sermon, the evangelist had taken up an offering. He had told the audience to give liberally. And then he had said that those who gave with a cheerful heart and, on this particular Sunday, if they gave cheerfully, they should believe God for a sevenfold return on the amount they gave.

"I am praying that God gives you a sevenfold return on your monetary gift today. All you have to do is believe it. But," he had explained, "you have to give willingly, and you have to believe that you are going to receive a sevenfold blessing. Believe it, not at all doubting."

For some reason, Reese had found the faith. He pulled out a twenty-dollar bill—the only twenty he had at the time—and with a glad and expectant heart had dropped it into the offering plate, with full faith he'd see a sevenfold return on his offering.

Within one week he had received a check for $140 and some change. The check had come from an unexpected source. To this day he couldn't recall where the check had come from.

"Yes, Bishop, I have seen God perform the unexpected for me, things that seemed to be directed by . . . an unseen hand, in response to my faith."

Padduck nodded. "We all have, brother Maxey. At some point in time in every believer's walk, God shows himself in some supernatural form. Often more than once for many. But even so, most of our walk with God is not by sight—not by supernatural events, but by our faith. 'The just shall walk by faith' is how the scripture worded it, prophesying about the church age hundreds of years before there ever was a church. So most of our day in, day out is by faith. It's not by magically seeing visions, or hearing voices, or cars healed. Our walk is with the Lord by faith, period."

Reese sat forward, elbows on the arm of the chair, hands locked together between his knees. He nodded. Padduck continued, "So when I hear the testimonies of members of the so-called Spiritual Church International about how they're being led to conjoint prayer to a hybrid god, and of unnatural miracles, well, I find it hard to believe. In fact, I don't believe it. And if by some chance those miracles are happening, I want to run as fast and as far away from them as I can. You know the biblical story of Jannes and Jambres, don't you?"

"They were able to imitate Moses's miracles," Reese said.

Padduck nodded. "The devil has power too, brother Maxey." He continued, "You know, I can almost—and I'm speaking hypothetically here now—almost see a Christian and a follower of Hinduism worshipping, or trying to worship together. Hinduism is kind of hard to define—it's real fuzzy around the edges, it doesn't have a specific leader, or an original founder. Its goal is to seek an awareness of God. I can see a Christian connecting a Hindu to Christianity.

And as far as Buddhism, it's more of a challenge. Buddhist follow on the teachings of Siddhārtha Gautama, it's one of the oldest religions around. Again they contradict Christianity in not knowing who God is, and in believing in good works to avoid continuous suffering and escape samsara. The Christian has an eternal relationship with Christ, but the Buddhist don't have a concept of an individual existing for eternity."

Padduck shifted in his chair, studied his clasped hands for a few seconds.

"The most serious error of Sky, brother Maxey, is trying to forge mutually exclusive religions together into one. And the most troubling of those attempted mergers is that of Christianity and Islam. They are mutually exclusive. And the latter can be dangerous—if you follow me."

Padduck stared at Reese. Reese let Padduck's words sink in and nodded, then said, "But of the religions you just mentioned, Islam is the only one of the group that makes reference to the God of Abraham, Isaac, and Jacob, which is the God that we as Christians serve."

Padduck nodded, gave a brief, slight smile.

"Sounds like one and the same on the surface."

"It does that."

"You take a closer look, though, and you find that the one very much important thing to our God is His wanting to develop a personal relationship with each one of us. In Islam, they tell you God is not that knowable, doesn't become that familiar with us.

"A closer look, we see that God is one. That the man Jesus of Nazareth was God and at the same time He was the Son of God. It's a distinction between God, the Father and the Son, and yet without a difference, something we don't fully understand, find hard to explain. Islam tells you Allah could not have a son—not a flesh-and-blood son. Yet we know that no man comes to the father, except by way of the Son.

"Both our faith and the Muslim's religion have a clearly defined leader. And both of us have a mission, unlike the other religions of the world, we compete.

"Allah comes from Muhammad, who came along six hundred years after Christ.

"Do you know, brother Maxey, how Muhammad got his message, how the Koran came about?"

"Not real sure about that," Reese said.

"No one is real sure. Supposedly through his revelations from Gabriel. We, on the other hand, know the authors of the Bible—we know who the books were written by. We know they were written by men, like you and me who were inspired by God. Without altering their personalities or their writing styles, God spoke through them and got one comprehensive and complete message of redemption to the world. Forty authors, over fifteen hundred years, and it all adds up, brother Maxey."

The Muslim sees Jesus as one of the greatest prophets that ever lived—out of one hundred twenty-four thousand prophets God has sent to the earth. Can you believe that?"

Padduck shook his head in disbelief.

"The book of John tells us, 'In the beginning was the word, the word was with God, and the word was God.' And that 'the word was made flesh.' And it tells us that 'He was in the world and the world was made by Him but the world did not recognize him.'"

Reese sat still. His chest felt tight, anxiety nudged him.

"We can—not can, we must—reach out to the Muslim, with genuine love, and witness to them. Then it is up to the spirit—to God—to do the rest. No man comes to God unless God draws him. We can't compromise, brother Maxey."

Padduck stood, started around his desk,

"The dangerous side, of course, is that there are factions of radical muslims, worldwide, numbering in the millions. We Christians, we tell the story, give the hearer the choice to receive it or reject it, and with a prayer in our heart, go on our way. Radical Islam will kill you for rejecting their beliefs."

Padduck paused, then went on, "You know, Reese, this Sky movement, and I've looked into it some, it appears to me it was started by those rich superclass elites that seem to be orchestrating a lot of our trends and laws these days. Ever occur to you that it might have been started because of their fear?"

"How so?" Reese asked.

"Radical Islam. They've taken a lot of peace from the earth in recent years, and they promise to continue doing so. If the powers that be can redirect religious fanatics into another, more peaceful path without blatantly disrupting their core beliefs, well, logically . . . peace would follow. Theoretically."

Padduck placed his hand on Reese's shoulder.

"You know what, coincidentally, I'm having a late lunch with two friends today—both of them are Muslim."

Padduck had a smile on his face, looked at Reese, waiting for a response.

"Let me guess who's converting who," Reese said with a smile.

Padduck laughed. "I'm for sure workin' on 'em, brother Maxey— for sure!"

"Let's have a word of prayer, brother Maxey." Padduck reached for a bottle of olive oil on his desk; he tilted the bottle, anointed Reese's forehead with the tip of an oil-moistened finger. He raised one hand upward.

"Heavenly Father, we come to you on behalf of our beloved brother . . ."

Reese heard the words, even as he himself prayed. Words of comfort. Lifting his spirit. Effectual words for forgiveness. For discernment. For decision making, for direction and guidance. For protection, for strength, and for service. Prayer from hearts of sincerity and of faith. Two gathered together in His name. Effectual, fervent prayer of righteous men.

Reese felt waves of relief wash over him and the joy of the spirit he hadn't experienced for too long.

"And, Father, let your angel of protection camp around brother Maxey, to protect him in all that he does, in every place that he sets his foot."

Padduck gave Reese's shoulder a warm, brotherly squeeze.

As Reese started to his SUV from Padduck's office, he knew what he had to do. And he knew it with peace and calmness, and even with joy.

From his SUV Reese used his cell phone to make reservations at the Doubletree Hotel on Metcalf in Overland Park, Kansas. He wanted some time alone after his session with Bishop Padduck, and before he called Al, or more likely Lou. And he wanted to stop at home, check the crib out make sure all was OK.

Everything was as he had left it at home.

He picked up some bills, a couple of items of clothing and drove to the Doubletree.

Breaking his contract would probably not be that easy. Al and Lou would not like it at all. At this point, though, it couldn't be helped because now it was a matter of conscience for him. He ordered a rib eye, baked potato, salad and went to bed.

CHAPTER

18

"You want to do what!?" Lou's voice screeched unpleasant surprise. He sat back rigidly, arms on both arm rests, fists clenching. Al looked at Reese with a pinched frown from the other chair facing Reese.

"I need to give you a resignation, get out of the contract," Reese said. His nerves were on edge, and he tried hard not to show it.

"Why?" Lou asked, incredulous at Reese's request.

"It has to do with my own beliefs, Lou, my personal faith."

"And you are just now waking up to this, you've been to some kind of tent revival or something?"

Reese detected the derision in Lou's voice.

"That's funny, Lou."

Lou didn't smile. He stared at Reese.

"You signed a contract, Reese," Al said matter-of-factly.

"I know. But that was before I fully knew what Sky was all about."

"What do you mean?" Lou asked.

"Sky—people take it seriously."

"They're supposed to take it seriously. What's your point?" Al asked—voice suddenly neutral.

"I mean—people are beginning to substitute it for church. They're beginning to see it as a real path to God."

"And your point is?" Al asked again.

"Well, do you two take Sky as real?"

"It is a real—and serious movement," Lou said. He was looking at Reese with very unfriendly eyes.

"A movement," Reese said.

Al and Lou shifted in their seats.

"A movement and a religion," Al said.

"But what if—"

"There's no *but what if* about it, Reese?" Lou said. "It is a religion. It is a movement, and a program. It does a lot of good. You do a lot of good, Reese. You and Sky, you've helped a lot of people to become better employees, become happier about their work. You've helped them lose weight, heal their marriages, become better friends of their spouses, you've even saved marriages." Al flecked an invisible speck of dust off a crossed-trouser leg. "Do you not understand the good you're doing?"

"Not to mention the miracles that have happened—that you've reported on," Al added.

Lou gave Al a quick, sharp glance, said nothing, continued to stare at Reese with hostility. He said, "What if we paid you more, Reese."

"It's not about the money, Lou." Meekness seeped from this voice.

"I mean a whole lot more."

"I mean, really, Lou, it's not about the money—you couldn't pay me enough to go on."

Lou and Al sat staring at him, silent with anger.

"You think about it some more, Reese. Before you make a final decision." Lou stood, studying Reese.

I thought I had made a final decision. Maybe Lou needed time to absorb this.

Lou's phone rang. He started toward his desk. "Al, will see you out—and Al, invite him to the party tonight. Your timing is great, Reese."

Reese and Al started toward the elevator in silence. Just before leaving him at the overpass leading to the mall, Al pulled Reese's arm.

"You know, we could sue you for breach of contract." He had a slight smile on his face. Reese detected duty on Al's part, not anger or hostility, unlike Lou, whose world Reese seemed to have shattered.

"Breach of contract, OK, what about my pastor, and a good lawyer arguing coercion against conscience, discrimination against my religion." Reese smiled at Al.

Al laughed. "Thought I'd give it another try. Come to our party tonight, be some interesting people there."

"Who, where, what, when?" Reese said.

"Right here, after work, sixish."

"Who's celebrating what?"

"Just a little get-together. We're inviting all the people we love and work with." Al smiled. "Some important out-of-towners, might be to your advantage. Wear what you have on." Al held out his hand. They shook hands before parting company. As he walked toward his SUV, Reese thought he would attend. Why not?

Reese arrived at the party at about the time the sun set. Signs from the parking lot on directed partyers to a room adjacent to Lou's office. Turned out to be two conference rooms with a partition that had been rolled back to make one large party room.

Jazz—American, Brazillian, and Philipino—played softly in the background of tinkling glasses, of mixing and mingling guests, ambienced with dim mood setting lighting.

In one corner, Reese saw a couple of execs—faces he'd passed and nodded to in the corridors of FCI—gently rocking to the sound of the music, ample drinks in hand.

A well-to-do crowd. Generally in business casual attire, a few suits, a few jeans. In taupe slacks, tasseled shoes, a blazer over a Tommy Bahama shirt that worked well in summer or winter. Reese felt at home—dresswise.

Reese wound his way to a refreshment table, picked up a glass of ice, poured Coke into it, and squeezed a lemon after.

"Aw, I don't know—not that big a deal. Lou puts on one of these two, three times a year, brings his international big shot friends in—he likes to show off."

Out of the corner of his eye Reese saw the speaker finish pouring from a bottle of Johnnie Walker.

"Yeah, I thought maybe I'd meet some more of the department—"

Reese moved a few feet into the crowd, scanning faces, wondering why he had accepted Lou and Al's invitation. He spotted Al near the door shaking hands with a new arrival at about the same time he saw Lou. Lou was talking to two dark-skinned men, one with Mideastern looks. Both men had an air of importance about them. One wore a cardigan sweater and looked familiar to Reese although his features were obscured by the dim light. The other man was nattily dressed in suit and tie.

"Hi."

Reese turned, saw an attractive young face behind the delicate voice. She wore a badge that said "Intern."

"Hi."

"I'm Jonie—it's a nice party."

Reese detected the nervousness behind the attempt.

"It is a nice way to end a day of work," Reese said.

"Which department do you work in?"

"I'm a contractor."

"Really?" she responded as if he had said he owned the company.

"That I am. Just an humble go-to for FCI—and what do you do?"

Before she could answer, Reese heard his name called. He turned and saw Lou and the two men he had been talking to earlier staring at him.

Lou was holding a drink and looked a little tipsy.

"Like you to meet some friends of mine, Reese."

Lou's demeanor and tone of voice were hard to read. Slightly slurred and glazed of eye was all Reese could discern.

He excused himself from the intern.

"Lacy, this is Reese Maxey."

The business suit took his hand.

"Pleasure to meet you, Reese."

Reese looked at the man's stick-on name tag wondering if "Lacy" really was his real name.

He eyed Reese with a faint curl of the lip and with curiosity. He was immaculate in a gray suit, blue tie, and white shirt, and the course features of indulgence screamed wealth and royalty.

"Pleasure to meet you," Reese returned.

"Lacy is from Saudi Arabia, Reese."

Reese nodded again and smiled.

"And, this is Fahzi Raheed. Fahzi, Reese Maxey."

Raheed shook Reese's hands in a noncommittal way.

"Nice to meet you, Reese," and a noncommittal cartoonlike voice, almost like he'd just inhaled laughing gas. TV studios must know how to control that, Reese thought. He said, "Very nice to meet you, Fahzi—seen your show, read your articles, many times.

"Yes—and I know a lot about you too, Reese."

"Leave you two to talk—come on, Lacy, somebody else I want you to meet."

Lou gave Fahzi an extended look before leading Lacy away.

"So how's it going, Reese?"

"It's going" Reese said and did an old Johnny Carson tiptoe. He really did not feel like talking about anything to do with Sky.

Raheed gave a slight chuckle.

"Kind of enjoying the party."

"Lou puts on a nice show—we had one of these six, seven months ago. People from all over the country were here then—and from Europe, China."

Reese nodded, took a sip of his Coke.

"I haven't seen any of your reports for some time."

And Reese hadn't thought much about them lately. Periodically he had directed marketing research projects to pick up audience impressions of various topics associated with Sky. Sometimes the studies were focused on the concept of Sky; oftentimes they were focused on reactions to Fahzi or another of his TV or radio guests' presentations.

"From what I recall, you have nothing to worry about," Reese said. And the marketing research studies had always confirmed that." Raheed was always well-informed, well prepared, articulate. A very excellent communicator, in spite of his off-putting voice.

"Your research keeps us with a finger on the pulse of public thought."

Reese only nodded.

"You did an excellent job on *Global Week*, Reese. I'm sure a lot of people were swayed to Sky by the testimonies of your guests. What we were hoping for—those were extremely important shows in our strategy, Reese—were reports on how the public at large reacted to those shows."

As Raheed talked, Reese recalled having seen one report—although he had only briefly scanned it—that showed the broadcasts to have been slightly influential in increasing Sky membership. By and large, a number of people had not been convinced though—not fully. Randy, his counterpart on the East Coast, had directed a study that showed the public needed, in a nutshell, new evidence from old literature—new scriptures, new Koran, something archeologists could find that proved divine desire for all religions to merge into one, and they needed to see a new "Messiah," someone who could show miracles, heal the sick, raise the dead.

"I believe there was a study and subsequent report after the last TV show. I believe it was—"

"I saw that report—tell me, Mr. Maxey, do you no longer believe in Sky?"

Reese wondered, with some anger, if Fahzi had been sent on this mission.

"Do you believe Sky will lead the world to unity and peace, Fahzi?"

"When people are no longer divided by religion, we will have a more unified—and safer—world, yes. Again, I ask you, Mr. Maxey—"

"Religious affirmative action and diversity, coupled with sensitivity training—in the workplace, yes, that will produce more productive workers—and happier employers."

"And what about the rest of society—Sky is not just for the workplace, what about places of worship—mosques, synagogues, temples, churches?"

"You're speaking to how people interpret God."

"That's right, Mr. Maxey."

"Or even if they believe in God."

Fahzi stared at Reese saying nothing for a moment, then, "Think about it, in the civilized world—and that's the part of the planet we are focused on—everybody works. And everybody worships. Increasingly they do the former in diversity and unity.

"On Sundays—we all go our separate ways. Especially in America.

"What if—if the whole world took time to work and worship together. What if this led the world to see that we all really do serve just the same God. Do you not see the advantages, the benefits of that, Mr. Maxey?"

"And what do you do with those who believe only the Bible is the way, and those who believe only the teachings of the Koran?"

"Our two biggest customers." Fahzi gave a faint, brief, unfelt smile.

"And those who don't believe in God at all," Reese continued.

"The testimonies, the persuasiveness—and the force—of Sky, overcome the stubborn, Mr. Maxey. You have been one of our effective apostles . . ."

Reese flinched.

"Eventually everyone gets on this bus, Mr. Maxey."

"There are a lot of militant Islamic and Arabic people out there."

"Lot's of 'em. You met Lacy a few minutes ago—we call him Lacy—we know a lot of Lacys, Mr. Maxey. And the Lacys of the world—of our world—they know the addresses of the car bombers—and Bin Ladens too, by the way."

Reese wondered if he meant that literally,

"There are a lot of truth-believing Christians out there."

"What is truth?"

"The Bible—the word of God."

Fahzi stifled his laugh.

"Well, Christians, they don't shoot back—excuse me, Lou is calling me."

Reese saw Lou across the room looking their way. Fahzi started in his direction.

Reese felt nature's call and started toward the exit to the nearest men's room.

"Oh, Mr. Maxey!" A female's pleasant voice, slightly slurred. Reese turned to see Marie—Al's secretary—disengaging a group of four and coming his way. The room was louder now and more crowded. The music had been turned up, and it seemed to Reese the lighting had become dimmer.

"Oh, Reese, so nice that you could come. I thought I recognized you—you were talking to Fahzi Raheed?"

"Glad I could make it, Marie. Yeah, Fahzi and I had a little dialogue. You lookin' good, baby—in your little black dress."

Marie smiled, took a sip of her drink, swaying into Reese. Reese grabbed her arm. Marie giggled.

"I'm fine, probably one sip over the line—I'll be OK." She focused her eyes on Reese.

"Mr. Maxey—you're such a nice guy, Reese."

"I hear a compliment there—or a little pity for nice guys."

"Well, it's got to be a compliment—I can't picture you finishing anything last."

"So I guess I did hear a compliment—or you heard me begging for one."

They shared a laugh.

"Give me a dance, Reese."

"I can't—I don't dance."

"Oh come on." Marie grabbed his hand firmly and led him with more strength than Reese would have expected to the front of the room where an improvised dance space had been carved out. Several couples were swaying to a now slow-tempo version of Etta James's "At Last."

Reese ignored most of Marie's nice fragrance and pressing breasts.

As they swayed to the music, Marie looked into Reese's eyes.

"Don't let them use you too much, Reese."

With twinkle and fun in her eyes, Marie still managed to convey the seriousness of her words.

"Well, they're paying me." He decided to not mention that he was terminating his contract.

"They're powerful, Reese. The world is changing—I guess it's always changing, always has been—but—I don't know . . . the world is changing, and they're part of the reason it's changing."

"What do you mean?" Reese tried to keep his voice light.

"Not everything is what it appears to be, that's all. But you—you're a big boy, you probably already know that." Reese heard a note of uncertainty now in Marie's voice. He wondered if she knew about the hundred-thousand-dollar invoice for Molly's and Ed's car repairs.

"I can generally take care of myself. But I do appreciate the heads-up."

Marie swayed a little more in his arms, but with control.

"You're so handsome, Reese. Several of my coworkers want to meet you. One of them said you were a cross between the Rock and Denzel and George Clooney." Marie giggled.

"And you keep her on your payroll?"

They shared a laugh. The music ended.

Reese leaned in, gave Marie a light kiss.

"You're a very pretty lady, Marie—and very sweet—I've got to go see a man about a horse. See you next time." He really did have to go. Two Cokes and a bottled water were trying to make their exit too. Just outside the party entrance, several people were in the hallway talking, mingling, drinking. He hoped there was no one in the crowd who recognized him. He started right, came to a door that said Men. He pulled; he couldn't believe it. It was locked. What the heck, with all the food and drink being consumed tonight, he'd think not only would this door be open but there'd be a Johnny-on-the-spot portable. Reese recognized he was near Lou's office. Lou had a private bath and toilet, as he recalled. Why not? He started toward Lou's office, hoping it was unlocked. It was. The room lighting was dim. The bathroom lighting was dim. And the bathroom was just as elegant as the office. Wall-to-wall carpeting, Gold faucets on beige-brown sink. An array of classy soaps on the shelf along with several men's colognes and expensive-looking deodorants—brand names Reese had never heard of. A shower furnished with plush towels.

Reese flushed. He reminded himself at this age he needed to be more strategic as to when he drank liquids. Maybe it was a prostate issue—

"He's a stupid fool!"

Reese froze. Unmistakably Lou's voice. He sounded like he'd had too much to drink.

"He's got the best job in the world, and he wants to throw it away."

Reese stiffened, his heart rate beginning to pick up.

"Well, good riddance, I say"—Reese couldn't mistake that cartoon character—like voice of Fahzi Raheed's—"because he doesn't really believe in Sky. His heart's not in it." Reese thought he heard Lou opening a desk drawer.

Fahzi continued, "You can find somebody to take his place."

"He was a good man. Good at research, good at interviewing. He knows how to put it all together. Now he's throwin' it all away. He's a fool!"

"Let him go, Lou."

"He said he'd take a day or two to think about it."

"Just let him go."

Reese heard another drawer open, papers shuffled.

"You've benefitted from his work too, Fahzi."

"He is getting too nosy, Lou." Fahzi's voice held less-casual note. Evidently Lou noticed Fahzi's change of voice too.

"What do you mean?"

"He's been snooping around. Places he shouldn't." For a few second, all Reese could hear were the distant voices of the party down the hall.

"Where has he been snooping?"

Lou's voice too seemed to have switched to a more sober note.

Heart racing, Reese tiptoed away from the door. To his left was a shower stall. Holding the shower curtain as still as he could he stepped into the stall, pressed back against the wall on which the shower head was mounted. He pressed back as hard as he could to the wall. His car and house keys were on a key chain along with a minirecorder—a gadget he had seen advertised on TV and had ordered via mail. It had served him well many times while at the grocery store—his voice recordings reminding him on the playback of his list of items to buy. Beat making a penciled list when he was shopping. He reached into his pocket, careful not to jingle his keys. He pulled them out. He pressed the On button of the recorder, put it carefully back in his pocket.

Fahzi coughed.

"He's been looking into things that he has no business looking into."

There was another moment of silence.

"Like what?"

"Like Vickery's Auto Repair," Fahzi said, his voice having lost a note or two of its cartoonish character. Whatever Lou had been doing, he stopped. The silence this time was three to four heartbeats longer.

"How would you know about Vickery's, Fahzi?"

Fahzi ignored the question.

"You need to let him resign, Lou—might be wise to give him a good severance package, in fact."

Reese heard Lou coming one step before he opened the bathroom door. Reese pressed as hard as he could against the shower wall. He ignored the tiny trickles of water dripping on his forehead. His heart pounding, he heard Lou's pant zipper.

"What about Vickery's, Fahzi?"

AN ANGEL FOR MAXEY

"You know—the car repairs."

Lou had left the bathroom door open, and Fahzi had moved closer, just outside the private bathroom entrance.

Lou cursed under his breath.

Reese heard running water and then paper towels being extracted.

"How do you know about Vickery's?"

Fahzi didn't answer.

"We are going to have to fix this situation," Lou said, as if talking to himself.

"One way or another," Fahzi said, as if talking to himself.

"You remember the two Davos guys, Brochman and Patterson—"

"They weren't really Davos guys—not really," Fahzi said.

Reese felt a real stab of fear. He remembered the names—and the case. Ehud Brochman, a Christian Jew and TV and radio host, and James Patterson, head of the Worldwide Church of the Bible. Both of them had protested Sky. Right after Azko Lee Britton's promotion of Sky speech. And they both had disappeared on the same day. Supposedly there was an ongoing investigation. But with decreasing news coverage. Reese hadn't given a lot of thought to the case. Now he was making visual connections that were pushing him toward an attack of panic.

"You resolved that problem," Lou said.

"We got rid of them, Lou." Reese heard the hard edge and not-so-cartoonlike irritation in Raheed's voice.

"Ain't no one monkey goin' stop this show here, you better believe that. I need a drink." Lou closed the door behind him. Reese took in several deep breaths. He heard Lou opening his desk drawer again.

Raheed changed the subject, "Keep up with the news coming out of Davos."

"I do—I read that Europe-American news, or whatever it's called—copy over there on the coffee table—"

"In the next few weeks you're going to see some interesting stuff." Fahzi laughed.

"Oh yeah?—What's up?"

"Our research is showing us we need to make Sky a little more convincing."

"TV miracles don't do it, huh?" Lou's voice reflected distraction to whatever he was apparently hunting in his desk drawers. Reese heard drawers being slammed shut.

"The world will be convinced soon, though."

Raheed's tone of voice got Lou's attention. He asked with more interest, "What's Lee up to, Fahzi?"

"You'll see soon. Just pay attention to the news—some new discoveries and some real miracles are on the horizon."

Reese heard the office door opened, and then an outburst of voices.

"Hey, hey, hey—get in here, guys!"

"Way to go, Lou!"

"Long way from college, Lou!"

Laughter and revelry filled the room.

"Where's she at, Lou!—gotta be a girl in here somewhere, probably ain't got no clothes on either!"

"Well, she ain't under my desk!" Lou's voice slurred again already. Raucous laughter followed and a few high fives slapping palm to palm.

Reese moved to the washbasin, his heart still racing. He needed a minute to think his way out of this.

Lou had already had his little boy's room visit. But drinking the way he was, he'd be coming back. And if they were all drinking, probably several of them would be coming in, in the next few minutes. If two or three of them came in at the same time, maybe he could fake it in the men's room when one of them comes in, and maybe blend in on his way out—the office lighting was dim enough—and if Lou spotted him, he'd probably assume he had come with the crowd, or at least after he and Fahzi had talked.

Might be a plan. Might not be. Maybe he should wait in the shower until the party was over. Maybe they'd all leave Lou's office together. From the laughter and voices, Reese guessed at least seven, maybe as many as ten, twelve people in the office.

He heard outside noise spill into Lou's office—the office door had opened again.

"Whuzzup!"

"Where's she at!" More loud laughter as two more voices joined the merriment.

"Hey, guys—didn't think you were going to make it!"

Lou's voice was leaning toward drunk, happy to be surrounded with what sounded like old college buddies.

"Just flew in. Plane was late, as usual," one of the new entrants said.

"You still got a shower in here?"

Lou made a crack Reese couldn't make out, but evidently a funny one as the room exploded with laughter.

"Kidding, guys—just drop those bags, plenty of liquor—right over there—shower's right through that door!"

Reese's heartbeat escalated again.

For a second his mind went to Brochman and Patterson; he wondered if any of Lou's old college buddies had anything to do with that. If so and if he were discovered tonight and Lou suspected he had overheard his and Raheed's conversation, he might not get out of the building alive. His heart thudded.

What about defending himself?

He'd had a few classes in the Israeli Krav Maga. And he had a gun. But he didn't have his gun with him. He never carried it. To him it was more of a toy—a hobby, good for target practicing on weekends with Jon. The idea of taking life repulsed him. Any life. He used to hunt with Reggie and a couple of other cousins. Today, though, he hadn't had a desire hunt in years.

"And you wash your feet, dude!" Another voice, more loud laughter.

Reese cracked the door less than an inch and peeked out.

Lou was leaning against the front of his desk, completely relaxed, drink in one hand. Eight men formed a semicircle around him, drinks in hand, listening intently to the alpha male. Raheed was not in the crowd. Lou entertained, "You remember ole—what'd we used to call him—the economics guy?"

"Old dollar scholar—yeah I remember him!" Another drunken voice.

"Yeah, I remember that old—"

"Well, his grandson put in an application here. Must love—"

Reese moved his head a fraction to see more of the room through the narrow vintage point. His heart skipped a beat. One of the guests had stripped to underwear. With a towel over his shoulder he was just a few steps from the bathroom door.

Reese scrambled to the sink, turned the faucet on just as the door opened.

Hey, hey! What's up, du—." Brown tusseled hair, bright blue eyes, the light went out in them, replaced with confusion, then a quick recovery.

"Oops—never mind, thought you was somebody else." Laughter.

"Well, I am somebody else."

Reese joined the newcomer's laugh. He finished wiping his hands, saw the temporary discomfort of the newcomer.

"I just work here." He smiled. "Leave you to your shower." He took a deep breath and stepped into Lou's office.

Lou was still entertaining his guests. Reese started diagonally across the room toward the back to the exit. Lou continued his show.

"I dropped three mil on him before—what the hell?!"

Reese noted the dramatic and sudden change of tone in Lou's voice. He saw Lou stand up abruptly, spilling some of his drink, mouth open, eyes wide. Lou looked at the bathroom door then back to Reese. He could see Lou doing the math.

"I thought I saw you leave, an hour ago, what the?—"

Lou tried to recover some grace, thinking as he dealt with the situation in front of his friends.

"Excuse me a sec, guys, right back."

Eight pairs of eyes scoping the situation as Lou grabbed Reese's arm and led him through the door, into the hall.

The party had spilled into the hall and had gotten ever louder. Lou led him to a quiet spot farther away from the crowd. He stared at Reese for a few seconds; anger showed in his glazed eyes.

"How long have you been in there?"

"Not long."

"What were you doing in my private bath, Reese." Lou's voice dripped venom.

"Somebody on your staff was stupid enough to lock the men's room. I had to go bad, knew you had a private bath. Simple as that."

"Somebody on my staff did lock the men's room, by mistake. I had them unlock it—almost a half hour ago."

Reese stood stock-still.

Lou glared.

"Sorry, it was locked—or I thought it was locked when I had to go—it was a real urgent call of nature."

Reese heard the Off signal of his mini-key chain recorder lightly sound in his pocket. He had forgotten he had left it on. And he had forgotten that the model he had, had a longer recording time than the model on TV, then shut itself automatically off.

Lou apparently heard the recorder too. He glanced down at the front right pocket of Reese's trousers, quick and in panic mode. In his stare, Reese saw anger, and a flicker of fear.

"Have you had time to think about your decision?"

"I gave you my answer, Lou."

"OK, Reese. Sorry to hear that."

Lou started back toward his office, stopped, turned, said, "You take care, Reese. And you be careful—very, very careful."

Reese started the trek back to the shopping center parking lot. When he reached the skywalk, fear hit him again. He could still hear the words of Lou and Raheed about Brochman and Patterson. These men, the respected men of the world. Upright—but only on the surface—good citizens, heads of multinational corporations of good citizenship, family men. Yes, they were capable of murder. He was just a peon to them. Brochman and Patterson carried far more weight than he did, by far, and look what had happened to them.

Reese was near the cross traffic of the mall. There was little traffic. The shops were closing in less than half an hour. Some had already half-closed their night security gates. Reese saw a couple hurrying to the parking lot ahead of him. Looking to his left and right as he entered the crosswalk, he saw only a lady with a shopping bag, small child in tow. On his right, a teenager, two bagsful. The lights were slowly being turned off.

He looked back, saw no one following him, but still quickened his pace.

"Sir."

Reese heard the gentle voice behind him and jumped. He turned. How in the heck?!—he had just looked over his shoulder and there had been no one there. Guy must have come out of thin air!

"Yes?" Reese slowed his breathing, watched him approach carefully. Didn't look like any of Lou's crowd, although he could have been dressed for a party. He wore a navy suit, plain white polo-type shirt, well-shined shoes.

He had reached Reese.

"Can you tell me where the Christian Bookstore is."

Startled, Reese just stared at the stranger for a second. He thought he recognized the face, but wasn't sure. It dawned on him, the face, the voice, the words—the man with the cane, only no cane this time. And there was something different about the face. Reese wasn't sure if this was their second encounter. But it was a déjà vu experience.

Reese swallowed. "the Christian Bookstore?"

"Yes,—I know it's late, but if you will . . ."

Reese thought he had never seen such a calm and serene face before. The man smiled.

"Sure—I'm going right past it. Better hurry—they're probably closing." Reese took another look at the empty hall behind him and started toward the bookstore.

"Here we are, sir. Looks like they are beginning to close."

"That's fine, won't take me long—I think I see the two books I'm looking for in the display case there." He pointed to a rack in the window holding two books. One was the Bible. The other looked like an ordinary book. Reese stepped closer to see the title: *Angels for Gentiles*. He didn't see any other writing on the book, not even the author's name. It was an impressive-looking book, in white cover with gold lettering.

"Thanks for your help." He looked at Reese's name tag—the stick-on he had gotten at the party.

"God bless you, brother Maxey. The Lord is with you. In your time of distress, call the chosen." He gave another brief smile and started into the bookstore. Reese continued toward the garage—at a slower pace—head full of forming questions.

Still perturbed about the encounter with Lou and keeping one eye on the exit into the parking lot, Reese sat in his SUV, motor running. Something was bothering him more about the encounter with the stranger at the bookstore. It was the same feeling he got when he knew he had forgotten something but just couldn't remember—then it hit him. The stranger had glanced at his name tag.

Reese snatched the sticky piece of paper off his jacket. It said "Reese." Simply "Reese." Yet the stranger had called him "Mr. Maxey"—no, not Mr. Maxey, he had said "brother Maxey."

His heartbeat accelerated. What was going on!?

Strange man, strange words. Twice. And the strange man knew his name—his last name. And the strange man was the same man he had met before—or not. The same and yet somehow . . . different?

And when he had come across the skywalk, he had looked back, checked his back every few minutes—seconds, fearful that Lou or one of his boys might be coming after him, and the skywalk overpass had been empty of traffic—there was no place to hide on it—and yet, a few seconds later, the man was behind him.

Reese shut the engine off, raced back to the bookstore.

A young salesclerk was bent over the counter, writing. Another young lady was turning lights off over a case, simultaneously replacing books back in their respective places, putting a couple in a canvas bag. Reese raced around the room to the last display rack, searching. Didn't seem to be anyone else in the store. He went to the counter. The young man was writing with concentration on a notepad.

"Excuse me . . . do you happen to have a men's room?" Reese gave a sheepish smile. The clerk looked up at him and then at his watch.

"Closing in less than five minutes—but, yeah, around the corner, back as far as you can go, left as far as you can go." He went back to finish whatever he had been writing.

"Thanks." Reese hurried to the men's room. He looked in every stall. Not a soul. He returned to the clerk.

"Excuse me, did you see a guy come in here a few minutes ago, blue suit . . . ?"

"I haven't had a customer for the last fifteen minutes—Trish!" he called to the other salesclerk—did you see a guy in here a few minutes ago, in a suit?"

Trish stopped, looked at Reese.

"Nope, sure didn't, not the last fifteen minutes."

"Sorry."

"Are you sure?" Reese asked.

"Trish, did anybody come in the store last few minutes?"

"I didn't see anybody." Reese went to the showcase, stepped outside to see the books that had been on display. The book the stranger had pointed out was missing. Reese returned to the clerk.

"Do you have a book titled—what was the title?" He hadn't paid much attention to it, being distracted by just the man's presence.

"*Angels and Gentiles,* or something like that?"

Both clerks looked up, stared at Reese for a second. Both looked at their watches. Trish looked at the other clerk, uncertainty on her face, wanting to close the store and go home.

"I don't think . . . the title doesn't sound familiar, to me," the man gave a sigh. "I'll do a database." He stepped over to the computer, started typing. A few seconds later, "Was it *Book of Angels?*"

"No—doesn't sound right," Reese said.

"*Angels and Demons?*—those are the only two books I'm finding."

"Anything *Angels and Gentiles*—I'm sure it had those two words in the title," Reese said.

The clerk typed some more, studied the screen.

"Nope, nada, sorry."

"Well . . . thanks . . . thanks a lot." Reese saw that it was five minutes past their closing time. "Appreciate your effort."

He started toward his SUV. Confused. What was going on? How could the stranger here know him? How could he have appeared, disappeared so quick?

His face strong, serene, calm, knowing eyes. And the strange resemblance—almost identical—to the man with the cane. Uncanny. This was real strange. Maybe . . . maybe he had seen Reese on the *Global Week* TV show. That would have to be it, or maybe he was at the party? Overheard his name? Reese felt a small sense of relief, a closure, with the explanation.

He drove out of the parking lot.

As he drove, with a jolt, his thoughts returned to Lou and Raheed. Like slap in the face his anxiety returned. He glanced in the rearview mirror. There was corruption in Sky, and he had evidence of it. He looked in the rearview mirror again, scanning the headlights as best as he could, looking for any evidence of being followed. He took Johnson Drive west from the plaza on into Johnson County on the Kansas side. He made the southbound loop onto Metcalf, looking carefully at the traffic behind him as he made the loop south onto Metcalf. On Metcalf he drove below the speed limit, checking the rearview mirror continuously.

Lou had been drinking, true. But he had sounded sober enough to mean what he had told Fahzi. Sky was too big, too important, too global, winning too many souls to let it be threatened by one man. Reese could feel the sweat of his hands. Fear was knocking again. He checked his rearview mirror as he drove into the parking lot of the Doubletree. He drove around the lot, around the building twice, looking at every parked car.

When he got to his room, he checked his messages. Nothing. He wanted to see Jan and John before he left town, made a mental note to call both of them before sleep tonight, or early AM. He checked the security bolt on the door, propped a chair against it. He went to bed and forced sleep to come.

CHAPTER

19

Early morning he called Jan.

"What's going on, baby girl!"

"Reese!" Reese heard the pleasure in Jan's voice. He smiled.

"Thought I'd give you a holler before I leave town." Reese thought about it—he had not had a lot of time, or mind, for Jan lately given all of the recent events. But she was always a pleasant thought when he did think of her.

"Well, you'd better had!" She laughed. "Where are you?"

"At the Doubletree."

"Nice place." She wanted his company.

"Uh-huh, let's do lunch."

Jan gave a few seconds of silence, then said, "OK, where?"

"Come out to Applebees?" She knew the Applebees down the street because it was where they had eaten on an occasion or two.

"Sure—maybe a little early, like eleven or so? I have to see a client early after lunch."

"Sounds good. Look for my car." Reese hung up and dialed Jon next.

"Special Agent Darrett."

Reese laughed. "What's so special about Darrett?"

"Who is—hey! What's going on, dude?"

"Nothin' but the rent, and the money I spent." An old-school college joke. They had shared decades ago back in the day, they both roared with laughter.

"You remember that one."

"For sure, dude," Jon said in old-school voice.

Reese said, "Come on out have a Coke with me."

"Where you be, dude?"

"Will be at Applebees, on Metcalf."

"About one?"

Perfect, Reese thought. "Perfect, dude." Reese hung up.

Reese paced a little in the Applebees parking lot waiting for Jan. A cold day, but nice and sunny. He saw Jan's car pull into the lot. When she got out, his heart did pitter-patter like a schoolboy's. She wore a tan suede jacket, sweater, denim pants, and boots. And looked lovely.

When they were close enough to each other, paces quickened, and somehow the chemistry, the mutual desire, the missing each other suddenly kicked in, and they found themselves in tight embrace, kissing deeply, for the moment, forgetting public diplomacy, oblivious to passing traffic.

They took a table by the window and ordered a simple lunch of burgers, salad, and Coke.

"I quit my job—broke my contract." Reese saw the light in Jan's eyes brighten.

"I am so glad to hear that, Reese—I've been praying for you."

"You've been praying for me?"

"I watched you on *Global Week*." She shook her head.

"Was I that bad?"

"You—your style and presentation were perfect. The message of the show was—was an abomination."

"I have to make a living, somehow."

"The Lord will provide, Reese."

Reese nodded, affirming Jan's words, but he was not as sure and as confident about it as she seemed to be.

"No job and, and I was just about to ask you to marry me." Reese chuckled, took a big bite of his hamburger to hide his nervousness.

Jan laughed, looked toward the ceiling,

"Lord, have mercy—that's about the most unromantic proposal—and no ring, Lord, have mercy! But if that is a proposal"—she looked at Reese—"the answer is yes!"

They shared the laugh. "But I did look into possibilities for a licensed master of social work in Dallas." Smile on face, one eyebrow lifted, she gave Reese a look.

Reese stared for a second, saw doubt creep into Jan's eyes, said, "I'll help with that if you need me."

She nodded.

They ate in silence for a while, both thinking of challenges in the future, both happy at the moment.

They parted in the parking lot with a warm embrace.

Reese found his same table in the restaurant cleaned and waiting, getting a smile of recognition from the waitress he had liberally tipped only a few minutes ago.

He would be glad to see his old friend, Jon. A side benefit of the friendship—he might need his help someday, especially with the situation with Lou and company.

He saw Jon enter the restaurant and inquire of the hostess, look in his direction. Reese waved.

Looking fit and trim, in a gray suit and tie, Jon joined him. "How's it goin'?"

"Aw, man, it's your world, I'm just tryin' to survive in it."

Old-school dialogue, and they both cracked up.

Reese ordered vanilla ice cream and pie, Jon a club sandwich and bottled water with a lemon slice. Reese knew Jon had to get back to work soon.

You remember when I was asking you about FCI?"

"Yeah—how's that going? Yeah, and dude, I'm proud to be one of your best friends. I watched you both times on *Global Week*, you did the part as good as any interviewer on TV." John raised his hand to do a high five.

Reese only nodded, gave a lukewarm hand slap. Jon looked closer. "Everything cool?"

"Well, I want to run some stuff by you, get your input."

"Well, that's what friends are for." Always a quick eater, Jon was all but finished with his sandwich. "What's going on with you and FCI—and Sky?"

"You know, Sky the spiritual aspect of it, kind of goes against my grain," Reese said.

"FCI, Sky—they're a dangerous group of people, Jon." Reese watched Jon's face for his reaction. As customary, he took Reese's words in stride, chewing his pie, nodding.

"How are they dangerous?"

"Sky, FCI, ain't what they're cracked up to be, lotta bad stuff goin' on there."

"We talked about that one time—years ago, right after college."

"I didn't know FCI right after college."

Jon laughed. "No—I mean, we talked about how none of the real world is what it's cracked up to be. I could say the same thing for the FBI—"

"This is a little stickier, dude—I'm talking about—about— maybe, maybe crime."

Jon stopped chewing for a second, looked at Reese.

"OK."

"What if I told you that the miracles, the so-called miracles that I showcased on *Global Week* were phony, fake?"

"I wouldn't be too surprised. But knowing you, I don't see you as willingly being part of something that unethical."

Reese realized that Jon had spent a career fighting crime. Something like fake testimonies in a religious context probably seemed lightweight to him. Although, Reese reminded himself, it was the kind of thing you sometimes read about in the news, particularly when the FBI was investigating it. He wondered if Jon cared about it. Regardless, though, he was very much concerned with his own safety.

"High crimes in high places, not always a way to correct that."

"What about murder in high places?"

Jon stopped chewing, sat back in his booth.

"Murder—what do you mean?"

"And I almost can prove it."

"You've got to be kidding."

"Serious business—serious as the pope on gay rights."

"Maybe this is something I shouldn't be hearing—at least not at this time."

"I might need your help."

Jon looked a little skeptical, but he nodded. "I got your back." Reese decided to not tell too much. Might be better to tell him in a limited way and talk to him off the record, as friends, not officially, although he wasn't sure that was legal. Jon was an FBI agent, not a reporter or a lawyer.

"Have you all made any headway in finding Brochman and Patterson?"

Jon had to think for a few seconds.

"You're talking about the religious leaders that disappeared."

Reese nodded.

"I'm not working on that case. I know it's still an open case." Jon swallowed.

"I overheard some stuff—by accident. Just happened to be hiding behind a curtain in a private bathroom."

He and Jon laughed. "OK," Jon said.

"I believe FCI and Azko Lee Britton had a lot to do with Brochman and Patterson's disappearance. You know who Britton is, don't you?"

"I think he's the head of the New World Bank, and one of those superrich people who control the planet from behind closed doors."

"That's him."

"You know something about him?"

"He sat in on my interview for the job with FCI . . ."

"You are kiddin'." Reese detected the awe in Jon's voice.

"Not at all."

"He was here in Kansas City, and he interviewed you?" Jon had put emphasis on the second "he" and the "you."

"For a fact," Reese said, nodding.

"You always were one too low-key in everything you do . . . I wonder how he came into Kansas City without making the press." You really are playing in the big league, Reese" His voice oozed awe and concern.

"And I want out," Reese said, face and voice showing anxiety, sincerity.

"You know, dude, some organizations you're either in or you're out, and once you're in, ain't no gettin' out. Knowin' too much sometimes makes you a permanent player." The two of them looked at each other in silence for a few seconds.

Reese decided his handling of this situation.

"Listen, Jon, I've got a tape, might, or might not be incriminating—people in high places. That and some more information I got on my own—my own detective work. It might, or might not be, useful to the bureau." Reese paused for a few seconds while Jon absorbed the information.

"What I want—what I want to be assured of, if I need your help, in any way, that I can call you, send you some information, whatever . . . can depend on you for help. Including maybe you introducing me to the right people at the bureau to listen to me."

"You got it, dude. I mean, you know, what are friends for?"

Reese saw Jon was not doing a rhetorical cliche, that he meant it—"we've been kickin' it a long time."

"And you, Reese, you have some credentials of your own. You're probably better known than you think you are. Just you knockin' on our door is going to get some attention—because it's you. Know what I mean?"

Reese nodded. "Appreciate that."

"You keep your tape and all the other info you've got. Organize it, put it in a safe place. You've got my home number, my cell, and office number. You get into trouble, call. I know a couple of agents in the Dallas office. But look, I wouldn't make any waves, though, not at the level you're dealin', not unless it was a matter of life and death. But if it gets dangerous—you call me."

Reese shook hands with Jon in the Applebees parking lot. Not wanting to drive back to Dallas this late, he took his room at the Doubletree for one more night. He was tempted to call Jan, remembered she was working late with her client tonight.

He caught a couple of movies at the Quivira Mall, turned in for the night.

CHAPTER

20

The next morning he checked out, started south on I-35. He was on the road early enough to beat the Dallas rush-hour traffic eight hours later if all went well.

As he drove home, he reflected while checking the rearview mirror at regular intervals.

His mind kept wandering to Lou, Fahzi, Lee, Brochman, Patterson; and each time it did, he felt a stab of fear. He didn't see how they could not come after him. He knew too much.

Lou and Fahzi had practically admitted to responsibility in the disappearances of Brochman and Patterson.

Reese recalled the look on Lou's face as he had heard the click of Reese's tape recorder. The look on his face said he wasn't sure, but he suspected something. Reese thought knowledge seemed to dawn on Lou's face. Suspicion—and fear. He had too much decorum to ask Reese what the sound in his pants pocket was.

Fahzi had already condemned Reese by telling Lou that Reese had been snooping in places he shouldn't be—Vickery's. Reese reached, unlatched the glove box. He saw the case. With one hand he opened it. The gun was holstered and in place. He had a permit to carry it. Thanks to his training and classes the short time he was in the competitive intelligence society. He would never kill, but the gun might come in handy.

He came into Wichita late morning. He took an access road exit. As he did, he saw a blue Taurus in his rearview mirror. Something in his brain triggered recognition, but he didn't know why. He felt the stab of fear again. He looked at the gas gauge. He had enough gas to get to Oklahoma City.

He exited to the frontage road, drove slowly, looking at the buildings on either side of him intensely, as if he were looking for an address.

The blue Taurus was still there moving slower, equivalent of two city blocks behind him. He came to the light. He saw the Interstate 35 sign and followed the arrows back onto the interstate. Just as he entered the entrance ramp he took another look into the rearview mirror. Two cars were behind him, but he saw no sign of the Taurus. Reese heaved a sigh. He made himself relax as he got into the fast lane heading south on I-35. Maybe it was all chargeable to his paranoid imagination. After all, he was just an ordinary citizen. A nobody in the eyes of Lou and his homeys. There was nothing he could do or say that would have any effect on the lives of people like Lou, Al, Lee, Fahzi.

He relaxed, turned on XM Satellite to the music of the '60s. The mellow rhythm of the Drifters' "Up on the Roof" floated in.

An eighteen-wheeler passed him. He looked at the speedometer, saw that he had slowed to sixty-five miles per hour. He looked in the rearview mirror. Reese's heart skipped a beat. Looked like the Taurus was back. Maybe, Reese couldn't tell, wasn't sure. The car was again about two to three city blocks behind him. Traveling at about the same speed Reese was. Which was noticeably too slow on an interstate where it seemed the norm was somewhere just under eighty miles per hour.

He slowly increased speed, set the cruise control.

When the speedometer hit seventy-four miles an hour, he was going just fast enough to be in the flow with his fellow travelers. The blue Taurus was keeping pace. He thought about scenarios and potential actions he might take. He didn't want to do anything that would let them know that he knew he was being followed. Second, any stop he made, he wanted it to be where there were lots of people. Third, h0e opened the glove box, pulled the gun case out with one hand, keeping a careful eye on the traffic ahead. He slipped the holster clip over his belt on his left side, back near his hip. Under his leather jacket. It wouldn't be visible when he stopped to get gas.

As he drove, he thought about the situation he was in. Maybe if he had done more research about Sky, he wouldn't have taken Al's offer, wouldn't even have gotten to the point of the interview with him and Lee and Lou. If he had been more faithful, he wouldn't be in this dangerous place in his life. If he had only studied the scriptures with more diligence. If he had studied the word of God like his parents had. And been true to it. If he had even known then—only a few months ago—what he knew now, he wouldn't be here, in this predicament. How could he have been a part of anything that watered down the Word of God? He thought about a sermon he had heard years ago. The subject had been on the prodigal son, "when he came to himself." When he came to himself, he had returned home, where he belonged, to the safe haven of his father's house. Reese had thought about that sermon many times. As a psychology major, it had intrigued him. That a person could consciously be engaged in something so wrong—consciously so, and yet, at the same time be blinded to the truth of his actions. Self-deceived and/or deceived by Satan. And remain in such a lost state until—and unless—God's grace brought him or her into awareness and repentance. He thought about the nation of Israel. Blinded to the reality of who their Messiah was. Blinded to the fact that He had come to them a little more than two thousand years ago and they had rejected Him. For thousands of years they had proved to be a "stubborn and stiff-necked people"—to quote the prophet—to the commands of their God. And God had dealt with them harshly, and justly so. And yet, they were still a blessed people. A nation that could not be destroyed, will never be destroyed, and a nation that the whole world will someday recognize in Jerusalem—as the seat of government for the planet and the earthly residence of the King of Kings. Israel's best days were yet to come. But not before their worst days. Reese's mind flipped to the book of Revelation. Not a pretty picture.

He was coming into Oklahoma City. He saw the tall buildings—the cityscape—such as it was on his left. He turn-signaled at Hefner road, to exit to the Fast Stop Conoco station, droved to the farthest aisle of pumps. A quick glance into the rearview mirror and he saw the blue Taurus, slow, make the same exit.

He pulled into the lot of the Conoco station. With his slouch hat and sunglasses on, he got out, pulled his credit card, inserted it, and pretended to look at the gas meter as he filled his tank. Behind dark sunshades he carefully scoped the Taurus. He made a mental note of the license plate—Missouri tags—the Taurus pulled up to the front of the store. Two men got out. Both of them looked his way. From their perspective, Reese seemed to be watching the pump meter. Reese glanced to his left, in just the opposite direction of the front of the service station. Reese carefully checked both of them out. Young men, tall, thin. Looked like late-high school or early-college age. The driver wore dreadlocks, jeans, a T-shirt that looked to Reese tie-dyed; sneakers, and a motorcycle-like black leather jacket. The passenger looked Hispanic, tall, a little heavier than the driver; he wore a button-up shirt untucked over jeans and tennis shoes and a three-fourths-length black jacket. Both men wore sunglasses to fight the glare of the early-afternoon sun. They went into the store, separated, one looking at a magazine rack, the other to the candy rack; both faced Reese's way. Reese put the hose back in place, closed his gas cap, and started casually toward the store, checking the station pedestrian traffic on either side of him. Fairly busy day, more traffic than Reese would have expected. But the more the safer.

He sensed both men tensing as he entered the store. He headed for the coffee station, then to the counter. He took one split-second glance at the man on his left—the Mexican. Reese thought he saw uncertainty and fear. The man on his right took his glasses off, glanced at and quickly past Reese, as if he hadn't noticed Reese any more than anybody else in the store. He looked at his partner,

"Hey, man, check this out." He held up a magazine. The voice betrayed false ease and confidence. A second split-second glance at him and Reese realized, with a heart skip, that he had seen him somewhere before. Handsome dark face with a thin mustache and goatee. Then it hit Reese he had seen him before.

"That's it, bud—cigarettes?—"

"That's it," Reese laid the required money on the counter, picked up his change, and started back to his SUV. An awkward moment or two, setting the roll and coffee down to open his door.

He started the engine and entered traffic toward the interstate. When he hit the interstate from the entrance ramp, he saw the blue Taurus following suit.

Reese felt fear return—and anger. The face of the young man—Reese had seen him briefly at the party. On his way out as he left Marie, or was it right after he had talked to Fahzi? The black man had been one of the wait staff. He was sure of it.

If this was true, Lou had sent a couple of punks after him. Reese again felt a stab of fear. He thought about Brochman and Patterson. But that had been Switzerland. Two strangers on foreign soil, a long, long way from home.

Reese settled in the slow lane, set the speedometer at seventy-four again. Fear morphed into anxiety and anger. He would take no desperate, drastic actions. He'd see this through, and he'd send the two punks Lou had sent to get him back home in defeat. And he might first whip their behinds good fashion, to boot.

He was coming into Dallas. He headed west on 635 hoping he had missed the brunt of traffic. Maybe he had, maybe he hadn't. It seemed to him the population in the Dallas metroplex spent an inordinate amount of time on the freeways and interstates. No matter what time of day, they were always crowded. A perpetual rush hour, the only thing he hated about Dallas. Once, looking at the metro map for a department store address, he had been amazed at the hodgepodge of streets. There didn't seem to be any through streets that ran true north-south or east-west. It looked to him like a random convolution of tangled, webbed streets that frequently changed names, or that had two different names, and that merged and morphed into confusion.

And the metroplex seemed to stretch forever. You could drive almost two hours across the greater Dallas area and never leave the city.

Reese slowed to join the stop-and-go traffic headed west on Interstate 635. He eventually hit 121 south and enjoyed a few minutes of seventy-miles-per-hour traffic—although everyone around him jumped over to the fast lane as they approached the rear of his SUV. That was again something he didn't like about the traffic. Everybody drove too fast. And paid the toll. Every day there were accidents on the metroplex's freeways—usually during rush hour—and every week, it seemed there were fatalities.

As 121 slowed and as he neared home, Reese checked his rearview mirror again. Dozens of cars behind him. He saw a blue car several car lengths behind. And one next to it and another several car lengths behind it. He couldn't tell the make of any one of them.

Reese pondered how to handle the situation he was in. As traffic moved ahead, he sped toward the 360 Highway juncture. He wondered if the two men following him already knew his address. If one of them had been a part of FCI's wait staff, he would have to be either with a catering company or with the in-house restaurant at FCI. If Lou knew him well enough to send him on this mission, the latter was possibly the case, but not necessarily. He might have given him a briefing on his target including his address. Reese would find out, or maybe better, why not lead them right to his apartment, let them show their hand, make the first play. Reese's heart beat faster as he neared home and skipped a beat when he saw a blue Taurus follow him off the 360 fork at 121. He would rather be at home waiting for them than for them to be at his apartment waiting for him. He wouldn't need to stop for dinner. He had a couple of TV dinners in the refrigerator. And the situation had killed his appetite. He pulled into the parking lot of his apartment complex, parked, retrieved his bags from the rear of the SUV. As soon as he had looked his door, he dropped his bags and rushed to the window overlooking his parking lot. Careful to move one slot of the blinds just enough

AN ANGEL FOR MAXEY

to peep through, he waited. In less than three minutes he saw the Taurus. They turned slowly into the apartment complex and cruised past his unit. Both men looked at his apartments. As they drove by, Reese saw them look at other units, scope the lay of the land. On the second drive-by, they seemed to have come to some decision, turned around, and drove out of the complex. Reese went to his office. He checked his gun, got some more cartridges. They would probably come after him tonight. He' be ready. He thought about calling the cops. But what would he tell them? That two men were out to get him? As soon as they saw no evidence of his story, they'd write him off as crazy, and even if the two men were stopped and questioned, they'd deny knowing Reese, and Reese had no way of proving otherwise.

He propped a chair against the door and prepared a TV dinner, drank a glass of orange juice. And prepared to wait pushing gloomy thoughts out of his mind. There were only two entrances to his apartment—the front door and the sliding patio door off the dining area. But there was a window in Reese's office. He went to the office and unlatched the window, raised it about six inches. He retrieved some electrical tape from his crowded, hold-all topdresser drawer. He sat in the dark and waited. His portable radio kept him company after prayer.

Sleep crept up on him around 10:00 PM. He went into the bathroom and slapped cold water on his face. Used to work on TV although he hadn't seen that cliche in the movies for years. But it worked. Fear was probably more of a wake-up factor, though.

By 10:00 PM, the neighborhood was usually quiet. Even on weekends. His observation and occasional hellos to his neighbors had shown Reese a professional middle-class neighborhood. Across the breezeway from him was a middle-aged divorcee who was an exec at the locally based American Airlines. One of the thirty-somethings above him travelled for IBM, in sales or service or something like that. Professionals who worked hard, recuperated on the weekends, braced for the grind on Monday morning.

Just after 11:00 PM, Reese heard the hum of an engine, and he peeped through the blinds of the bedroom window. He watched the blue Taurus park three park spaces from his SUV. In a few seconds, dreadlocks went around to the south side of his apartment as the Mexican walked slowly toward the front breezeway. Reese hurried back to the front door, made sure the chair was in place, and then headed to his office where he had set the file cabinet just to the side of the window. He checked his gun, bent low behind the file cabinet. Waited. A few seconds later, he heard the screen being removed, heard window raised; dreadlocks was crawling in, horizontally, using the bay window shelf as support. Reese, his heart beating fast, saw the intruder's hands touch the floor for support. He could hear him, breathing hard. Reese sprang, his left hand slapping precut electrical tape tightly with his hand pressed over the intruder's mouth, and almost simultaneously he showed his .9 mm into the base of the man's skull, pulling up, hard. The man started to struggle, tried to holler, but Reese straddled his back, pressing his pistol hard in the man's skull.

"Shut up and relax!" Reese whispered harshly in the man's ear. The man went dead still.

"Do you understand me?"

The man's head shook violently, in spite of Reese's restraining hand, that he did very much understand. Reese grabbed the back of the man's shirt collar and slid him into the room. He patted him down quickly, found a .45 caliber, slid it under the bed.

"Both hands behind you—now!" Reese's voice was a harsh whisper. The man immediately complied, resting awkwardly on his chin and shoulders. Reese hastily wrapped both wrists, turn after turn of the tape until he was confident the man couldn't get free. He then put another piece of tape around his mouth, two complete turns, and taped his ankles. He bent down.

"Do you want to come out of this alive?" His harsh whisper, right in the man's right ear. The man nodded, his fear palpable. Reese dragged him to his desk and added more tape—taping his wrists to the desk legs.

"If you stay quiet, and if you stay still, you might live. Do you understand me?" Reese shoved the .9 mm hard into the back of his head. He groaned and shook his head.

Reese, with speed, went to the front door. He heard a light knock—*tap, tap*. He looked through the peephole; the Mexican was sweating, looking around, his eyes full of fear and apprehension.

Reese slowly started to unlock the door. He saw the Mexican push his coat aside, revealing an automatic pistol. Before his hand touched it, Reese yanked the door open, pulled hard on the Mexican's gunhand, downward, shoved his knee hard into his solar plexus. He immediately pulled the Mexican's gun out of his belt before he hit the floor.

"What—owww!!" The pain of his dislocated arm registered. Reese pulled him in the room, slammed his foot in the man's back, showed the .9 mm into the back of the Mexican's head.

"Completely quiet! Comprende?"

"What the!—"

Reese stepped back, kicked him in the side.

"Did I say quiet? Just nod your head." The man nodded emphatically.

"Hands behind your back!"

Reese hastily taped both hands and both feet. "Stay still—and quiet!" He then dragged dreadlocks into the room, closed his apartment door. He patted them down, the Jamaican for the second time, removed the tape from his mouth. He took their wallets, put the chair he had used for a prop in front of both men, straddled it, his gun in hand.

"Both of you want to keep breathing?"

"Please, mister . . . d-d-d-don't shoot . . ."

Reese studied the two criminals, both on their stomachs, ankles taped, hands taped behind their backs. Dreadlocks was trembling, his partner grimacing in pain. *There but for the grace of God*, thought Reese. He felt a stab of compassion for his would-be killers. But he couldn't afford to go soft on them.

He pulled out his cell phone, activated the camera.

"Wiggle your nasty behinds over against the wall facing me." Reese felt compassion for them, but he also felt anger. The anger was apparent in his voice. Breathing hard, they were finally in place. Fear on the black man's face, pain and an edge of fear now on the

Mexican's face. They avoided Reese's eyes and stared at the floor under their noses.

Reese dialed Jon's number. He answered in a sleepy voice, "It's me."

"Who—hey . . . what's going on . . . what time is it?!"

"Middle of the night."

Jon laughed, good-naturedly, hiding his annoyance.

"And we should all be sleeping."

Reese got to the point. "I got two thugs in my apartment—want you to take a look at them."

"That's right—two thugs. Tried to break in and kill me." Reese paused. "Square biz, my man"—Reese took a chance—"Lou, you know, the one at FCI sent them."

Reese saw the surprise, with even more fear on the black man's face. Reese pulled the phone away from his ear, looked at the two, and said, "I'm talking to a friend at the FBI. You two are going to regret this night—if you live." He pointed the gun at them, watched them cringe, turning their heads away as if to avoid the impact of an expected bullet. Both were breathing hard and now showing a lot of fear.

"I'm going to send you their pictures."

"One is named David Marley, lives on prospect in KC, Missouri."

He picked up the other wallet.

"The other is Rono Hernandez, lives on west Twenty-ninth Street, KC, Kansas. Hold on a second, Jon." Reese looked at the two men. "Mug shot—look into the camera!" Both men looked into the cell phone, defeat along with fear showing clearly on their faces.

"I'm sending this photo via cell phone—you can do whatever you need—or whatever the FBI needs to do. But hold up before you do anything. Want to see what kind of dialogue the three of us have. Let me call you back—No, I'm fine, nah, don't need the police." Reese saw both men flinch, uncertain what Reese was going to do to them.

"Yeah, sure . . . if anybody dies tonight, everything is well documented, I understand that." Reese watched the level of fear accelerate on the faces of his captives. He had faked the last line with Jon, but Jonathan had gotten it.

"Good tactic, be very, careful, very, very careful. You should call the police, Reese." Reese heard the concern, and maybe a little fear in Jon's voice.

"Gotta go, but will call you back." Reese flipped his cell off, sat looking at the two men.

"OK, what did Lou tell you to do?" Silence.

Reese stood up.

"He t-t-t-told us to get you." Reese noticed the black man's accent—seemed Jamaican, Bahamas, somewhere in that vicinity. And he couldn't tell if the stutter was fear or natural.

"And you were stupid enough to sign that contract."

The Jamaican was nodding. The Mexican said painfully, "I just came along for the ride." Reese walked toward them. Both men cringed. Reese stooped down, still out of reach of them.

"Go to church. Find God." They both looked confused, trying hard to comprehend what he meant.

"You have a life ahead of you. A good life if you seek the Lord— and I mean, the Lord—find a Bible-believing Christian church once you find the Lord, a good church . . . it is not boring . . . otherwise, what happened to you tonight is what you have to look forward to the rest of your short lives. You are just one trigger pull from death. You realize that, don't you?"

Both men shook their heads affirmatively.

"Yes . . . sir." Almost in unison, apprehension and uncertainty, fear etched on their faces.

"And . . . ," Reese continued, "if you go back to KC, mission not accomplished, Lou will kill you." Reese watched the expression on the dreadlocks face—wheels turning, brains tabulating Reese's comment.

"You ever failed the test with Lou before?"

"I've never done anything like this before," the Jamaican blurted out.

"Nothing, only delivered messages for him before."

"You from the Bahamas?"

"Jamaica."

"Did he tell you why he wanted me dead?"

"He just say to follow you, and . . . first chance . . ." The Jamaican looked away, not finishing the sentence.

"How much did he pay you?"

"Five thousand." The Jamaican realized his mistake too late.

"You said it was twenty-five hundred!" his partner said with anger.

Reese said, "Here's what we're going to do. You've lost your guns, you've lost your driver's licenses." Raised both of them, threw their wallets back to them.

"The FBI has your pictures—and the story of what happened here tonight. And you've failed a job for a very powerful man. At the first chance he gets, he's going to have you killed—he cannot afford not to. And I have this whole show on tape." Reese let it all sink in, continued, "You are in way over you heads."

My four-one-one for you is to leave KC. And you better not hang around Dallas."

"Do you understand me?" Both heads bobbed up and down.

"Get outta Dodge." Reese threw a pair of dull scissors to them. "One wrong move and I will shoot you."

"Leave, tonight. Don't ever come back. And remember what I said about church."

Reese watched as they freed each other and slunk out of his apartment. When the door was closed, he latched it, hurried to his bedroom window, and watched as they sped out of the apartment complex. He would FedEx the intruders' guns to Jon's office, first chance he got.

CHAPTER

21

By 10:30 AM on a bright sunny, but cold Monday morn, Lou Maez had finished most of the telephone calls he intended to make that day. He lit an H. Upmann cigar, pushed back, propped his feet on his desk, ankles crossed. He felt pretty good. Talks with his accountants all but assured him the quarter would reflect healthy profits. Projections for the fiscal year end sounded almost too good to be true. Even if they were a little exaggerated—and Lou suspected they were—he would take home double digits in the millions as his bonus. He had come a long way since the early days.

His father had struggled as a haberdasher in New York. He had managed to service and sell to all five of the organized families and to the Irish without ever having incurred the wrath of any of them. His mother had come from blue blood money. How they ever got together Reese had never had explained to him. Early on his father had changed the family name from Maezetti to Maez and had determined that his son would finish his post-high school education at Yale. And Lou had done so; while in school, he had made friends—in a sort of crude way. He never quite fit in, but on the other hand, he did well enough.

Lou looked at the small scar on his right hand. Happened at a drunken frat party. Lou recalled it too painfully well. Big Mike. He had hated Big Mike. The fraternity had rented a house for the party. Lou had had one of the sexiest, finest sorority girls in his grasp. He had been rappin' away. Lights were low, music turned up, everybody was havin' a good drunk time. Big Mike—all six feet five and 260 pounds of him had jumped into the play.

"You can do better than that." Leer on his face, voice slurred.

Lou had turned to him and said, "Beat it!"

"Who you talkin' to?" Rage had flamed Big Mike's complexion.

"I said beat it."

Beet Red Big Mike said, "Step outside—I'm going to turn you into *it*." Lou had paused for a second. He wasn't sure he could whip Mike. But he hadn't wanted to look bad in front of the girl. Both men made their way to the front lawn, several party goers having overheard the exchange trailing them. As soon as Mike had turned to face Lou, Lou had hit him hard, in the mouth. And he had had to stifle the sear of pain he felt from Big Mike's teeth. And then Mike hit him, and he went down. And he had had no fight in him after that. When he was getting up off the ground, he had heard one of the partyers—they were supposed to be his friends—say "kick him." Lou had never forgotten that. Lou had slunk away with what seemed like hundreds of eyes laughing at him.

Two weeks later, Big Mike had been killed in a hit-and-run off campus.

After the accident, his friends seemed a little ill at ease with him when in his company. Even when they were getting drunk and doing fun frat stuff, some of them were unable to look him in the eye.

At first this bothered him. He adjusted to it eventually, wrote it off as his imagination. Soon he learned to use the leverage it provided him, with both his college buddies and the college girls.

No one ever hinted at a connection between his fight with Big Mike and Big Mike's death. At times he referred to it in an oblique way when it was to his advantage to do so. The truth was he—and his family back home—had had everything to do with Big Mike's death. A man needed to know who to dis and who not to dis.

Eventually he had shared a couple of business classes with Azko Lee Britton, and the two, connected by a kindred spirit, became close friends. Weekend drinks with Britton and the Symingtons and he had laid a path for a career and future at FCI Incorporated.

He reached for the news memo in his inbox. Something about the Spiritual Church International. Again, Sky. Sky brought Reese Maxey to mind with an uncomfortable jolt.

He hadn't heard from the Jamaican.

He lifted the receiver of his in-house phone, dialed the extension for the company's dining service.

"Dining."

"Bert?"

"Speaking." It irritated him that he never recognized the chef's voice.

"Lou here—any of those cinnamon rolls you do so well?"

"Got a few left, Mr. Maez, still fresh and warm."

"Send up a pot of black coffee and a couple of the rolls, and send 'em up with David."

"He's not here, Mr. Maez."

"When is he due in?"

"Well, I'm not sure . . ."

"It's unlike him to not call in or something."

That was unlike him, Lou had vetted him months ago.

"Maybe he's ill."

"He hasn't shown up for—for the past three days, not like him at all."

Lou was silent. He watched a large cloud block out the sunlight. The day had started sunny; now it looked threatening outside.

"Did you try to reach him at home?"

"Tried several times. His cell has been turned off, and his home line has been disconnected. I'm afraid I'm going to have to let him go, Mr. Maez."

"Do what you have to do. Send the coffee and rolls up." Lou clicked off. He swore.

He should have known better! Never send a boy to do a man's job. How many times had he heard his father preach that?

He sat brooding for a few minutes, anxiety building, the chef's news confirming a fear he had pushed to the back of his consciousness.

Two major mistakes. All about Reese Maxey.

How could he have been so wrong? They had thoroughly vetted him, checked his history, his credit, his relationships, had their own men—the best there were—follow him, search his car, search his home. And they knew him; he'd been interviewing top FCI execs for years.

The problem was his religion. He actually believed word for word whatever the Bible said. He took it literally and refused to compromise.

Well, that was going to cost him. But he'd have to be careful. He didn't know fully what Reese Maxey knew. And he didn't know what had transpired between the Jamaican and Maxey, didn't even know where the Jamaican was.

This was going to cost him too. He'd have to put six figures into the Davos pot to get this mess cleaned up.

He picked up the phone again, dialed. "Marie? I need you to get me a secure line to Lee Britton's office."

CHAPTER

22

Reese thought about the future on the way to his job interview. He forced himself to push the thought of Lou out of his mind. Last night's prayer and church yesterday—both had lifted his spirits. The sermon had come from Psalms 55. For those who trust in God, those of upright heart, when the enemy turned on you, God had already determined that the righteous would not be moved. By faith in those words, Reese proceeded on to his job interview, with hope in the future. He would take a day at a time, and he would deal with the enemy's attacks—one at a time until this situation was resolved. He thought back on the attack of the two thugs. His fear had subsided as he took charge of the situation that had been designed for his death. He had had some periods of anxiety—and fear—since then. But not a lot. The scripture came to him about the peace of God that surpasses all understanding.

He pulled into the mental health center parking lot. With the money he had saved—from FCI and the very little he had saved prior to FCI—he could make a solid down payment on a nice home. Like those he had seen in Colleyville and Grapevine. He couldn't afford Southlake or Highland Park, but then his taste didn't run quite that high anyway. And with this job—if he got it, and just a little bit of

Jan's help—she wouldn't even have to work full time; they could make the mortgage and enjoy some of the things they liked to do. He didn't need to make a lot of money—the job he was interviewing for today certainly paid a modest salary.

Another good thing, if he got this job, it would be a job fitting the helping aspect of his master's degree in psychology. Training social workers and other community behavioral workers how to market themselves and their clients' skills to the job marketplace appealed to Reese. Helping people with psychiatric diagnoses find employment in the competitive job market was what he would be doing. Not an easy task, but Reese felt we was up to it. The HR director had said they might even consider hiring on a contractual basis.

As Reese waited for his interview in the lobby seating area, he studied the surrounding people. He felt a little tense—it had been a long time since his intern/practicum days in a mental health setting. Back then, working with, interacting with, mental patients had become his comfort zone. He had even dated a couple of them after they had been discharged. They were called patients back then. Today, at this center, they were "consumers." Reese looked around. He felt way overdressed and out of place in suit and tie.

"Mr. Maxey." The receptionist's eyes finally rested on Reese; she started his way.

"Hi, I'm Bernice." She extended her hand and led him into the office area. She wore jeans, tennis, and a simple sweater.

Reese and the HR director exchanged pleasantries and began the interview.

When Reese exited the mental health center, he left with a good feeling. The interview had gone well. He had given honest and straightforward answers about his feelings about the task of the mental health center. Questions regarding his understanding of the concepts behind the job tasks he had answered well, and he thought he had seen appreciation on the HR director's face. Supported employment was the name of the game here. And it was an altruistic and worthy game. He had applied Maslow's and Carl

Rogers's concepts about, self-worth, self-actualization as needed in the interview. The how-to of marketing the center, the services the center offered, and the clients, Reese had explained with skill at the appropriate times during the interview. Reese thought as he talked, this was right down his alley. Why hadn't he looked into this before? With a stab of guilt, he realized he hadn't because it didn't pay the kind of money he had wanted.

"If the Lord wills, that will change," he mumbled to himself—but, he corrected himself, whether he got this job or not, that had already changed. Vibing with the aftermath of the interview, a little euphoric, he paid no attention to the Hummer that followed him.

When he got back to his apartment, Reese went through more help-wanted ads on the Internet. His focus had been on health care and marketing-related advertisements. He responded to two by e-mail, made a note to call one, and typed a cover letter and resume to two others.

Since the incident with the two intruders, he instinctively scoped the parking lot of his apartment complex on a frequent basis. His brain cataloged make and models of his neighbors' and their visitors' cars. On the second peek out, Reese saw the Hummer. Again somewhere in his brain, recognition fired. He had seen this Hummer before; there were two men in it. He couldn't see the details of their faces because of the tinted glass. With a faster-than-normal heartbeat, Reese checked his gun, placed the chair he had used before against the door. He checked the windows, patio door. He placed the pin bar safety on the patio door. When he went back to his spy gap, he saw the taillights of the Hummer waiting to enter traffic at the apartment entrance. Reese breathed easier. The Hummer had looked familiar, but it could belong to another apartment. But then, thinking about the predicament that Lou was in, Reese couldn't picture him just sitting and hoping all was forgiven, and forgotten. Had the two men reported back to Lou? Whether they had or not, Lou had committed and exposed himself. And it was unlikely that he had forgotten the encounter the night of the party. With a feeling of gloom, Reese again realized Lou couldn't afford to let him slide. Still, he had to take this one day at a time. And not worry. Have faith in the One who knows the end from the beginning. On this thought Reese eased into a light sleep.

CHAPTER

23

"Tell me what you liked most about your previous jobs?" The interviewer sat back in his chair and made notes on his notebook as Reese related the highlights and high points of his career. Marketing research for a food product maker. Reese left the interview only lukewarm about the job. Too much electronic research and data tabulating. He preferred old-school face-to-face interviewing: Interviewing real people, in the flesh. That method of interviewing seemed to be going the way of public pay phone booths. He was feeling an increased pull toward an occupation with duties that were of direct help to people who needed what he had to offer. He'd keep looking.

It was three cars back, but Reese was certain it was the Hummer he had seen yesterday evening outside of his apartment. The traffic coming out of downtown Dallas on I-35 was heavy this time of day. Reese drove along at a below-speed-limit pace with the flow. As he switched lines to merge in 183 traffic, abruptly jumping in front of a Honda Civic, he saw the Hummer slow down to let a couple of cars in front so it could make the same lane change onto 183 Highway.

OK, Reese thought. He was determined to see this out.

By the time he was three-fourths of the way home, he was convinced the Hummer was following him. He wanted to see their faces, but he wanted to do so in a large crowd of people. Lou probably had not made the mistake of sending amateurs the second time.

He got back onto 183 and headed toward Northeast Mall. Should be a lot of people there. And the mall had cameras everywhere.

He merged 183 into I-820 and immediately exited.

As he waited forty-five seconds later at the light he saw the Hummer coming onto the exit ramp. He got into line—the parking lot was crowded, crowded enough—even on a workday.

He parked near the Dillards entrance. He grabbed his slouch hat and entered the mall. Just inside the tinted-glass store entrance, he watched the Hummer park. He watched as the two men started in fast pace toward the same entrance Reese had come in. He felt his heartbeat speed up. They were big men. At least six feet four, one slightly taller than the other. One white, one black. The white guy had long white blond hair, thick, over the ears, and long in the back. The black guy had a short Afro. They both wore suits and ties. The thought that hit Reese startled him—could they have been sent by Jon? He hurried into the store, began browsing the men's clothing section. He looked at the shirts—Roundtree & York—Dillards house brand, Daniel Cremieux—not a bad line of product. He picked up a lime-colored button-down and surreptitiously scanned around him. He saw one of the men checking the pants rack, the other browsing through the stacks of jeans on display.

"Finding everything all right?" Reese turned. Pretty and smiling.

"I'm just looking."

"Anything in particular?"

"Nah, just want a look at some of the shirts."

"OK, let me know if you have any questions—"

"Thanks," Reese said.

He noticed that both of the men had moved closer to him—like they were closing in, like a vise. Reese wondered if they'd do anything violent in a place as public as this. He noticed several other shoppers, but still, unfortunately it was not as crowded as he would have liked—two young men looking at jeans, a couple browsing the hanging shirt racks.

"You are Reese Maxey." The big blond was holding a couple of pairs of jeans in his hand, smiling at Reese. More of a tight, menacing grin than a smile.

Reese controlled his breathing.

"Guilty." He attempted a humorous tone and smiled.

"We would like to talk to you."

The man had stepped in closer. Reese could feel the tension and toughness of the man.

"And who is we?"

"Both of us." The black man's voice hissed cool, calm, professional venom on Reese's neck. Reese took a look. He reminded Reese of the football player Jim Brown. And he wasn't smiling like his thug partner.

"Come on, what's up, guys?"

Reese tried to squelch the tremor in his voice.

The blond man said, "I said we need to talk. And I said not in here." Controlled violence with a smile on its face.

"Talk about what? I don't believe we know each other."

"Are we doin' this the easy way or the hard way?" Reese could feel the impatience in the black man's voice. He thought for a second.

"What about coffee—in the food court?"

The blond man grabbed Reese's arm.

He had a firm grip, but up close Reese detected some softness in him. Not as tough as first impression.

"You come with us peacefully or we'll drop you right here. And we've got badges in case you have any idea of trying to make a scene, your choice."

"OK, you just want to talk, right?" He had to struggle to breathe.

They started toward the exit. Reese saw a salesclerk stare. Probably noteworthy, three big six-footers walking side by side.

When they got to the exit, the big blond stepped ahead of Reese to open the door. Reese took a deep breath, and before the blond was out of reach, Reese extended his foot. The man stumbled on Reese's foot, started to fall with the opening of the door.

Reese leaped, grabbed the man around the waist. As he cleared the door, he twisted violently to his left, his arms tight around the man's middle.

As they fell toward the sidewalk, Reese slid the man's gun out of its holster. They hit the ground, Reese, his back to the ground, the man on top of him, both facing skyward.

Caught off guard, and with bulk, the black man came through the door a little late. He reached for his gun.

Reese fired, deliberately aiming not to kill.

Thud! The bullet found it's target—the man's kneecap. Fired from a silenced six-shooter, the gun made less noise than the man's cry of pain.

"Ayyyy!!" He immediately grabbed his knee, dropping his gun.

Reese shoved hard, rolling briefly on top of his assailant.

But the blond was not quite ready to throw the towel in. He twisted, and Reese ended up again under the man. The man pressed his back against Reese's chest trying to pin him down. He was reaching for the gun.

Reese had a mental flash of a Krav Magaa lesson he'd once had. The instructor had been teaching him tricks of last resort.

He bit down hard on the man's ear.

"Owww—oh!" The man's hand went instinctively to his ear.

Reese rolled again, and using the mans back as leverage, he was on his feet in a second.

He ran as fast as he could to his SUV.

At a dangerous speed accelerating out of the parking lot, Reese saw in his rearview mirror the two men helping each other—both running, one limping—as fast as they could way from the onlookers who were beginning to gather at the entrance.

As he sped along 183 toward home, Reese wondered how close he had come to dying a few minutes ago. For some reason, he was not feeling any fear now.

He hated to shoot his assailant. Instinct had kicked in and he didn't see any other option at the time. As he took the northbound loop onto 360, he realized he must have dropped the gun right after he'd fired it.

After he had secured his apartment, Reese turned on the TV, wondering if there had been any news coverage of his adventure at the mall.

From 5:00 PM to 6:30 PM he switched from channel to local channel. Nothing about the shooting.

"The shooting." The expression did not sit well with Reese. He recalled the expression on the man's face as the bullet tore into him. Surprise and severe pain. Reese guessed excruciating pain. He took no pleasure in that.

He turned the TV off, threw together a salad and a smoked turkey sandwich and, with his favorite drink Coca-Cola, ate in the living room, thinking reflectively as he ate.

Here he was, alone and on the run from people who were trying to kill him. He let that sink in.

And were trying to kill him. The Jamaican hadn't denied that fact. And they were powerful people. Globally powerful. He pushed back the fear and looked briefly at his .9 mm sig-sauer lying on the sofa next to him. He knew how to use it—had had lessons. He practiced with Jon at the firing range on a fairly regular basis. And he had a permit to carry the gun.

At one point he had been a member of the Competitive Intelligence Society. He had joined on a whim, influenced by an old college friend. He had been trained how to use a weapon. He had had Krav Magaa instructions in self-defense, and as part of the organizations program, he had been trained as a private investigator and had acquired a license to carry a gun. All of this had been extracurricular, for him. A social group to pass time with (but not too often) and an acquisition of some more skills and some plaques and certificates to hang on his home office wall along with his college degrees. At the moment he was glad he had taken the time.

How had he come to this messy point in his life?

By backsliding, for one.

If he had stayed close to the church, stayed close to God, his life would have taken a different path. He thought about his pastor cousin, Reggie. Reggie had gotten away from the fun life—the so-called fun life—early on, returned to the Lord. And he had done well as a pastor. And he was not looking over his shoulder in fear of losing his life.

Maybe too much pride and desire for worldly things was part of it too. To be honest, he had wanted the FCI job. He'd wanted the TV show and the celebrity that went with it. And that was self-deceit, or not knowing self well enough, because he had always thought that he preferred life in low-profile mode.

And compromise. Reese flinched at the thought. As much as he feared God, how could he have compromised the faith? His fear of God exceeded his fear of FCI, Al, Lou, Britton and—well, any man. And yet, he had found himself publicly promoting a church—quotation marks—he didn't even believe in. And more fearful was the thought that he had helped lead others astray.

Again, a sermon he had heard Bishop Padduck preach flashed in mind. It had to do with the prodigal son, and the emphasis had been on five words: "when he came to himself." In his backsliding, the prodigal had been aware of what he was doing. Consciously aware. And yet, unaware. It had taken loss and hard times to bring him to his senses. That seemed to be a pattern among believers. Couldn't see the light until God made you feel the heat.

Well, he was feeling the heat—now. There had to be hope for him.

Maybe he could talk to Lou.

He entertained several dialogue scenarios with Lou Maez. None of them worked. Maez had too much at risk as long as Reese was breathing.

Getting away—as far from the Midwest as he could—might be a solution. Or not. From what he knew and read about Sky and Azko Lee Britton and the agenda at Davos, there was no safe place on the planet—maybe deep in Angola.

Conclusion: He had one source of help—his faith in God. Maybe an angel—he thought about Padduck's prayer for him.

An angel.

He had a mental flash of the men he had encountered at the FCI shopping center.

He felt something stirring inside. The two men he had encountered.

He mentally revisited the two occasions. There had been something. Something otherworldly about them. In fact, the *them* now seemed to him one man.

He sat down, took a sip of Coke.

He didn't believe in angels. No, that was not true. He did believe in angels. The Bible told him they were real. He just didn't believe in visible angels.

And yet, he wasn't sure. He knew that *angel* meant *messenger*, but—

What did he recall about those two encounters that might be considered out of the natural realm?

Both of the men had made sudden appearances. Not like "poof," right in front of his eyes, but both had suddenly appeared unexpectedly. And the second time, well, as afraid as he had been that night of the party, and as frequently as he had looked back over his shoulder on his way to his SUV, no one could have gotten close to his back without him having seen him coming. But the strange man—one second he was not there, the next, he was. And his not materializing in the Christian Bookstore. And the vanishing book. Was it possible?

Reese stood, paced a few steps. And what had been the message for him?

Something about, in his time of stress, call the chosen?

The chosen. For some reason, Zonman came to mind.

Reese felt the increase of adrenaline.

And Zonman had told him to call him if he . . . was ever in trouble or something to that effect. And he had made the invitation in a meaningful manner.

Why not? He was in trouble, and he needed help. Zonman had impressed Reese as being sincere about his Christian faith. And he certainly had been opposed to Sky.

He went to his desk, searched through an array of business cards he had accumulated, and found Zonman's card. A New York address with office, cell, and fax numbers.

He was tempted to call his cell number now. He wasn't exactly sure what he'd say, though, wasn't sure about how to approach him. And he wasn't 100 percent confident he'd be received well. He'd call him tomorrow. He felt better already. He secured his apartment and went to bed.

On waking, Reese's thoughts went to the call he intended to make. He was nervous about it, not sure how Zonman would respond to his call. He checked the apartment complex. A sunshiny day and only four cars at home. He recognized them as belonging to residents of the complex.

He had a glass of orange juice, sat down, and dialed Zonman's number from the business card.

"Mr. Zonman's office."

A professional female voice, Reese was a little surprised, encouraged by the fact he wasn't talking to a switchboard receptionist.

"May I speak to Barak Zonman."

"May I tell him who's calling."

"This is Reese Maxey . . . in Dallas."

"I believe he's on his way out of town, Mr. Maxey—is he expecting your call?"

"No, but I suspect he will take my call." Reese had to smile at his own boldness.

"Hold a second, I'll see if Mr. Zonman is available."

Reese waited through two minutes of dead silence. Not even any static on the line. Maybe this had been a mistake. Hang up before embarrassing himself.

"Mr. Maxey, how are you?"

"Uh, fine, doing good—I take it that you remember me—"

"Of course, I remember you."

Zonman gave a friendly laugh.

"The blue Sky guy."

Reese joined the laugh.

"Blue Sky is right. And in fact, Sky is why I'm calling. Don't want to bother you while you're busy, but the situation with Sky—the people I've been working for—well, I would like to get your advice."

"You gave me—"

"Are you in New York, or in Dallas?"

"In Dallas."

"Do you know the Radisson Hotel—in Austin?"

"Think I could find it."

"Can you meet me there tomorrow, say around 11:00 AM?"

"I certainly can."

"Looking forward to seeing you again, Mr. Maxey . . . maybe we can take a few minutes to finish our last conversation. See you at eleven." Zonman clicked off.

Reese returned the telephone receiver, breathed a big sigh of relief.

CHAPTER

24

Zonman had taken a small pedestrian room. Reese was surprised. He had had a better room himself the last time he had moteled out of town. Shaking hands, dressed comfortably in a long-sleeve rust-colored polo shirt, khakis, and desert boots, Zonman led Reese to a small table by the balcony. The two big men with him nodded to Reese and left the room quietly.

"This is one of the properties we control," Zonman said. "For sentimental reasons that I won't go into, I happen to like this particular room."

Reese could understand Zonman's need to explain the austere quarters. Reese looked out over the balcony—fifth floor. Nothing to see but the shopping center next door, and the busy traffic on I-35; Zonman poured coffee.

"So you and Sky . . . Sky's not so blue anymore, I take it?"

Reese saw a twinkle in Zonman's eye as a smile played around his lips. He smiled.

"Blue Sky."

They both laughed. Zonman waited. In a more serious tone Reese said, "The organization is . . . fraudulent. And their people are dangerous." Zonman was nodding.

"They are dangerous, Reese."

Reese was surprised. He had a quick mental flashback to the article he had read about Zonman, about his mystery and his connections to the intelligence community.

"So . . . you are aware of them—of how they operate."

"Let's say that perhaps I know quite a bit about the who and what's behind sky—maybe more than the average person knows." Zonman paused, continued, "You said that you wanted to talk to me about some trouble you are having . . ."

Reese swallowed.

"They are out to kill me."

He felt silly, little boyish. And he felt relief at the same time.

Zonman looked at the traffic whizzing along I-35. He turned back to Reese.

"Tell me, Mr. Maxey, how much did you believe in the speech you gave at the business luncheon, how much did you believe in Sky?"

The question caught Reese off guard. But he knew his answer.

"I didn't believe in Sky. Oh, you know, somewhere there was some rationalization in my mind that perhaps a unity of faiths could come about—that it would be good . . . to see people work together, to like and cooperate with each other better, to be more productive workers . . . but the spiritual part, I was, and still am convinced that you can't obtain eternal life—life beyond this life, beyond the grave, without the Lord."

Zonman studied Reese for a few seconds.

"You actually believe that?"

"I'm fully persuaded of that, Mr. Zonman." Reese said, looking Zonman full force in the eye.

"What do you think of the Muslim?" Zonman continued to watch Reese carefully.

"I love people, Mr. Zonman, all people, of all religious, ethnic, etc., backgrounds."

Reese thought for a few seconds, continued, "I admire and love people who are devoted to a cause a . . . I believe Judaism, Islam, and Christianity, all of the adherents to those faiths all are looking . . .

I don't know, are trying to look to, the same God—the God of Abraham, Isaac, and Jacob—but the true path to God is through Christ. So one of the three has it right."

"You're sure about that?"

"I'm 100 percent sure. In fact, by faith, I know that to be true."

Zonman leaned back in his chair.

"How is Sky trying to kill you?"

Reese told Zonman about his initial suspicions about the miracles televised with Sky members, about his own personal investigation into them. About his overhearing Fahzi and Lou talking about the disappearances of Brochman and Patterson and his taping of the conversation and about the attempts on his life.

Reese, a little bit amazed, watched Zonman take all of his story in stride. Nodding as if the events he was describing were everyday normal events. When he finished, the room was silent for a few seconds. Reese was even more surprised as he heard Zonman ask, "How do you feel about Israel?"

Reese thought for a few seconds, then, "I think most Christians have a love for Israel." From her, the world got the knowledge of our creator. Israel is here forever, and those who bless her will be blessed, and those who curse her will be cursed. That's a promise God made way back then, to Abraham." Reese paused, then continued, "I do believe her worst day is yet to come—the period of the great tribulation—but her best day is yet to come after that, the one-thousand-year rule of Christ on earth."

Zonman leaned forward.

"Yes, it will get worse for Israel before it gets better for her. It's too bad our people did not accept the Messiah when He came the first time." Zonman winked at Reese. Reese processed what was coming at him; he asked, "Are you a believer?"

"Long story there, Reese, but yes, I went to a church one night, heart wasn't right, but before I left, I saw the light." Reese laughed; Zonman smiled. "True story."

"I believed first, then I studied our history, biblical view."

"I saw how God has had trouble with Israel from the Red Sea days. Israel has been a very stubborn, rebellious, and stiff-necked people—a continuous pattern of backsliding—into idolatry, and sin in general. Full of doubt even after God had repeatedly delivered them from numerous troubles. And then, when He finally came down here to visit them, they rejected Him, crucified Him."

"They were blinded by God. At least partly," Reese offered in defense of Israel.

"So that you Gentiles could be saved too," Zonman supported, "set aside for a short term until the completion of the number of Gentiles called by God are brought into the church."

Zonman stood up. "So, Mr. Maxey, maybe you could come to work for me."

Reese didn't follow the segue, and the question startled him. "I—"

Zonman continued, "Maybe we could be of mutual benefit to each other."

Reese was not sure what Zonman had in mind, but he was warming to Zonman's words. He said, "Maybe so," uncertainty in his voice.

The next statement from Zonman threw him for a loop.

"You have a permit to carry a gun, and you were once a member of the competitive intelligence society, I believe."

As surprised as he was, Reese felt neither fear nor resentment.

"That is true," he said in an even voice.

Zonman walked a few paces, turned, hands in pocket, looked at Reese.

"I'm going to share a few things with you, Reese, information that is never to leave this room . . ."

Zonman was studying Reese with intensity.

"You have my confidence, Mr. Zonman."

"My friends call me Mr. Z."

"OK . . . Mr. Z."

"I am a truly successful businessman." Zonman paused, and continued, "Do you read *Forbes*, Reese?"

"I don't subscribe, but I did see that article about you—your profile."

Zonman seemed pleased.

"Good." Zonman sat back down. "So you know about my business activities."

He paused. Reese nodded.

"I am government approved. I work with the Mossad and the CIA, occasionally the FBI. Kind of like a contractor, but under the table—so to speak. I very much love Israel, and I love my country—America. And I love God—by way of Christ. That's who I am, Mr. Maxey."

He paused again. He continued, "And we have been keeping an eye on Sky—you don't need to know who 'we' is at this time."

Reese took it all in, gladly, and, for some reason, not too surprised.

"Do you have any legally binding ties in your contract with FCI that would prohibit you from working for another organization?"

"None. I work as an independent contractor, not limited to one company."

"Good."

Zonman stood again, took a few paces, turned, faced Reese.

"How does the following scenario strike you. You come to work for me—you'll have the title of field liaison and/or investigator/reporter or some such for one of my business divisions. You investigate Sky. Particularly, get taped testimony from one of the fakes they had on your TV show. And in time, you present evidence on our—that's right our own program. I am in talks with the people behind Brochman's Christian Jew TV program, and it's just a matter of time—a short time—until we begin broadcasting with his replacement. You investigate for us. Testify to the world about our true faith. You'll have a better contract with us, we'll match what FCI paid you and then some, with some benefits to boot. And we protect all of our people, Mr. Maxey."

Reese could hardly believe his ears. He stood, walked over to Zonman, grabbed his hand,

"You have a deal."

"Great!" Zonman shook his hand, and Reese saw the pleased look again in his eyes.

"Can you come to Rockville, Maryland, for a week? A little training and orientation we require of our employees and contractors."

"Sure. Just outside of DC/Baltimore as I recall," said Reese.

"Right, call my office—the number on the card—have the secretary book you, next session is four, five weeks from now. And she'll send you some papers to sign."

As Zonman walked Reese to the door, he said, "We will keep an eye on you, Reese. Know one thing, we are very good, the best. If you spot someone following you—if you are able to detect you are being followed, you can bet it's not one of ours. One other thing, wouldn't hurt to start by getting some kind of confession, at least some taped information from one of those guests you had on your TV show."

"After you sign our papers, start sending your expense bills to us."

Absolutely nothing but a blessing from the Lord, Reese thought as he drove toward Dallas. To walk out of one job—a job he should never have taken—under a cloud, a dangerous job, really, and to walk into another job most compatible with his lifestyle, both secularly and spiritually, and one that paid a lot more, nothing but a blessing.

In high spirits, Reese called Jan to give her the good news.

"Hallelujah!" Reese could see the smile on her face as they talked.

"A better job, Reese, and you will be on TV witnessing for the Lord too. Honey, that is a blessing, I mean a real blessing!"

After he signed off, the reality of Sky—of Lee, Lou, Al, Molly, and company—set in again. A real spirit-dampener situation. Reese mentally chastised himself again for even taking the job with FCI.

He checked the rearview mirror again. His heart did a flip. He could swear he had seen the black Hummer behind him more than once since leaving Austin. He thought about Zonman's words. If he could spot a tail, it wasn't one of theirs. Lot of traffic between Austin and Dallas. What should be a three-hour trip was closer to four at times because of traffic slowdowns.

He drove on a few miles. At the next rise in the road, on the down slope, just a few seconds out of sight of the following traffic, Reese hit the brakes to cut the cruise control and slowed to fifty-five miles per hour, moved to the slow lane. The Hummer gained on him slowly.

He watched as the black Hummer passed him. Out of the cover of his eye, Reese checked the occupants, three men. All looking straight ahead, seemingly oblivious to the slowpoke SUV they were passing. Probably his paranoia, but Reese had the feeling they were very much aware of him. An unusual three men. The glass was tinted, but from the silhouettes, it looked faintly like two of the men wore ponytails. Reminded Reese of characters he'd seen on the TV show *CSI Miami*. As they passed, Reese made a mental note of the Hummer's license plate number.

Florida plates. Didn't see many of those around here. Plates fit the occupants, though. As the Hummer continued moving farther and farther ahead, Reese's fear subsided some. Occasionally he did see Florida plates in this part of Texas.

He thought about Zonman. Rich, well-connected power in low-key form—mystery man associated with both the CIA and Israel's Mossad intelligence. And a Christian. Reese was impressed. He could feel the eagerness rising in anticipation of going to work for such a man. And the icing on the cake, what would make it even doubly, no, not doubly, triply—if there was such a word—nicer, he would be serving the Lord.

It felt right to Reese, and it was far more exciting and comfortable than the temporary euphoria he'd had starting up with FCI.

Meanwhile, he had an investigation to conduct. He thought about the guests he'd had on the TV show. He thought he could handle Molly. And he had more incriminating evidence against Molly—Vickery's repair order.

He had a sudden thought, why not just take all of this evidence, Molly's, the testimonies he'd taken from the two intruders would-be killers, take all of it to the police and be done with it. Marry Jan, buy a house, take a job as a social worker, settle down. "Settle down." An old-school word. Old-fashioned word and concept.

The reality was the direction, the opportunity Zonman had offered him felt like a calling to him. It felt right. More than any other job he'd taken. He had a feeling that to go otherwise would be stepping outside of a path supernaturally made just for him. And going to the police, that would be a mistake. They would do nothing. They would have to do nothing. Reese was certain that this situation would have to be handled at a level that transcended government and the criminal justice system. It would have to be handled at the level of Davos. And that's where Zonman operated. And with the Lord's help—Reese flash backed to the two angels? he had encountered at the FCI mall—he would come out of this alive and well and in the will of God, on both feet.

The investigation. Molly. She would be the one to go after. He would go home sit-down with a Coke and a sandwich and figure out how to get a freewill verbal confession out of Molly. He was curious as to how FCI or Sky, or whoever, had gotten Molly Reed to bold-face lie on public TV.

Reese turned into his apartment complex parking lot, breathed a sigh of relief.

He secured his apartment and sat at his bedroom curtain peephole. His fellow apartment dwellers slowly filled the lot, dragging themselves tiredly from their SUVs, near-luxury sport cars, and Hondas into the comforts and retreat of home. Not one strange ride in the lot.

He was about to vacate his peephole when he saw a black Hummer slow down near the complex entrance. Reese's pulse raced. The Hummer slowed below speed limit; Reese thought he heard a couple of horns blow as traffic went around the Hummer. He couldn't see clear enough, but it looked like three occupants in the Hummer. Clearly there were two in the front seat. In ponytails? Reese wasn't sure. In a few seconds the Hummer joined the rest of the traffic again and disappeared. Reese's heart slowed down. Just

a driver slowing down in rush-hour traffic, for whatever reason,—
hundreds of reasons possible—not at the remotest related to Reese,
or perhaps a crew from Zonman, making sure Reese was safely
tucked in. Zonman's men—the two he'd seen—didn't seem like the
ponytail type. Or it really was more sinister people from Lou and
company planning another attack.

He continued his peephole vigilance for another thirty minutes.
He didn't see the Hummer again. He rechecked his apartment's
security, thinking security he was glad he hadn't taken a lease at one
of the properties FCI owned when he had moved to Dallas. And
further thinking of security he wondered if the apartment complex
had a night guard.

He looked at his watch; if he called now, he just might get the
property sales agent before she left for home. He dialed the complex
number. He felt some relief when he hung up. A recent car break-in
in the last week, so happened, had prompted the complex to hire
an on-site security guard. He felt a little more secure but not a lot.
Not much protection there, especially if Lou had hired professionals.
His ultimate confidence and peace was in his faith. He had prayer
as usual before a sound sleep.

CHAPTER

25

Reese drove carefully, matching the pace of the rush-hour shift exiting the Exxon building. He had spotted the big brown Chevy and was following it at a discreet distance. As he drove, he kept one eye on the rearview mirror. He had not detected anyone following him.

Reese followed Molly at almost a continuous undetectably safe distance. I-635 into Highway 21 south into 183 Highway west. Molly took the Brown Trail Road exit. A few more minutes north, Reese watched the taillights brighten as a right-turn blinker started. He sped up, turned right. He saw the brown bomb pull into a two-car driveway halfway down the block.

It was a neighborhood of lower-middle-class dwellings. Neat lawns, with flower beds, two-car front-facing garages that took up half the width of a house.

He made a mental note of the house location—the brown house matched the color of her car. He cruised past as Molly's garage door was descending. He cruised to the next stop sign thinking. He wanted to catch Molly, confront her in a nonthreatening way, sit down with her, and talk. And do it before she had time to call whoever her handlers were. A public place might be his best shot. He drove past her house several times before heading home.

That night before going to bed, he found the apartment complex security guard walking the grounds. It was just dark enough to be called dark.

As he approached, he saw the guard's hand move slightly toward his gun.

He watched Reese suspiciously as he turned from the apartment he was about to enter.

"Hi, ya doin?" He'd try a friendly approach.

"Good," the guard answered curtly.

"I live in apartment 1G—Maxey. You're the new security guy?"

Reese saw the guard relax. He stuck his hand out.

"I'm the one." Gray haired, mustached, pale skin, sixtyish. But he looked fit enough.

"Heard we had a break-in the other night?"

"Happened before I got here—but that's what got me hired. Hope it wasn't your car," he added hurriedly.

"Nah. Thank goodness. I was wondering, though, have you seen a black Hummer in here anytime?"

"I haven't gotten to know all the residents' cars—what's up?"

"Long story," Reese said. "But if you do see one, driver or passengers wearing ponytails, you should keep an eye on them—and let me know. Make it worth your time." Reese winked. The guard looked at Reese, slightly questioning look on his face.

"I'll keep that in mind, keep my eye open—where did you say you lived?"

"I'm in apartment 1G—Reese Maxey."

"And no, I'm not crazy. Check my background sheet in the office. I'm trying to give you a heads-up." Reese walked back to his apartment. He felt a little foolish but thought that his mission had been accomplished.

AN ANGEL FOR MAXEY

The next day Reese again followed Molly in hopes that she would stop and shop someplace. But she didn't. He'd get an early start Saturday. Surely that would be shop day for her.

On Saturday he parked on Brown Trail Road near Molly's house. Too much traffic and too many no parking signs. He cruised past her house a few times. Fourth trip he decided that was too obvious. He didn't need the neighbors calling the police. He parked west of her house, far enough away to see if she exited but too far away to arouse any suspicion in her block. Next he did the same east of her house. He drove past her house again. Just as he passed, he saw the garage door sliding upward.

His heartbeat hastened as he drove to Brown Trail Road. He continued west across the Brown Trail Intersection. He pulled into a driveway and, holding his breath, waited until he saw Molly head north on Brown Trail Road. He backed out of the strange driveway just in time. He saw the put-upon homeowner's door open just as he was beginning to retrace his tracks back to BT Road.

He headed north. He sped up. No sign of Molly. She must have turned. At the next light Reese looked east, saw the brown Chevy speeding along the major thoroughfare.

He turned, stepped down on the accelerator hitting passing gear. Within a block and a half, he felt he had gained a safe distance behind the Chevy. He slowed down, reminded himself that Molly had no reason to think that she was being followed. Speaking of which, he glanced in the rearview mirror again. He had detected no déjà vu traffic behind him.

After a few miles, he recognized the entrance to the Wal-Mart where he had examined Molly's car. Coming from the west, he hadn't recognized the location until he was near the Wal-Mart parking lot. On a couple of turns he had wondered if Molly was lost. Or worse, had spotted the SUV following her. Seemed like she was driving in a circle. But that was easy to do in the Dallas metroplex. Seemed like none of the streets ran in a true easy-to-travel north-south, east-west grid. He had too many times found himself driving in circles.

Molly parked, lucky enough to have found a parking spot near the entrance. Reese kept an eye on her car from the east end of the parking lot. After she entered the store—she seemed to be in a hurry—Reese drove around until he found a slot two aisles almost directly behind her car. She wasn't gone long. He was glad to see that she didn't seem to be in quite the hurry on exit as she had been going into the store. He wanted to talk to her when she had enough time to sit down and talk face-to-face.

He timed his approach, arriving at the rear of her car as she settled into the driver's seat.

He pulled close to the rear of the Chevy, blocking her in. Aware that the parking lot was camera monitored, Reese casually approached the driver's-side door. Molly had not looked up; she looked like a soccer mom in a dark coat and khaki pants. Reese saw her twisting the cap off a prescription bottle. She popped two pills and took a swig of ozarka bottled water before she noticed him. Her look was startled. And then fear, and then faint recognition. She relaxed and put on a what-in-the-world-are-you-doing-here expression. Her window went partway down.

"Hi, Molly," Reese spoke softly and smiled. His portfolio in hand, tape recorder in pocket. He felt relaxed. It was kind of a warm day for late winter. In a sport coat, jeans, ankle boots, he felt overdressed but had thought his attire might increase his influence and authority with Molly.

"Hi, I know you." A big smile, not fully comprehending who he was. Reese thought about the prescription bottles he had found in her glove box, wondered what she had taken a minute ago.

"Yeah, well yes, you should remember me." Reese laughed. Molly laughed. Window all the way down now. She turned a little more toward Reese trying to remember.

"You . . . you're, oh, hey! You're Reese Maxey!" Her face lit up with a big smile. Reese felt a stab of guilt and compassion for Molly.

"Guilty," Reese said, still smiling.

"Well, how've you been? How's the TV show going?"

"Well . . . that's what I wanted to talk to you about. I followed you here, Molly."

"Oh." Some of the smile left Molly's face as she pondered the meaning of Reese's words. She sat still, watching him for a second.

"Well . . . I guess we can talk." Reese detected uncertainty, reluctance in her voice.

"Won't take long. Can we go somewhere—McDonald's right down the street, on, I believe it's Harwood?"

Molly glanced at her watch.

"I guess." A growing caution in her voice. "What do you want to talk about?"

Reese hesitated, then said, "I need some information about Sky."

"Well, you're more of an authority on Sky than I am."

"Not really."

"What do I know about Sky that you don't, Mr. Maxey?"

"Can we go—and talk. Better yet, why don't you let me buy you breakfast?"

Molly looked straight ahead for a few seconds, thinking.

"Oh . . . why not . . . what about Denny's? There's one up off of 114."

"Sounds good. I'll follow you."

After a friendly waitress had settled them both in with coffee at a booth, Reese was almost sorry he had suggested sit-down dining. The place was too crowded and too noisy.

"You know, somebody told me once to never eat at a restaurant that had a menu with pictures of the food on it." Reese laughed. Molly was much more relaxed now. A little more glazed of eye too, Reese noted. Maybe the pills would help this go easier.

"Well, I can think of three reasons to eat at a restaurant with pictures on the menu—it whets your appetite even if you're not so hungry. You see what the food is supposed to look like on your plate, and . . . the price is right." They shared a laugh.

Reese ordered scrambled eggs, sausage, pancakes, and orange juice.

"I'll have the same, only make mine over easy." When their plates came, Reese said, "Plate looks better than the picture. Not bad." Another shared light laugh.

They made infrequent small talk between bites. Mostly about the weather and Texas life compared to previous lives. Reese ordered coffee for both of them. Sitting in the last booth back to the wall, he was glad to see the booth facing theirs empty as the table's foursome left their tip.

Reese looked over the crowd. Still noisy, but the late-morning crowd seemed to be thinning. He looked back at Molly.

"What I say to you today, Molly, is not going to be pleasant. You're not going to like this conversation." He gave a weak smile.

Molly sat very still and stared at Reese, lips slightly parted and headed toward a frown. For a second Reese thought she was going to cry.

"Am I in trouble, Mr. Maxey?" Reese thought ahead, projecting future scenarios if in case, somehow—unlikely though—what he hoped to get from her ever came to public or legal attention. He thought about Zonman and company.

"I don't think so, Molly. I think this case—if I might use the word case—will be handled behind closed doors and at a higher level than local authorities."

Molly nodded. Her spirit seemed to lift.

"OK. What do you want to know?"

Reese turned the tape recorder in his pocket on and leaned toward Molly. He placed the recorder on the table, placed one of the Denny's tent top merchandising plaques near it to shield the recorder from public view. Molly looked at the tape recorder and said nothing.

"Tell me how they got you to fake your story."

"They made me an offer I couldn't refuse." She attempted a feeble laugh.

"I can understand how that could happen. Kind of the way they got to me too." Reese smiled.

"Go back to the beginning, how did you get into this?"

Molly sighed, leaned forward on the table, hands holding elbows. Reese detected nothing of resistance in her.

"HR personnel, at work, they called me in one day. They were supposedly recruiting for Sky. I signed up and started to attend the Sky sessions. A few weeks later—could have been a few months—I don't know."

Reese saw the regret in her eyes. She continued, "Two guys, very sharp, tall, thin, well dressed in business suits—looked like corporate execs to me—they asked for me in the lobby one day."

"Company men?"

"I thought they were. I don't know—looking back at it now—they showed up in the lobby one day . . . I guess they could have been outsiders."

"Did they show you credentials?"

"Well, come to think of it, I don't know . . . they had a small conference room reserved in the building there. That's where we talked." Reese nodded. Forming Molly's scenarios in his head.

"What did they want?"

"They wanted my help with Sky."

"Your help."

"The way they put it, Sky was becoming a great organization. Dream fulfillment of world unity. Unity of home, work, of religions, of nations. Those were their words. For some reason I recall that part if word for word."

"How did you get from that to . . . to, well, to my TV show?"

"They said that there were some obstacles, that there were a few things in the way, something like that. The point was some people in parts of society needed to see stuff that was supernatural before they'd believe in Sky, before they'd join. I got the impression somebody somewhere was doing a lot of research, all over the world, not just in America, finding out on a regular basis just how to make Sky a religion people would like and support."

Reese stared at Molly a few seconds.

"Go on."

"Well, bottom line, they convinced me that I would be doing humanity a service if I provided a miracle, prove that there was a real spiritual life to Sky."

"And they paid you."

"Yes." Molly swallowed. "They paid me."

"In money and in car repairs."

Surprise showed on Molly's face.

"Yes."

Reese waited.

"I told them—they came out to my house several times. That's where we talked about the money—I told them I needed cash and I needed to have my car repaired."

"How much did they pay you?"

"Quite a bit, quite a bit for a working girl," Molly said sadly.

"And Vickery's." Molly stared at Reese for a second, nodded.

"Vickery's repaired the car for free."

"What do they want you to do next?"

"Nothing, I guess I'm not sure. I guess I have no assignment." Molly gave a small, sour smile. She continued, "They came to the house after the TV show I did with you and thanked me, gave me more money, and told me to go back to life as usual . . . and to stay in Sky. End of story." Molly sat back, stared at Reese.

"Quite a story." Reese turned the tape recorder off, repocketed it, sat back, looked at Molly and smiled.

"Don't worry about any of this, Molly. You did the right thing here." In reality, Reese wasn't sure how this taped story would be used or even if it would be used. But this was damning evidence against a false religion, and that fact alone made Reese happy. And he would help Molly if the need and appropriateness arose.

"Do you believe in God, Molly?" She looked startled by the question.

"Well . . . of course, I do. I am a Christian. I had a lot of reservations about Sky, Reese. And I felt guilty about the lies. And I asked God to forgive me. But . . . I don't know . . . I guess I thought maybe Sky was truth too. I don't know . . ." She looked down at the tabletop.

"Molly, there is one God, one faith, one baptism. You cannot mix faiths. Jesus said He was the way, the truth, and the life. He said that no man—no man, mind you—comes to the Father except through Him."

Reese felt his passion rise. A little embarrassed, he said, "Sorry, Molly—don't mean to preach to you."

"That's OK, Reese. I needed to hear that. It encourages me to know you are a Christian—I wasn't aware . . ."

Reese saw the beginning smile on her face.

"I guess we both strayed for a while there, Molly."

"I'm glad we did this, glad we had this talk."

She smiled broadly. A genuine smile of relief and of hope.

A few minutes later, Reese waved good-bye to her in the parking lot.

CHAPTER

26

They fell in behind him on the freeway. On Monday, coming out of downtown Dallas, Reese recognized the black Hummer, and its occupants in the rearview mirror. At sixty-eight miles per hour, his heart rate almost doubled for a few seconds. He calmed himself and maintained the speed, which was the speed of the surrounding traffic.

Over the weekend he had allowed himself to half-believe Lou and all of his bad company would evaporate. Simply lose interest in him and go away.

He continued driving as if he hadn't seen them. But they were not hiding. Too close to his rear end. Reese pretended to ignore them as he drove. He wondered if any of Zonman's friends were following the bad guys. Probably not. He was not quite a part of the Zonman family yet.

He said a silent prayer as he accelerated. He left the Hummer behind for a few seconds, but they soon caught up, this time not so close to Reese's SUV.

He drove another five minutes, taking 183 toward 360 north. When he looked in the rearview mirror again, he saw the back-row passenger of the Hummer leaning forward talking to the driver and front-seat passenger. The Hummer slowed, letting a couple of cars ahead of it. Reese accelerated and, in a few minutes, lost sight of the Hummer.

But not for long. Like a fighter jet on the tail of an enemy, the Hummer seemed to drop out of nowhere in his rearview mirror. Reese for a second froze, expecting them to crash into him.

He sped up. The Hummer sped up. Did he try to outrun them to his apartment? Or should he lead them to a very public place where there were lots of people and maybe some help? What about doing all and getting police help while he was still driving? Where were the cops when you really needed them?

He reached for his cell phone. Before he could dial, he felt the slam of the Hummer into his SUV. Just enough of a slam to make him drop the cell phone and grab the steering wheel with both hands. He made a mental note to look into Bluetooth. If he survived.

He sped up, left the Hummer three-fourths of a mile behind. He drove north on 360 until he saw the opposite southbound lanes free of traffic for a quarter mile. He braked slowly, did a left onto the grassy median between the south and northbound lanes, started back south on the opposite side of the highway. His maneuver had caught the driver of the Hummer off guard. But it took him only a few seconds to recover. Reese saw the Hummer climb out of the grassy median and follow him in southbound traffic. Of all times, there was little traffic.

This time of day, this far from downtown, the nearest place with the highest concentration of people would be the Northeast Mall, but it was too far away. More logical would be the Wal-Mart Super Center.

Reese took the midway exit and headed west, pushing zoom speed, recklessly passing all traffic, slowing just enough at the lights for safety. The Hummer followed suit. Reese felt around the floor with his left foot, trying to locate his cell phone.

Apparently it had slid under the seat. He crossed industrial street, swerved into the uphill lot of Wal-Mart, raced to the store entrance. He parked abruptly in the entrance, blocking pedestrian traffic. An elderly lady with a sack of groceries stopped, threw him a hostile glare for blocking her path. As the store automatic doors started open, he leapt from his SUV, started toward the open door, he felt a viselike grip on his right arm, almost snatching him off his feet.

Three seconds later, another hamlike hand grabbed his left arm, and he was lifted off his feet. Lightning fast he was thrown on the floor of the Hummer. He heard the rubber tires on his SUV burn as it was quickly hustled to a parking space. He felt his hands being tied behind him as the Hummer sped off. He felt the cold steel of a pistol at the base of his neck.

"You behave and you'll live. Any aggressive move, Mr. Maxey, and I'll put a bullet in you."

An accented voice. Very cold and in control.

Reese silently prayed.

CHAPTER

27

The private jet landed at the Chippewa County International Airport in Kinross, Michigan, on a bright sunny and cold day.

Fahzi Raheed slipped on a newsboy cap and sunglasses. In denim pants and peacoat, he looked more like a Hollywood celebrity than the journalist the public was so familiar with.

The mackinaw shuttle limo glided smoothly north on Interstate 74. Raheed relaxed and closed his eyes and enjoyed the float of the luxury car as it headed toward Sault Ste. Marie, Michigan.

The meeting would be brief, but it would be one of the most important for him in the Sky project. And thank goodness it was to be a brief meet. Professor Adolph Sunhauser was such an unpleasant man. Very smart, but not enjoyable to be around. Raheed suspected Sunhauser did not like him very much. In fact, he had been told Sunhauser didn't like any people of color—black, brown, red, yellow. Basically a skinhead with a PhD. A doctorate in the field of archaeology. A very smart—and crooked—professor. Someone in Davos had found him—Raheed wasn't sure who. And he hadn't asked. At the time, he seemed to be exactly what they needed.

"Sir, you said a block away from the Cup of the Day?"

"Yes—I need the walk."

The limo pulled to the curb.

"It's right down the street—you can't miss it." The driver pointed.

"Great. See you here, this same spot—twenty minutes."

Raheed walked the down Ashmun Street and turned into the Cup of the Day Coffee Shop. It had advertised as the place to read your morning paper, and Raheed would have described it the same. Very quiet. A couple sat huddled together back from the entrance. Seemingly oblivious to their surroundings. They hadn't even looked up when he entered. Good. He didn't want to draw any attention to himself.

He took a seat near the expanse of window facing the street. Just as he sat, he saw his guest approaching.

Raheed moved to the far end of the coffee shop, took a booth at the rear. The couple didn't look up.

The waitress, college young, a pleasant face, slightly overweight, approached.

"One pot-black coffee, two cups." Raheed tried to modify the singsong quality of his voice.

He had learned to do that. Once, traveling incognito, he had been meeting with a friend at restaurant. In the heat of good comradery, their voices had raised. A woman in the next booth had turned around and asked if he was Fahzi Raheed, a big smile on her face, pen and a piece of paper in hand waiting for his autograph. She had recognized is voice.

"I hope you can carry this."

Sunhauser stood, looking down at Fahzi, breathing hard. Average height, white hair, thinning and receding. He wore a Nor'easter commuter coat—the kind you found in the L. L. Bean catalog—and corduroys.

Raheed looked down at the briefcase on the floor. Large and bulky, in leather.

"It looks like just another leather case—there's more to it than that, though." Sunhauser sat down without offering his hand.

"You ordered?"

"Right behind you." Raheed looked over Sunhauser's shoulder as the waitress approached. She poured two cups as Raheed and Sunhauser looked on silently.

"Well, there it is." Sunhauser kicked the briefcase. "I've done your dirty work for you."

Raheed felt a quick stab of anger and immediately killed it.

"Why not think of it as your contribution to world unity and peace?"

"If you say so. Got any questions?"

"Did you have any trouble—run into any problems?"

Sunhauser laughed.

"I could antique those papers at my kitchen table, no problem there."

"What about a site—where these papers will be . . . found?"

"On my trips to the Mideast—and to Europe, I've found a number of sites you can use. I think somewhere near where the Dead Sea scrolls were found would be appropriate."

"You found some prospects in that area?"

"Yes. There are details in the briefcase."

"I can study what you have here"—Raheed moved the briefcase to the space beside him—"and begin a plausible story? I mean it's—"

"Everything you need—it's all in that case," Sunhauser spoke sharply, pointing to the briefcase.

An angry, bitter man, Raheed thought.

"I will need to study the contents tonight on my way to Europe."

Sunhauser looked at him with incredulity.

"You're not going to carry that—let alone open it—on an airplane, are you?"

"In a private jet Dr. Sunhauser."

"I was going to say—"

"You were going to say what?" Raheed stared bullets at his guest.

Sunhauser looked away, looked at his watch.

"I have got to get back to class."

"How are things at Michigan Tech?"

"Things are good. Should be much better when I am department chair."

"We are working that."

Sunhauser caught the "we," stared a second, and nodded.

"I would think with the money you're going to get from this, you'd think in terms of retiring."

"Well, I like academia, but who knows, I might do just that."

Raheed wondered how a man of Sunhauser's ethics and personality had gotten as far as he had. A brilliant mind had to be the only answer. He stood.

"I'll need the combination number."

Sunhauser stood, reached into his billfold, extracted a small slip of paper,

"Guard it with your life. Only one way into that briefcase."

Raheed pocketed the piece of paper, left a ten-dollar bill on the table, and they started toward the exit, Sunhauser leading the way. Sunhauser turned, jabbed a finger in Raheed's chest.

"You wait a few minutes before you leave."

He turned and left the restaurant. As he was opening the door, Raheed said, "See ya."

Raheed fumbled with some loose papers in his pockets and then exited the restaurant.

He started the short trek back to the corner to meet the limo driver. A couple more stops and he would be on his way to Europe.

CHAPTER
28

Evidently, they had drugged him. When he awoke, he felt groggy. He attempted to move his hands. The rope was too tight. Arms pinned back, he raised his head in an attempt to get sensory bearings on his whereabouts.

He surmised he was in a small room, about the size of his apartment bedroom/office. He could hear soft music nearby. Would be soothing music if it wasn't for the circumstances. He was sitting in the clothes he had worn earlier, and he consciously could feel no pain anywhere in his body: small comfort. He could feel fear rising again. He prayed again silently.

The door suddenly opened, and light from the adjoining room blinded him. He felt a hand grab his chin and snap his head up.

"Open your eyes!" An accented rough voice. He painfully opened wide, not really seeing anything as a penlight probed his eyeballs, encouraging the giant headache he had.

"He's OK." The unfriendly hand let his head go and gave him two mild slaps.

"You'll be OK—at least for a while."

He heard a course laugh, footsteps, and he was suddenly back in darkness. Whatever they had given him had not quite worn off, and he felt sleep overtake him again.

When he awoke again, he was sitting in the middle of a large rectangular room still strapped to the chair. He saw three sets of black shoes. Military looking, thick with tire treadlike soles. His head came slowly up to three sets of eyes, emotionally neutral staring at him. Two big guys, dressed in black pants, dark gray shirts. Football-sized people. A rough hand grabbed his chin. This time a little gentler than the first time.

"You awake?" An American voice. Reese looked at the man. Slightly smaller than the other two, but still over six feet and muscular. In khakis and gray sweater. He wore a crew cut. Salt-and-pepper hair. Tinted rectangular-rimmed glasses, which somehow made more acceptable the ugly scar tissue that ran from his left eye downward toward the lower rear of his jaw, fading as it descended.

"You OK?"

Somewhere inside, Reese found his sense of humor.

"Under the circumstances?" All three men just stared at him.

"If you need to go to the little boys' room, now's the time. We got a lot of talking to do."

Reese heard the seriousness, the coldness in the man's voice.

"I'm OK." He took in his surroundings. On his left was a wall. Two doors at each end. Wood floors, a "kitchen" ahead: sink, microwave, fridge, small portable TV, cabinets. Two rectangular windows on his right showed a high wooden fence outdoors boxing whatever kind of structure they were in. Every few feet, trees landscaped the perimeter. Reese had the impression they were in a rural setting—farm country or perhaps a semirural setting. Occasionally he heard the sound of passing traffic. Very sparse traffic.

"Where's the tape?"

The crew cut guy pulled up a chair, straddled it, elbows resting on its back. He stared coldly at Reese.

"What tape?" And for a minute Reese had no idea what the man was talking about.

"The tape you made at FCI—Maez and Raheed—ring a bell?"

"Of Lou?"

"The tape you made of Lou and Raheed—in Maez's office."

Reese was too scared to dwell too long on how the man knew. "Who?"

The man stared at Reese for a few seconds, then said, "I know you're smart enough to know you're going to tell us everything we want to know before you leave this room."

The man continued to stare at Reese with coldness. The two ponytails, standing on either side of him, looked at Reese impassively. Reese felt his fear increasing and tried to bolster his mind to withstand any pain they might inflict. He knew that he could take some pain. Reese silently prayed and returned the men's stares.

The man continued, "The harder we have to work at this, the more painful it's going to be for you," stated matter-of-factly.

"Please." Reese heard the note of desperation in his voice.

"I don't have any tape for you—what's this all about anyway?"

"Have it your way." The man stood, nodded to one of the ponytails.

Reese felt the ropes come off as they lifted him off the chair.

"Ooomph!" He felt and heard the air go out of him as the ponytail landed a solid punch to his gut.

The pain seemed to accelerate as they sat him back down, slapped tape on his wrists.

For a minute he thought he was going to die. Maybe they had stabbed him. He looked at his stomach through blurred eyes. No blood. He tried to catch his breath, tried to not focus on the pain.

"You can make this easy on yourself, Mr. Maxey—we don't enjoy this either."

Reese looked at each of the three men through watery eyes and took some small amount of comfort and hope in the fact the man seemed to mean what he had said. They didn't look like they were looking forward to beating the living daylights out of him—or worse. Reese spluttered, "Let me get my breath and think. I don't make a habit of going around eavesdropping and bugging people's conversations. What is it you really want from me?"

Reese saw the flicker of doubt and uncertainty in the crew cut's eyes; he said, "We want—the—that tape."

"Please! What tape?"

Without untaping his hands, the ponytail hit him in the same spot again.

He saw stars. He felt nausea. He couldn't ignore the pain radiating from his midsection. He thought he was going to pass out.

"We'll give you time to think about this some more."

The three men went to the kitchen area. One of the men opened the small fridge, tossed a can of beer to the other two. They sat down, kicked back, turned the small TV on, volume up. Like they had completely forgotten Reese.

Reese sat, hurting, praying, thinking. Maybe he should just tell them, give them the Lou Maez recording. It was in his pocket, on his key chain. They hadn't bothered searching him.

And the recordings and cell phone pictures of the Jamaican and Mexican. Evidently they didn't know about that. Kind of amazing, though, how Lou had guessed right about his having a tape recorder—of sorts—in his pocket.

Reese heard the scrape of a chair, saw the crew cut stand up, drain the last of his beer, and start toward him. He felt his body tense involuntarily. The man stopped at a dresser drawer. Reese watched the man pick up what looked like an old-fashioned cop's billy club. As he walked slowly toward Reese, the man smacked the business end of the stick into his left palm several times. He watched Reese as he approached. He shook his head, making sad noises.

"You were probably one of those little boys that learned everything the hard way."

Thwwwop!

For several seconds Reese wasn't sure what had happened. He saw the man in front of him stagger backward a foot, then forward, then slump to the floor, blood seeping from his left temple. He heard a tinkle of glass and, out of the corner of his eye, saw a glass mirror on the dresser just ahead of him on his left shatter. Partial reality dawned on him, and he shoved hard with his legs, pushing himself over on the floor. As he went down, he saw the bullet hole in the rectangular window to his right.

"Enemy fire!" One of the ponytails screamed. From the floor, Reese saw both men produce guns that looked like Uzis or MAC-10s, and he heard the boom-boom-boom of guns, the rat-a-tat of bullets being sprayed wildly at the rectangular window with the bullet hole as the two men dove for the skimpy cover of the kitchen table.

"Let's get out of here!" Reese heard the fear in the accented voice. Crouching low, the man started toward the door to the left of the kitchen. He reached to unlatch the lock. "Ooww!" the man's hand splintered, and he sank back down just before a bullet slammed his crouching body into the door. The man sank to the floor, rolled back on his back, legs up, bent back as if he were about to do a back-over flip. Reese saw his body relax in death, legs stretching out, pushing the door closed.

"Oh, Mama . . . please."

Reese heard the third man crying. In panic and fear, balled up under the kitchen table holding his head between his knees. For a few seconds there was nothing but silence. Reese heard a loud crash, saw the door splinter, then shoved hard, slamming the dead body at the door aside.

Two men, dressed in black military garb entered. In a second they had surveyed and analyzed the results of their attack.

One of the men went to the kitchen table, kicked it over, looked down at the whimpering man.

"Get up!"

"Please . . . please don't shoot me."

"Get up!"

The man stood, eyes wide, imploring, filled with fear. He trembled uncontrollably.

Four more men entered the room, semiautomatics at the ready. One carried a sniper rifle.

"Get him out of here."

Two of the men grabbed the whimpering man, led him out on wobbly legs.

Reese lay breathing hard; the pain had subsided some. Head raised a few inches off the floor, he tried to take it all in, hoping that the new guys were good guys and on his side.

Two of the men lifted him, and in a snap, his arms were free.

"You good?"

Mustached, shadow bearded, the man's voice exuded friendliness. For some odd reason, he seemed to be slightly amused.

Wobbly and in pain, Reese managed to nod.

"I'm good—be OK."

"How bad they hurt you?"

"Just a couple of punches to my—my stomach. I'll be OK."

"Feel like traveling?"

"Like to get outta here."

"Good, 'cause Mr. Z would like to see you."

"That would be 'Z' as in Zonman," Reese said.

"Only one Mr. Z, sir."

Reese smiled as they led him out of the house.

CHAPTER

29

Lou Maez was worried as he made his way to his car in the underground parking lot of FCI.

This level of parking was underground, and it was specifically designated for the brass at FCI.

Still, it seemed to Maez—the outside lot—the corporate lot on the east side was closer to his office. He should make a note to have two parking spaces reserved for his car, one there, one here.

He had far more important things on his mind today, though.

He was worried because he had not heard from the people he had sent to Dallas. They should have checked in with him no later than yesterday.

He felt a surge of anger. If that Jamaican had lived up to all his braggadocio. That was the first mistake. Sending an amateur to do a pro's job.

He wondered what had happened to the Jamaican. It was like he'd dropped off the face of the earth. He'd still have to deal with that. Another loose end in what he was beginning to wonder, and worry was his own world coming unraveled.

He reached his Mercedes S550, slipped out of his gray windowpane suit jacket. Nothing more uncomfortable than driving with a coat on. Even during Missouri's cold winters, he frequently drove in shirt sleeves.

He looked diagonally across the garage lot. Looked like Symington was still here. Not a typical time of day for his visits.

Out of habit and almost unconsciously, he glanced up at the garage security camera. In his subliminal preconscious mind, it registered that there was something different about the camera today. But overriding that was a consciousness of and a worrying of things related to Reese Maxey. In spite of that worry, he was looking forward to the comfortable ride home. The Mercedes was a joy to drive.

He opened the back door, placed his jacket on the hanger.

"Lou!"

Startled, Lou looked up. He hadn't heard the van approach, his mind preoccupied with events in Dallas.

Window down, the driver of the van smiled. A friendly bearded face. Lou didn't recognize him.

"Hey, Lou."

Startled again, he looked behind him. Two men were approaching. Again smiling faces. Engaging men, masculine, one in a three-quarter length jacket and khakis, the other in a blazer and khakis.

"What's up, guys?" Lou answered, feeling on unstable ground, not exactly sure what to make of an unusual situation.

"Need to talk to you."

He hesitated. The fact that they were in this parking lot gave them some credibility, but still.

"Talk? About what?"

They continued toward him, just a couple of yards from him.

The image of the security camera suddenly kicked into consciousness. He had a growing sick feeling.

"Sure." His voice warbled fear.

"Sure. Let's go to my office."

Something was very wrong here. He pushed the rear door of the Mercedes closed with a hand that trembled uncontrollably.

Before he could turn fully to face the men again, he felt himself being lifted off his feet.

"Hey—what are you doing?!" For a couple of seconds he thought—he hoped—it might be a joke set up by one of his frat brothers.

"Come on, guys!"

He felt his body turned horizontal in the air—what were they doing?—the rear door of the van was opened. He felt himself catapulted into the back of the van. His head slammed against the back of a passenger seat, stopping forward travel. He felt the pain. He heard all of the van doors close.

He heard the van start out of the garage. He lay there, resigned to his fate. He was through.

As the van eased into city traffic, he knew he had seen his last day at FCI Incorporated.

CHAPTER

30

Reese followed his rescuer into the Crescent Hotel in downtown Dallas. They proceeded to the elevator in the opulent hotel. In a few minutes, Reese found himself sitting in one of the rooms of grandeur with Barak Zonman. Beige, light furnishings. The words *plush*, *lush*, and *oversized* came to Reese's mind as he quickly surveyed the room.

Reese sat in a plush, stuffed chair next to the patio door overlooking downtown Dallas. Zonman sat on the sofa at a right angle. They both sipped coffee. They were both dressed comfortably. Reese in an argyle sweater and chinos, Zonman in a brown blazer, open collar shirt, and khakis.

"My people took good care of you." Whether a statement of fact or question, Reese nodded affirmatively.

"I'm very grateful, Mr. Zonman."

"They're good men," Zonman said.

Reese nodded. Zonman's team had brought him to this luxurious hotel after stopping at his apartment to pick up clothes and toiletries. They had also installed a very secure alarm system at his apartment. A phone call was all it had taken to get it done.

He had spent a couple of nights at the Crescent, paid by the Zonman's organization.

He had been looking forward to seeing Zonman again.

"I'm glad you're leaving Sky. That's a real hornet's nest. You're lucky to have escaped with just a few stings."

Reese nodded. "Thanks to you, Mr. Zonman."

"All things work together for good . . ."

"You know"—Zonman seemed reflective—"they're trying to save the world, the Davos people—Azko Lee Britton, the people behind Sky. Britton's vision is of a world saved by world religion from itself—from the religious fanatics. He likes to see himself as the world savior, surrounded by beck-and-call people of his ilk. A planet safe and controlled by his people—by the super rich elite that's his vision."

"I can almost understand why," Reese said, thinking as he envisioned the theory, "they're rich—the wealthiest on the planet. They are the best educated, the best informed. Arguably, the most intelligent. They are the most influential. They possess the know-how of leadership. Arguably, they are the most qualified to rule this world, and the world has shrunk. With the advances in computerization, automation, transportation, communication. With globalization, the world has reached a point where it can be managed by a small group of people—maybe even one man, theoretically."

"Your description of this point in history is accurate, Reese. But we both know that a peaceful, human-governed world is not possible. It's not in our future." Not until Christ reigns.

"It's not in man who walks to direct his steps," Reese quoted Jeremiah 10:23 from the Bible.

"And the government will be upon his shoulder," Zonman said, quoting Isaiah 9:6, referring to Christ's future worldwide rule.

They sat silently for a moment. Reese watched the mad rush of traffic stories below.

"How did your investigation go?"

Reese had to think for a second, then realized his "investigation" referred to Molly.

"Molly and I met, had breakfast together. She told me she had lied on air, and why she had."

"Good work, Reese. We want to talk about that later."

A cell phone rang, and both Reese and Zonman reached for their phones.

"I believe that's mine," Zonman said and lifted the phone to his ear. He answered, walked to the stationary desk, scribbled some notes, folded the paper into his pocket, and returned to the sofa.

"Tel Aviv. Situation there." He sighed in a reflective moment, poured more coffee.

"You know, my people—Israel, the Jews—we lost out. We had the Messiah—the Savior of the world, and we didn't recognize Him." Zonman paused for a second then.

"We've suffered. And still, our worst day is yet to come. But in spite of that"—he turned a half smile at Reese—"the most glorious day any nation will ever have on this earth is in Israel's future."

"Mr. Maxey, I've made millions—not millions. I've made billions. I've built a lot of businesses, and I've been very successful."

Reese noted the absence of conceit and self-congratulation in Zonman's matter-of-fact statement.

"My priorities have changed though. My businesses practically run themselves." He paused.

"As I see it, there are two beacons of light on the earth—and this is just my personal view, Mr. Maxey—America, because of her Judeo-Christian orientation, and Israel, because of the promises God has made to her. Outside of that, the world seems a pretty dark place to me. And getting darker.

"The great tribulation is coming, that is fact. No way around that fact. And according to the fourteenth chapter of Zechariah, eventually all the nations of the earth will turn against Israel.

"But while I live, I intend to defend America—as long as she reflects her Christian character and supports Israel—and I intend to support Israel against her enemies.

"It bothers me sometimes to see America's light dimming."

Reese said, "Do you think we are getting near the end of time?" He felt awkward asking the question.

"Just look around, Reese. And look at what the Bible says about the last days. Earthquakes, wars and rumors of wars, pestilences, famines, etc.

"Look at what the Bible says about the control of commerce in the last days. All of the world buying and selling by a number, for example. Until the twenty-first century, that wasn't possible. And the part of Revelation about the whole world seeing the two witnesses. That certainly wasn't possible when John wrote the Book of Revelations. Has not been possible—until now.

"Read Paul's second letter to Timothy—third chapter. Look at the personality traits of the latter-day man—today's humanity— described there. And then add modern man's technology. Oh, we've got the technology down pat, we're able to do whatever we want— weapons of mass destruction and all. Add that all together, Mr. Maxey, and you've got what Paul refers to as 'perilous times.' He wrote that 'in the last days perilous times will come.'

"We're continuously learning and yet never able to come to the knowledge of the truth.

"We've steadily and upwardly progressed in learning the chemistry, the physics, the materials of the world around us, and how to harness them into making what we want.

"We've got all this ever-new technology.

"But we've got the same old heart of Cain when he slew Abel.

"Makes for a dangerous world, Mr. Maxey. And the Lord himself told us in the twenty-fourth chapter of Matthew that if God didn't intervene, eventually, everyone would be destroyed by 'that man of sin' who is coming and by the great tribulation."

Zonman stood. "We're talking about something I'm very much interested in. Mr. Maxey. Sorry, I didn't mean to bore you with a sermon. The last days—well, that started with Christ's first advent over two thousand years ago. Right now, this minute in downtown Dallas, we've got a lot of living to do." Zonman chuckled.

"It's something I'm interested in too," Reese said. "In my Bible studies lately, I've been coming to the same insights—the same illuminations—you have."

Zonman had gone to the desk again to scribble another note to himself.

"I am glad to hear that. The people in my organization see things pretty much the same way to a large degree."

Reese had another issue on his mind.

"I'm coming to work for you. I'm a little concerned though. I'm not sure I'm up to the—the kill ability of your, your, special forces, I guess.

"You don't have to be, Reese. Those men are called to that work. They are soldiers."

"You are a communicator. And something of an investigator."

Zonman returned to the sofa, took a sip of lukewarm coffee.

"We are a secret organization, Mr. Maxey. We are sponsored by intelligence sections of the US government and the Israeli government. We will train you to defend yourself. Not to attack others. And you will probably never have to use any of the training we give you." Zonman paused. "Hopefully."

Zonman smiled at Reese.

"You've already completed your first assignment for us."

"I have?" Reese's eyebrows lifted.

"Molly. You drum up some expenses for that and send us the bill.

"Another thing, I'm going to take up where Brochman left off. I'll probably use your help with that. One of my missions is to convert every Jew I can to Christianity."

"Speaking of Brochman—and Patterson," Reese said, "what are your thoughts about that?"

"We're looking into that in our own way. You have to remember that Sky is a worldwide movement, it has a lot of support. Remember, we are a select group. A secret group. But not everyone in government—supports us.

"Tell me, Reese, what are your near-term plans?"

"I believe I am going to move to Dallas." Even as he spoke, Reese was making that a final decision.

"Good," Zonman said. I like to keep close to every operative in my organization. I'm in Dallas frequently. I hardly ever have a need to go to Kansas City. Have you found a house yet?"

Reese shook his head.

"Have you been looking?"

"I kind of like the area my apartment is in—the midcities and areas around it."

"Great area. Look in Bedford, Euless, Hurst, Colleyville, Grapevine, anywhere around there is usually good."

"Your house up for sale?"

"Not yet."

"Someone from my office will contact you. We'll help you sell and get relocated."

"What do you plan to do with that lovely social worker you're dating?"

"Well, I—"

"You don't have to answer that." Zonman grinned.

Zonman stood, Reese joined him. They both looked out of the balcony window to the street below. The traffic was even more hectic than earlier Reese noticed. They watched two limousines pull up, discharge two passengers.

"Probably a celebrity or two," Zonman said. "A lot of them stop here."

Zonman glanced sideways at Reese briefly.

"I've noticed your taste in apparel, Mr. Maxey."

Reese made a humorous note to himself to try to catalog Zonman's use of "Mr. Maxey" versus "Reese."

"Thank you, sir. I try."

"I like a well-dressed man. I encourage that with those who work for me—says a lot about how a man feels about himself and those he comes in contact with. Also speaks to his character."

Zonman pointed, "See that BMW turning in the lot? It's parked right next to Stanley Korshak's. They sell extremely nice threads. Get a chance, stop in, and let them know you work for me."

"I will do that."

"I'm glad we had this visit, Reese."

They started toward the exit.

"I wanted to see how you held up after the ordeal—the stresses you've been through, wanted to confirm my opinion. And I wanted to confirm our relationship."

"I'm your man," Reese said.

They gave confirming handshakes and parted company.

CHAPTER

31

The Gulfstream G550 climbed to it's designated altitude and settled into a northeasterly stream toward Helsinki.

Azko Lee Britton was proud of his new fifty-five-million-dollar jet. He took another congratulatory sip of premium whiskey.

He sat alone in the large cabin. He looked out the porthole. A cloudy day. But soon, they'd be soaring above the clouds he hoped. Partly sunny was the forecast. Maybe they'd fly high enough.

The meeting in Stockholm had gone well, although truthfully, Azko had had little interest in it. He had been accommodating a good friend—a high-ranking and still-rising exec at the New World Bank. He owed him one.

As it turned out, the meeting had more to do with planning festivities surrounding the awarding of the Nobel Peace Prize than anything of serious substance.

He had sat and listened while his friend used the silent influence of his presence.

In reality, he hadn't even listened to the proceedings.

Mundane dronings. His mind had been on his future and the future of the world. The two were intertwined after all.

He was fully persuaded that he had the solutions the world needed. At least some of them.

In the club of Davos, his mission was to do his part—a major part—to bring peace to the world through the merging of world religions.

The Spiritual Church International was the path. So far, Sky had made stupendous progress.

In his work, in his building of the Sky church, it pretty soon dawned on him, as he progressed, what the religions needed were tangible proofs that a new day had come upon the world. A dawning of unity via religion and spiritual life combined with work life.

And also needed was a new leader. A new leader of faiths. And some visible miracles.

He thought about the recent gay leader of the Episcopalian Church—Bishop Gene Robinson. Robinson had tried to make the point that his homosexuality, his gayness would have been a sin in the time of Sodom and Gomorrah. But it wasn't so today. Because of new revelations. In other words, just because the Bible was not being extended with new writings today didn't mean there were not new revelations and interpretations.

Azko Lee Britton was determined to make the world see that. If they could get the Muslims to see the new pastor at Sky as the new and final prophet, they'd be more than halfway home.

The Jews. Another problem there. And too much a source of the world's anxiety.

He took another sip of whiskey.

He would have to placate Arabs. Ahmadinejad had perhaps been right. There really was no place for Jews in the Mideast. Or perhaps, even on the planet.

"Another drink, Mr. Britton?"

He jumped. The soft, delicate voice had startled him, so deep in thought he'd been.

A seductive tall slim brunette with an intoxicating fragrance.

"Yes, please." Britton recovered his composure and handed his empty glass to her.

"And, Jeannie, ask Fahzi to come forward and to bring the briefcase."

A few minutes later, Raheed and Britton faced each other over a table in the forward cabin.

On the table were their two drinks in supports and the heavy briefcase Raheed had picked up in Sault Ste. Marie.

Raheed pulled out several pieces of paper.

"Those are some of the locations Sunhauser recommended."

Britton studied the pages for a few minutes.

"Makes sense," he said, looking up.

Raheed nodded. "I think it does."

He continued, "In time, these will be discovered on an archaeology dig. Discovered by the right people—our people, although there won't be any visible connection between us and them—and they will be validated as credible, legitimate scriptures and verses of the Koran, dating back to the point in history that we want. And our communications people will see to it that the world—"

"Good, good, Fahzi—what about the miracles?"

"Chezlewski—"

"He's still asleep back there. He's going to give me a brief. I want your take on it."

Raheed shifted in his chair.

"Well, I think it's going to be more effective than the TV testimonies we've used.

"Chezlewski is going to do a series of TV programs, worldwide coverage—big, big productions—make the pope's stuff look like a tent revival in Omaha.

"In one of the programs—we haven't pulled all of this together yet—Chezlewski looks into the camera, he calls six different names. Ordinary Joes—and Janes,—real people. Sick in different hospitals around the planet. He prays for them. They get up out of their beds, healthy as an Olympic athlete, go home, this—"

"Love it!" Britton had a broad smile on his face.

"Still needs a lot of work," Raheed said.

"We're getting there. That's the important thing. We've got time."

"You've got more in that case."

"Leave me alone with it for a few minutes, then the three of us can talk."

Raheed left the cabin as Britton started an overview of the contents of the briefcase.

Twenty minutes later, he was satisfied.

He took another sip of his Chivas Regal Salute 21.

In time, he perhaps would come to be seen as the most important man on the face of the earth. That was not too much of a stretch. He had the right people with him—working for him, in fact. He would come to be known as the architect, the founder of the universal church.

He looked out of his porthole. Still cloudy, and they weren't flying as high above the clouds as he would have liked.

He took another sip of the Chivas and started to play his private cloud game. A kid's game that he had continued privately into adulthood.

What could he find in the clouds today?

Over there, down below their level of flight. He wondered how many miles away it was. A bank of clouds forming into . . . into what? Reminded him of the Michelin Tire Man. He chuckled quietly, took another drink.

And over there, a little farther away, looked like a man, looking his way.

Britton stared down at the "man," imagining they were looking each other in the eye.

Almost felt like it too.

He looked back at where the Michelin man had formed. No longer there. He had morphed into an ordinary mass of clouds.

But the man was still there, looked like he had a stick in his hand now. Just a few miles away, starboard, and below them.

Britton looked away for a few minutes, then looked back.

"He was still there, same position ahead and below the Gulfstream." Britton smiled, fascinated.

"The man and the stick" Britton started to laugh out loud and caught himself. Wouldn't do to have Jeannie or Fahzi or Chezlewski walk in see him half drunk and laughing to himself. He looked around, no one in the cabin. Probably wouldn't have heard him anyway. The G550 was a quiet plane, but the BR710C4 Rolls Royce engines made noise enough.

He looked out of the window again. Still there. The man with the stick—not a stick, it looked more like a cane.

Britton leaned closer to the window, more than fascinated at the unusual phenomenon. He watched the cloud slowly change shape. It looked as if the "man" in the cloud had pointed his cane right directly at him.

This time, he did laugh out loud.

And what was that? Looked like something had come out of the tip of the cane.

It looked like—like a rocket?

And it looked like fire—real fire coming out of it's tail. And it was rising toward his Gulfstream.

He wondered if he had drunk too much, and for a second, wondered if he was hallucinating. Maybe Jeannie had slipped something in his drink.

It was coming fast.

It looked too real.

Britton stood up. Too unsure to embarrass himself with a scream. Surely it wasn't—

"Couldn't be!" he heard himself holler. A second later, he heard a loud thud. Felt like the plane had hit a brick wall in midair.

He screamed. He heard another shriek and a wail coming from the rear of the aircraft.

The wounded plane did a steep tilt downward.

On the floor, Britton felt himself leaving consciousness as panic took hold of him.

A few minutes later, the Gulfstream disintegrated into the ice of the Gulf of Bothnia.

The next day reports of the crash circled the globe. The crew, Azko Lee Britton, the pastor of the Spiritual Church International,

Ferdinand Chezlewski, and the journalist Fahzi Raheed—all had perished in the crash.

The final investigative report of the catastrophe placed blame on a Captain Jurno Pystynum of the FAF (the Finish Air Force) who had been piloting a newly modified McDonnell—Douglas FA-18 Hornet. Flying out of Tampere Air Command, he recalled having fired rockets in a test flight at about the time the Gulfstream crashed.

And he had been in airspace in proximity to the Gulfstream.

How he had strayed so far from his flight plan neither he nor his air command could explain.

CHAPTER

32

Reese slowly came out of his slumber and checked his watch. They would be landing soon.

"That's a very nice watch."

Reese looked at the passenger sitting next to him. Young, dark-skinned, straight black hair. He looked Mideastern. Coincidentally, they were dressed alike in sport coats and jeans. The title of the magazine in his lap read, "Islam's Growth in America."

Reese raised his arm, looked at the oyster perpetual on his wrist.

"Thanks." It had been a gift from Zonman's organization. Zonman's policy was to give a Rolex at sign-up time, not at retirement.

"It's a very fine watch. It was given to me by a friend."

"We should have friends like that." He gave a friendly laugh. Reese smiled.

"You look familiar."

"Excuse me?"

"You look familiar. Like maybe I've seen you somewhere before," an innocent, accented voice.

"Probably not. I'm rarely in the DC area."

In fact, this was his first trip to Washington in several years. And this was a business trip. He was interviewing a defector from Sky. She too had been enticed to lie about a miracle, and she was willing to testify against Sky on air. Zonman had been successful in continuing the TV and radio show that Brochman had started.

"What do you do?" Brash, intrusive, inquisitive in kind of an unoffensive way. A man after his own heart.

"I am an interviewer, a researcher, a writer, an investigator—I wear many hats." Reese laughed. He glanced at the magazine on the young man's lap.

"Interesting article you're reading there."

"Yes—Islam is growing in America."

Reese thought about a recent article he had read that gave some support to the man's statement.

The Asians, Africans, Mideasterners who migrated to America were made up of a large number of Muslims. And they were Muslims who didn't believe in birth control, unlike Americans.

And the church in America was weakening. America's fixation on wealth, and pleasure had weakened its spiritual strength.

Islam, with its strict demands, its intensity seemed to give more meaning to religion and the spiritual side of man.

"In sheer numbers Christianity is growing faster. But you're right, percentage-wise. Islam is the fastest-growing religion in America."

"I take it you are a Christian."

"I am."

"Islam is a wonderful way to live."

If you like regimentation, Reese thought. He said, "So is Christianity. True, Christian living is clean living with a lot more freedom. With a guarantee of eternal life."

"You're not one of those Christians who hates Muslims and Arabs, are you?"

"Not at all. I don't believe Christians hate Muslims. We witness to them. We don't attack them or try to hurt them. Fact is, Arabs are a blessed people."

"Really?" The man looked at him with eyebrows lifted. "You really believe that?"

Reese nodded. "I do."

"We are blessed because of Allah?"

"You are blessed because of Abraham—and the promise God made to the mother of Ishmael."

The young man looked at Reese with a little more intensity.

"If you believe that, I'm curious about your take on Jews and Arabs."

"Jews and Arabs—they're both the offspring of Abraham. They're both blessed."

"And yet they fight."

"It's a conflict that will one day be resolved."

"When Allah rules—"

"No." Reese paused, thoughtful for a second.

"Take a look at the biblical story of Jacob and Esau. Jacob had to run from Esau for a long time—many, many years. But in the end, they embraced each other in reconciliation. It's a story of—"

"Ladies and gentlemen, please fasten your seat belts."

As Reese reached for the strap, he said, "Are you staying in the DC area?"

"Relocating. Just finished college. Just finished a training program. Just got married."

"A season of firsts for you," Reese said. "Those are major life milestones. Congratulations."

"Thank you. Listen, maybe we could continue this talk sometime. I—I'm—well you didn't ask if I was Muslim. You just assumed that."

Reese lifted his eyebrows for a second.

"Guilty. You know what they say about making assumptions."

"No—I don't—"

"You don't want to hear it then." Reese laughed.

"But I apologize. I shouldn't have made that assumption."

"But I am leaning that way. I'm learning about Islam—"

"Maybe we can do lunch sometime—I'm here for a few days," Reese said.

"I was going to suggest that. In fact, I just finished a training program for Buffet's International—ever heard of it?"

"Umm—it's a restaurant chain, I believe—a new one."

"Exactly right. I'm opening the one in Rockville, Maryland."

"Great!" Reese said. "I'm staying in Rockville."

A few minutes later, they shook hands after deboarding. Reese looked at the young man's business card. He would have that lunch with the young man. The sooner, the better.

Reese did a lot of thinking as he drove his rental car through the semirural beauty of Rockville. He had just talked to Jan, and he felt good. They would marry. Her call had to do with some of the purchases they would jointly make for their wedding. She had been ebullient and spirit lifting as usual.

Things had gone well the past few weeks. His upcoming interview—the lady was relieved and eager to tell her story. Maybe the TV broadcast and the radio show would allow Reese to undo some of the damage he might have done in his support of Sky. He was looking forward to that. Sky seemed like a bad dream now.

He wondered what had happened to Lou Maez. The last time he had been seen was on videotape, a video of him getting into his car in the underground executive parking lot at FCI. During the investigation, he and Al had watched the police video together. They had had nothing to contribute to the investigation, nothing the police didn't already know.

After the interrogation that day, Al had walked Reese to the elevator. They shook hands. Al had looked at him, a look of revelation in his eyes,

"You know what Reese—"

"I just realized what has been bothering me about that video we just looked at. Lou never, I mean never, drove his car with his suit jacket on. We used to kid him about that."

Reese had thought back. He couldn't remember what Lou had had on in the video, but he was certain he didn't recall him taking his jacket off.

"Maybe it's something you should tell the police," Reese had said.

"Not at all the thing to do, Reese, not at all. Listen, I know how you feel about Sky, but here—if you ever need a favor . . ."

They had shaken hands warmly again and parted company.

He wondered about the plane crash. Azko Lee Britton, Fahzi Raheed, Chezlewski—all had died. And there had been nothing to recover. Everything had burned on the ice and then sunk into the frigid waters of the Gulf. They were still looking for the bodies.

The FAF captain had not been able to explain his flight. It was if he had been in one airspace one minute and in another—hundreds of miles from his flight plan—the next. He had admitted to firing a missile only because it had been obvious one had been fired. The reality was, Captain Pystynum had no real recall of having fired any weapon that day.

As he drove, Reese found himself giving praise to the Lord. He would begin teaching once-a-month orientation class for newly saved members at his church when he returned to Dallas.

He felt the progress of his Christian life. He was making his calling and election sure. He now realized that was not a one-time event, but a process that would continue the rest of his life.

AUTOBIOGRAPHY

Ronald Winters is a part-time teacher and writer. He holds a master of arts degree in counseling psychology. He has held professional membership in the American Marketing Association, the Society of Competitive Intelligence Professionals, and Associate membership in the American Psychological Association.

His work background includes field rep positions with three Fortune 500 companies and a community mental health center.

The predominance of his work history has been as an industrial market researcher for the publishing community.

He has worked as a volunteer with the counseling department of an Assemblies of God Megachurch.

He and his wife attend a nondenominational church in the Dallas-Forth Worth metroplex. This is his first novel.